Praise For *THE WALLPAPER F*

For his forty-ninth birthday, Ka…
band, Henry, . . . an eighteenth–century handpa…
wallpaper depicting a fox hunt. They are an American
couple who have everything: money-position-looks-taste,
friends with the same . . . Why, then, does this fulfilled
man risk everything, needlessly? . . .

A superior entertainment for the thoughtful, as well
as a swift, no-fudging narrative by a writer it is always
rewarding to rediscover.
—Sophie Wilkins, *National Review*

The Wallpaper Fox is the ideal introduction to Philipson's
sequence of novels about America's upper-crust professional and managerial class: people in secure positions
who have everything but a moral sense and nothing to
lose but their souls. Philipson is not only a good writer,
but an important one. . . . [His characters] evoke a whole
society and a whole country, an America adrift.
—Stephen Vizinczey, author of *In Praise of Older Women*

Not just an expose of what *really* goes on behind the well-
groomed facades of the affluent, but a thoughtful explo-
ration of character and the efficacy of moral action in
forming and reforming it.

Morris Philipson . . . writes with grace and amplitude.
. . . The novel raises disturbing and complicated questions about the capacity of family life to mitigate an
increasingly barren modern experience. . . . Philipson's
characters do manage to break through to some essen-
tial sense of reality and communion—and they seem to
do so through the power of human love.
—Jane Larkin Crain, *New York Times Book Review*

A civilized, entertaining novel . . . At [its] heart is Henry's relationship with his wife, Kate . . . As the couple faces up, first separately, then, at last, together, to the emotional crises overwhelming them, Philipson gives us a very believable portrait of a marriage. He also gives us no easy answers, . . . and, best of all, real storytelling.
—*Publishers Weekly*

Moral dilemmas are all over the place in *The Wallpaper Fox.* . . . It's the intelligent kind of novel that makes the reader ask himself what he'd do under the same circumstances.
—William Cole, *Saturday Review*

Lucid and engaging prose, incisive social insight, high wit, ironic brilliance, narrative urgency, the puzzlement and poetry of human life, above all an elegantly stocked *mind:* Morris Philipson's novelistic signature comprises all of these. To allow his work to go undiscovered—and unacclaimed—would be to miss a significant and resonating literary presence, one with the power to enchant and energize new generations of readers. For admirers of E. M. Forster's *Howards End,* say, the novels of Morris Philipson are an American fulfillment.
—Cynthia Ozick

An extraordinary novel, fascinating, compelling, and totally disconcerting.
—*Fort Worth Star-Telegram*

All of Morris Philipson's novels are stamped with his special style of wit and razor-sharp psychological observance, the nuanced tragicomedy of manners that takes the reader deep into some world . . .
—Wendy Doniger

The Wallpaper Fox

The Wallpaper Fox

A Novel by
MORRIS PHILIPSON

The University of Chicago Press

The University of Chicago Press, Chicago 60637
Copyright © 1976 by Morris Philipson
All rights reserved. Originally published 1976
University of Chicago Press edition 2000
Printed in the United States of America
05 04 03 02 01 00   6 5 4 3 2 1

Library of Congress Cataloging-in-Publication Data

Philipson, Morris H., 1926–
    The wallpaper fox : a novel / by Morris Philipson.
        p. cm.
    ISBN 0-226-66748-0 (paper : alk. paper)
    1. Friendship—Connecticut—New Haven—Fiction. 2. Family—
Connecticut—New Haven—Fiction. 3. New Haven (Conn.)—
Fiction. I. Title.

PS3566.H475 W35 2000
813'.54—dc21

                                                    99–087635

♾ The paper used in this publication meets the minimum requirements
of the American National Standard for Information Sciences—Perma-
nence of Paper for Printed Library Materials, ANSI Z39.48-1992.

For Iris Murdoch
with gratitude

The Wallpaper Fox

After drinks and lunch at the Quinnipiac Club with his oc-
togenarian uncle—who gave him, as a present for his forty-
ninth birthday, a Bible that had been in the family for six
generations—Henry Warner, slightly euphoric, returned to
his store, to Warner and Son, popularly known as the Tiffa-
ny's of New Haven, and found a "For Sale" notice stuck to
the door of the men's room in the corridor of the top floor.
He tore it off and crumpled it in his fist. It was for a studio
couch in good condition. Holding it in one hand and the
Bible in the other, as he walked through his secretary's office,
he asked her to take a memo. Mrs. Wicks picked up a stenog-
rapher's pad and followed him into the handsome office that
looked out on the Green.

"Just say," he began, " 'To All Department Heads,' and ask
them to post it. Then the text should read:

> " 'Let us be more discriminating. A door is not a bulletin
> board. A wall is not a bulletin board. For Sale Notices and
> other signs should not be posted anywhere but on actual bul-
> letin boards. If we are going to be both purveyors and leaders
> of good taste, let us practice it ourselves. Propriety, as well as
> Love and Mercy, begins at home.' "

Mrs. Wicks snickered. "No comment, please," he said, smiling. "I'm to be forgiven almost anything today. This is the
first day of my fiftieth year."

Mrs. Wicks stood up. She was close to sixty; a faithful friend
who had worked for Henry Warner for seventeen years; a
dumpy body with a cheerful face; a woman divorced, and
abandoned by an ungrateful son. "I can't imagine what difference that makes," she said. Her view touched momentar-

ily on the box of cigars on his desk—her birthday gift to him.

"It means that I pass from being a hard-nosed bastard into becoming an aging eccentric."

"Mr. Warner," she said, in the peremptory tone they used freely with each other, "you are indulging yourself!"

And why not? he felt, when she'd closed the door behind her. I have survived. I've come to earn what I inherited. His large window on the fifth floor gave him the view of the Green above the level of the tree tops: the three churches in the center, the library and the courthouse on the right, the shops and hotels on the left, bordered in the distance by the bastion-like buildings of Yale College. I have made a better thing of a good thing. With his back to the desk, he looked out over the table in front of the window and noticed the Bible his uncle had given him. He took the thick red buckram-bound volume up in his left hand and held it against his left side—as he had been taught to carry his Bible to Sunday School nearly half a century before—and with his right hand dropped the cardboard box and the tissue paper into a wastebasket.

The Warners, like the Pardees and the Davenports and the Winthrops, had been among the earliest settlers of New Haven; and for three centuries they had bettered themselves. Farmers and carpenters to begin with, they had used their skills wisely and began to go into trade on the side, then into professions and into state government. There had been a store named Warner and Son at this same site on Church Street since 1801. As it was rebuilt, enlarged, changed with the times, so had the family adapted to the character of their generations, but none had made so radical a break with tradition, taken so risky a gamble, as Henry Warner. He had married a Jew. He put the Bible down on his desk, thinking of the spelling of his wife's name which he would inscribe there. Marrying Kate had been the best decision of his life.

He looked around the office at the trophies of that life.

Facing him on the mahogany desk were the photographs of his wife and the three children; the crystal vase incised with their names given to his parents on their fortieth wedding anniversary by his brother and himself; the gold-plated golf ball to celebrate membership in the Hole-in-One Club; the antique carved jade urn that held his pen and pencils, a present of the City Council for participation in the Advisory Committee that planned the redevelopment of New Haven. With his archaeological view of life, he could see the events that resulted in the objects. The carpet was not only a beige rug of Isfahan, with its subtly woven design of flowers; it was a bazaar in Constantinople where he had bargained like a native and Kate and he had gone staggering through the humid streets in the dark, giddy with laughter, carrying the heavy roll on their shoulders up to the impassive doormen at the steps of their hotel. The sofa and the armchair were covered with upholstery fabric based on a design by William Morris which he had found in the British Museum—never before executed—and he had successfully urged the head of Sanderson's in London to bring it out. On the mahogany credenza stood the pictures of his mother and his father, not in their old age—each had died at seventy—but in the fullness of life as they had looked to him when he was an adolescent. On the ivory-colored wall behind them hung his three degrees: from prep school in New Hampshire, from Amherst, and his Master's in Art History from Harvard. Next to that stood the citation for service in the Navy of the United States during the Second World War.

Mrs. Wicks came in with the memo to sign. "You're sure you want to send it?" she asked.

"You don't think my internal censor is working today."

"All of us can use a little extra help now and then."

He read through the message and initialed it. "This is not my only indulgence of the day. I'm taking off the rest of the afternoon. If the ad for this Sunday's paper isn't here before

I leave, it'll have to wait until the morning. Then I'm going to play golf, go home and play with my children, and go out to dinner—for a birthday cake and ice cream."

Mrs. Wicks said, "Shameless!" as if she were genuinely shocked, and left him alone. To the right of the door opposite his desk, the side wall was covered with a Venetian mirror in a gilded frame of stalks of wheat. He stepped to the right of his desk in order to look at the reflection. He thought of himself as plain: well made but undistinguished. His lips were thin, but his square jaw somehow sensual in the round-ness of the chin. His eyes were his best feature: hazel, with a circle of pale blue around the iris. His children called them "tiger eyes." He laughed. Just this morning Kate had said, "For years I've loved you for the crow's feet around your eyes; but you're beginning to show the whole crow's leg." Only Kate had ever made him feel handsome. His dark-chocolate-colored suit, the light blue shirt, and the gold woven necktie fitted him well. It was Conrad Taylor's second wife, when they'd first become acquainted with each other, who had said to him, "You're one of the few men I know whose life seems to fit him perfectly, the way your suits do." Sometimes a near stranger can sum up everything you have tried to understand for years—because strangers know nothing of what else might have been; they see only what is.

"I *have* survived!" he repeated to himself. After his parents' initial opposition to his marriage—Kate was a widow and pregnant when they met—they gradually accepted her. But in the division of their estate, they gave his brother all the stocks and bonds—at face value very much greater than the worth of the store, which, with the house in Woodbridge, the summer cottage in Maine, and the rest of the real estate in Connecticut, went to him. He owned them outright and he remade them and enhanced them, whereas his brother lived on a yacht harbored at Palm Beach, did nothing, cultivated nothing, and would leave nothing to anyone. Even now he was beginning to make noises on long-distance phone calls from Florida about the possibilities of a loan—noises that Henry chose not to comprehend. It was not that he wished him ill; his brother simply meant nothing to him.

Henry had his own financial problems. Business was down twenty percent this year, and expenses were up thirty-three percent. Between the costs for the renovation of the ground floor and the second floor and the needs of the payroll for this month, he was borrowing more heavily from the bank than he had in ten years—twelve years, he corrected himself. And the Internal Revenue Service had just served him notice of a review of his personal income tax return for two years before. Jonathan had just finished his first year at the University of Michigan, and the two young children were in Roger Sherman Day School—which cost almost as much. The house in Woodbridge needed a new roof. Everybody needs new clothes; I need a vacation; and Kate needs—ah, he thought, Kate needs—a bouquet of the most beautiful flowers, so that if I die this afternoon, even if not everything is perfectly in order, this at least she will know: that she is the love of my life.

He sat at his desk and buzzed for Mrs. Wicks as he began to unwrap the first of her gift cigars. "Mrs. Wicks," he said, lighting it in her presence, "is there anything more I have to do before I leave today?" She smiled at the sight of his smoking.

"I hope you like it."

"You are a dear person. I hope you know how grateful I am to you for all your kindnesses." Am I behaving as if I expect to die soon? he wondered.

She brushed aside the compliment with a wave of her hand and a pleasant sigh. "There are the last of the letters you dictated this morning. They need to be signed. And Hopkins in Jewelry just this minute called to ask if you'd talk to a customer."

He looked at his watch. Two forty-five. Could he get in eighteen holes of golf? "Do I have to see him? Do you know what he wants?"

"Hopkins kept saying the man wants a personal discussion."

"Have him come up." Efficient. Available. I am a good administrator, he thought.

He looked around the room: like touching wood or throwing salt over his shoulder, a superstitious reaffirmation of all he was, to prepare himself for each new encounter. He looked out again at the Green. Then he went into his private bathroom for a minute.

Hopkins came in, while the customer waited with Mrs. Wicks. He was white-haired and round-shouldered; he had sold much of the most expensive jewelry at Warner and Son for twenty-five years. Henry thought he must look like a salesman even in pajamas. "At your service," Henry said.

Hopkins held out a calling card with the name Robert Stanton engraved on it, an address on Wall Street, and a New York phone number. In the other hand he showed a hard black jewel box. Henry took them both and placed them on the desk, then snapped the box open.

"Why a plain box instead of one with our name on it?"

"The customer's explicit request. Mr. Stanton is insistent on talking with you personally," Hopkins said. "Pleasantly but firmly insistent."

Henry looked at the earrings, the twin gems lying side by side on the black velvet: the square-cut emeralds were the essence of green, without depth, all internal, infinite, as if to attempt to look through them would result in seeing green forever; and the three pear-shaped diamonds dangled beneath each of the emeralds radiated eternally imprisoned starlight. "The list price is fifty thousand dollars," Hopkins continued. "The wholesale price, of three years ago, was twenty-five thousand dollars."

"Thank you, Mr. Hopkins. Will you show him in now, please." Hopkins did. He was very good at introductions. And at retiring gracefully.

Robert Stanton was well over six feet, and broad, heavy, but only with the contained weight of a long-time athlete growing older; a man of about his own age, Henry presumed, but bald on the pate and shaved bald about the rest of his head; heavy-lidded, shadowed eyes under bushy eyebrows; his nose sharply marked like a three-dimensional triangle. Teutonic, from the Prussian Baltic States, Henry imagined, or Scandinavian. His sandy-colored moustache, shot through with white hairs, was neatly brushed. A commanding man, in a pin-striped suit with a silk bow tie like a large domesticated butterfly against his white shirt. "Do you always do business," he asked, "with your fingertips on a Bible?"

Henry laughed self-consciously. "It's a gift. From the past. I haven't decided where to put it yet." He gestured toward the sofa. "Won't you make yourself comfortable?"

"I'd like that," he replied, and lowered himself into a corner of the plush cushions.

Henry snapped the jewel box shut, set it on the coffee table between them, and then seated himself in the armchair at Stanton's right.

"I hope you don't mind," Stanton said, "but I'm accustomed to dealing primarily with owners or directors of things. You are—?" he left the question incomplete.

"Both," Henry answered.

"Splendid!" Stanton brought a silver case out of his breast pocket, offered a cigarette to his host, who lifted up an agate lighter from the table. The base of the lighter and the large milky blue agate ashtray on the table embodied Rio de Janeiro, those ten days of summer in Brazil during the winter of his tenth wedding anniversary.

"What can I do for you?" Henry asked.

Stanton smiled. "You can save me money. I need a gift for

a special friend this afternoon. I'd like to give her those earrings. But I wouldn't like to pay fifty thousand dollars for them. I've often found that one is able to pay somewhat less than the asking price if one deals with the man in charge— and if one offers cash."

Henry said, "There is the problem of accurate information for insurance purposes."

"That is the problem of the next owner—who can arrange for an objective estimate to be made, if she wants to handle it that way. But there must be no bill of sale, and I am to remain anonymous."

"I see."

"No record; just an exchange of goods for goods." He smiled. "I have found that there is sometimes mutual advantage in dealing with the man in charge. Cash is so—how should I put it?—fluid . . ."

Henry had met men like this before; they would buy and sell the air they breathed if there was profit in it. "You are—" he began, looking around for the calling card.

"Interested in a lower price."

"No. I meant . . . you're—"

"Ah, yes. I'm from New York. What brings me to New Haven occasionally is that I'm on the board of a southern New England utilities company, and—my special friend."

"How much of a saving did you have in mind? You realize, of course, that emeralds are the most fragile, the most costly, and the most difficult precious stone to obtain today."

Stanton regarded him with detachment as if to say, The *last* thing I'm interested in is a hard sell.

Henry smiled. He took a different tack. "Perhaps, I should put it another way: How much discretion are you in need of?"

"How well are you able to keep a secret?"

"Perfectly," Henry felt himself uncomfortable in answering, "as long as it doesn't hurt anyone."

Stanton laughed. "What others do not know—is as if it never occurred."

"The price of the earrings . . ."

"Let me offer you thirty-five thousand dollars—cash."

"Let's say forty-five thousand."

"Ah," Stanton sighed, "then it's forty thousand, is it?"

"Agreed."

"All right." His voice expressed no emotion. Stanton stood up and pulled out his billfold. He laid three ten-thousand- and two five-thousand-dollar bills next to the jewel box. Then he opened it, confirmed the contents with a nod of his head, and slipped the box into his right trouser pocket. "It has been a pleasure to do business with you."

In a peculiar way, Henry thought, he is trying to express some kind of enjoyment of me and not just satisfaction with himself. "Would you like a drink?" he asked. They were both standing now.

"Put the money away," Stanton said in a paternal manner. Then, shaking his head, "Thank you anyway. I must be going." He moved toward the door. "I can see myself out." Then he paused. "What a good-looking office, Mr. Warner. You must be very happy here." With his hand on the door- knob, he added, "Perhaps we will have occasion to 'exchange goods' again someday. Good-bye."

An impressive man. Forceful. Probably ruthless. Worldly, Henry thought, but without envy and without distaste. He gathered up the cash and placed it in his central desk drawer.

Mrs. Wicks brought in the copy for the Sunday newspaper ad—"You Eat The Apples And Not The Leaves" was the headline—which he read and approved. She stood there while he signed the few remaining items of his correspon- dence; just before she left with the folder in her hand, he said, "By the way, will you have Hopkins record the sale of the earrings he brought up here?"—taking an envelope from the drawer and placing bills in it—"for cash. Thirty-five thousand dollars. Buyer unknown." He handed her the envelope.

When she had gone, he took the remaining five-thousand-dollar bill out of the drawer and slipped it into his wallet.

Henry almost never took the elevator down. To descend the stairs meant to look through the glass walls of the stairwell for the sight of each floor: linens, then crystal and silver, porcelain, and then jewelry; he would fondle the thought of each as he passed them, slowly, as a collector of rare books might stroke the bindings of the treasures on his shelves, reminding and congratulating himself: This is my first edition of Hume; this is the full-morocco Byron; here is my elephant-folio Audubon. We are together in this. We complement each other. We care for each other. What Henry never ceased to marvel at was the inventiveness of the human spirit, the imagination. To think that the simplest, most basic necessities—a plate, a knife, a glass—could be transmuted into a work of art by the quality of the material, the craft of the designer, the sense of beauty of the decorator. That was the Midas touch of the mind. That was the purpose of life: to take the ordinary daily needs and means of fulfilling them and transform them into ends in themselves.

He nodded to the salesmen on the ground floor as he walked down the central aisle; he waved to Hopkins at the far wall, as he reached the front door. The doorway itself was a favorite conceit of his: the black marble pillars supporting a pediment broken in the baroque manner to enclose an urn in porphyry; but as if that weren't sport enough, for it obviously couldn't hold up a roof, there were no walls for it to appear to hold together either; it stood proud of the glass walls around it. Like a Japanese archway near the edge of a lake which says, by its merely being located there, Here is a frame; the view of the world that you see through it depends on how near or how far away you are, at what angle, and what you are looking for.

Kate Warner had had enough. By five thirty she was attacked by another migraine. She had wanted everything to go right, and for the most part it had, but she'd completely forgotten about the paper hangers. The breeze of the early June morning that had woken her filled her with joyous anticipation. She rose and dabbed drops of perfume on her cheeks and, silently, slipped into Henry's room, lifted a corner of the sheet that covered his body, and lay down next to him. He woke to the stroking of her fingers along his shoulder, his neck, his earlobe. His eyes still closed, he reached up and took her wrist into his hand. "What delicate bones you have," he said, "what bird bones." He felt her pulse through his thumb. "My caged wild bird," he whispered. "Don't wake up," she replied in a soothing voice. "You are dreaming. And into this sweet dream . . ."

"A little rain must fall." They both laughed. He opened his eyes. She covered them with the palm of her hand and nestled closer to his warm body. He pulled her closer to his naked body and he fondled her playfully until the pale filmy nightgown was a mist caught about her breasts. They made love, comfortably, carelessly, as only long-time lovers may do, knowing the doors are shut, the children not yet awake, old grudges closeted if not settled, the day's schedule planned in advance; without the desperate anxiety of imminent loss or the tentativeness of discovery, but with the fullness of good fortune and gratitude.

"What a marvelous way to start the day," he exclaimed.
"Happy Birthday, darling!"
He smiled; he kissed her passionately on the lips.
"I still love you," she said with mock amazement.

The family breakfast went off well, with the pretense that the children had forgotten what day it was; and then they all surprised Henry with their birthday presents. Even Jonathan was on time, although he was on vacation, and gave Henry a cigar cutter. Peggy presented him with a pale brown bowl she had made in ceramics class; it looked woven, from a distance, but up close it was a warp and woof of her little fingerprints. Gabriel gave him a crayon drawing of a smiley face as the sun making all the flowers smile. He was delighted; he hugged them each, even Jonathan, who was as big himself as Henry now, and lavished kisses upon Kate's brow. He was a head taller than she and whenever he kissed her on the forehead she felt it as a benediction. He would be back by six, he said.

Then there was a bad half-hour in the kitchen. The younger children were dilatory about making their lunch.

"Why do we have to go to school, when Johnny doesn't?" Peggy whined.

"Don't whine," Kate said. "He has to work a lot harder when he's in school, so he doesn't have to be there as long as you."

"Harder? Do you know how hard we have to work? Do you know we have to *memorize* our parts for the Pilgrim Pageant?"

"Yes. That part's hard. Gabriel, tuck your shirt in. Jonathan, do you ever stop eating?"

"All right with you if I take your car?"

"Where are you going?"

"I'd like to go to the club: play golf in the morning and swim in the afternoon."

"But you'll be home early, won't you? We are going to Dr. and Mrs. Connolley's for dinner this evening."

"Oh, don't do that to me!" he pleaded. "There's a new rock group at the Road Side and a bunch of us—"

"You've been home five days and you've been out three

nights. It didn't occur to me to ask you about tonight because I took it for granted you could put yourself out for your father's birthday."

"Put myself *in.*"

"Don't sulk. You're too old. Forget it. I'll see if Helen will stay; or I'll get a baby-sitter. Peggy, what the devil are you doing to the African violet?"

The nine-year-old girl was sitting on the edge of the sink with one arm supported on the hot-water faucet, leaning toward the window and fingering the leaves of one of the many plants on the glass shelves across the wide window.

"These leaves are different. They're tough but they're springy. Like a trampoline for an ant."

Kate felt an instant of beatification—You are exquisite, I adore you—but said quickly, "You are a poet. But did you ever hear of a poet who was late for school?"

"Where's the peanut butter?" Gabriel demanded, puffed up with frustration.

"You're looking right at it," Jonathan supplied. "A seven-year-old who can't find his own peanut butter'll probably starve to death."

"You're eating all the coffee cake!" was Gabriel's reply.

The Siamese cat came shooting in and leaped up onto the white formica table in the middle of the kitchen. The rust-colored cocker spaniel bounded in after it, yapping.

"Poor pussy," Peggy commiserated, jumping down from the sink.

"Poor Spanny," Gabriel said, reaching for the dog's tail.

"Poor *me,* goddamn it," Kate said, reaching out for the cat, who bounded down to the dog's back and springboarded from it off to the dining room in a flash, leaving the spaniel disconcerted, with Gabriel hugging his neck. "To hell with her," Gabriel said.

"You're talking about *my* cat," Peggy complained.

Jonathan laughed. Kate closed the door to the dining room.

"You will all leave," she said calmly. "I do not know if I will ever see you again. But it has not been only nice knowing you." The lunches were in paper bags; the smaller children were in red checked shirts and maroon overalls; the big boy was in a University of Michigan tee shirt and tan Bermuda shorts. All three of them wore sneakers. "Go with them to the road," their mother said to Jonathan. "The bus will be here any minute." In a day or two Jonathan would go off to Martha's Vineyard with friends of his for a sailing trip, in a few weeks the younger children would go off to summer camp in Maine. In about a minute I'll slit my throat, Kate thought.

"Good-bye, Mom," echoed twice and the three of them were out of the back door—precisely at the moment that the front doorbell rang.

Helen, the maid, very neat, always dressed in uniforms of her own choice, today looking like a nurse in white nylon and white shoes with thick rubber soles like gum erasers, stopped vacuuming in the living room and let the three painters into the front hall.

How could she have forgotten? Her own birthday present to Henry. They were here to paint the woodwork and put up the wallpaper in the front hall. It was nine o'clock. Could they finish by six? There had been so much secretiveness about it that she had deluded herself into being surprised as well. Last February, when she and Henry were in Paris for two weeks—he on a buying trip—they had visited a shop on the rue Jacob where he found sixteen rolls of hand-painted eighteenth-century wallpaper, a scene of British fox hunting as imagined by a French studio artist working in gouache: a slightly foggy morning in a great expanse of softly rolling hills of English countryside, pistachio green with a dawn of pink and azure, stallions at the gallop and foxhounds long and low to the ground, imaginary trees of overarching grandeur and the fox as swift and wily as he was terrified. Henry savored the possibility of it. He calculated that it would fit exactly the two walls of the entrance hall at home. He weighed the price, the freight, the customs duty, the difficulty of having it hung; he went back twice, but ended by deciding against it. He enjoyed himself enough with the porcelain and crystal makers he made wholesale arrangements with. It was with a childish glee that he would go off to the rue du Paradis in the mornings. Old colleagues, good business transactions without excess. Kate went back to the shop on the rue Jacob alone. She left a down payment and promised to send the rest of the money in a couple of weeks. The shipment had cleared customs; the painters had been engaged; the paper was hidden in her sewing room. Today was the day. And she had forgotten. She awoke in the morning thinking only of making love with her husband and dressing for dinner at Quentin and Ellen Connolley's that evening. But here they were, quite properly. And it meant moving the hall tables, putting down drop cloths, calculating the sequence, offering them coffee in mid-morning, beer to go with the lunches they had brought. It meant keeping the dog in the garage and the cat in Peggy's bedroom, reminding Helen that there was work to be done, that she was not to be simply the audience for the three workmen in the front hall during the day; it meant the noise. The waves of sounds they brought with them mounted and broke steadily, incessantly. They had each other to talk with and still they kept a transistor radio on the floor at their feet humming continually. They talked with each other the way old ladies in rocking chairs, who see each other every day, tell the same stories over and over again: "Did I ever tell you about the time . . ." and do not wait for an answer.

In Peggy's room, Kate found the dress she had worn yesterday as well as the pajamas of the night crumpled up at the foot of her bed. The cat nestled on them, with one paw on shriveled socks. Kate made the bed but left the clothes where they were. Gabriel had left his record player going. She went from one room to the next hardening her heart with anger.

Jonathan's suitcase lay open on the bench at the head of the bed, where he had left it five nights ago. Kate began to put things away: two shirts in a drawer, a pair of slacks on a hanger in the closet, and then she came upon a pornographic novel heavily illustrated with photographs of youths and girls in strenuous positions of sexual intercourse but not enjoying it. Their faces were uniformly impassive. What a way to make a living! She replaced the book, covered it with the slacks, brought the shirts back from the dresser, and left the room, thinking, At least they're normal. *Spoiled*—but normal. It wasn't much consolation; she wanted them better than that.

Helen brought into the spacious kitchen the clean clothes in a wicker basket from the laundry room and set up the ironing board. Kate began the dinner to be left for the children that evening. Helen talked; Helen chatted whether Kate was in the room with her, out in the pantry, over in the breakfast room. It didn't matter; she was content with an occasional "Uh huh" or "You don't say" or "Isn't that too bad." Helen had been their maid for six years—more a baby-sitter filling her time while the children were at school rehearsing to be a maid. But she was good with the small ones; she called herself "a skinny Mammy."

"Oh, Helen—" Kate interrupted, looking up from the casserole, "will you be able to stay tonight?" Helen hesitated; Helen ruminated about a cousin and a possible Bingo game and whether "you folks" might be early or late; Helen resisted.

"It's all right." Kate was brusque. "I'll make a few calls." Something else to waste time.

The painters needed attention. The woodwork was dry. They had finished their lunch. They were ready to put up the paper. In what sequence? Kate thought of the old joke about Michelangelo in the Sistine Chapel, looking up at the ceiling and saying to Julius II, "What color you want it, Pope?"

The gardener's truck swung into the driveway and

stopped in a clamor of dry brakes. Kate went out along the covered walkway between the kitchen and the garage. "Hello, Pete," she called. "How are you today?"

"Okay. How are things with you?"

"Hectic. Tell me—do you think your daughter could baby-sit for us this evening?"

"Lucy? Sure. I'll have to call her to make sure, but I think so."

"Oh, good. Come in when you'd like a cool drink and you can use the phone then." She waved and turned back to the kitchen. Henry allowed Pete to mow the lawns of their four acres, take care of the trees and the bushes, but he did all the gardening of the flower beds himself. "If you want an hour of complete solitude guaranteed," he would say, "all you have to do is ask your children if they'd like to weed with you."

In the warm air of the kitchen, Kate felt the presence of Helen bent over the iron more vividly than she actually saw her. I am surrounded by phantoms, she thought. Silhouettes. Abstractions. A maid. A gardener. Three painters. The cook was on vacation for the month of June. Cardboard characters. Every day spent in the company of people I do not choose to be with, whom I know only in the most superficial way. Could I even describe them? We make our transactions: goods for services; money for work rendered—and not always rendered well at that. All this *doing* just to keep fed and neat and clean, without any feeling for it or for the people involved in it. The thought began to stifle her as if she were trapped in a telephone booth and saw near her people who could not hear her voice when she'd suddenly found the door wouldn't open. She left the casserole unfinished, lit a cigarette, and walked through the dining room, then through the French doors out onto the flagstone terrace. She looked to the west. The clear blue sky was flawless; the lawn that Pete was mowing lay like a lime-green carpet from the house to the border of evergreens, elms, and birch that hid the nearest neighbor's house from view. New grape leaves were growing on the fences at each end of the tennis court. This island of beauty and peace—all bought at the price of turning into a phantom myself. Drained. Paled—like a snapshot left out in strong sunlight too long.

Where was the center where adult life took place? Not the endless series of trivial scenes, picking up or putting together or being helped out where only fragments of the self are used to carry out the actions and the gestures that you could do with one arm tied behind your back. Where were the times when you were all together—in Living Color—when you were at your best? She was aware that within a radius of ten miles from where she stood she could count on three good friends and twenty worthwhile acquaintances. But to get from the condition she was in to spend an hour with any one of them felt as if it required a passport and six hours on a jet plane. High above her head, she watched a silverfish of a plane chalk a trail across the clean sky.

"Foolishness," she said under her breath, dropped the cigarette into an ashtray, and returned to the kitchen to make a Bloody Mary.

The phone rang. Ellen Connolley wanted to confirm that they would arrive at seven, that Henry would wear black tie, and that a chocolate soufflé would, truly, be a permissible substitute for a birthday cake. She cheered up Kate. "Quentin is at the hospital delivering a dozen babies this afternoon and Raymond is cramming for an exam." He was a year older than Jonathan and a sophomore at Yale. He lived at home. "I tell you, Kate, if that boy doesn't get out of the house next year, *I'm* moving into the dorms." But, then, kittenish, "Do you think he has a mother fixation?"

"Not on you for a mother," she laughed. "Don't worry. He'll find an indecent woman who can make him happy."

The wallpaper hangers finished; the front hall was transformed: as if the walls had become windows for a vista of half a mile in both directions. They had been praised and tipped and waved good-bye to just at the time the little children, having gone to after-school play for an hour, got out of their bus and ran in through the kitchen door. Gabriel ran right out again to bother Pete. Peggy wanted to know where her Siamese cat—"Simey," of course—was. Helen let the dog out of the garage. Pete came in for a lemonade and Lucy would be able to baby-sit. "Chicken-shit," Kate muttered to herself, finishing up the children's dinner and putting it all in the refrigerator. "Chicken-shit!"

Peggy came back to the kitchen holding the cat in her arms. "Can I have an apple?"

"Of course!" Helen said while Kate's mouth was opening —although no answer had yet bubbled up to her mind.

"Mommy," she began, holding the cat in one arm and polishing the apple against her overalls with the other hand, "why does Simey catch mice if he doesn't eat them?"

"He doesn't need the food."

"Then why does he go after them?"

"It's an instinct. It's something a cat is born knowing how to do. We feed him and he likes the food he eats, but he still has that instinct. So every time he sees a mouse he goes after it *as if* he needed it, even though he doesn't."

"Is that what an instinct is?"

"I believe so."

"Too bad for the mice."

"But then, if we weren't able to take care of Simey and he had to become a wild cat, living on his own, he'd need that instinct to keep himself alive."

"Simey is not a *wild* cat." She hugged him and took a bite out of the apple at the same time.

"Right," said Kate, knowing when a conversation is over. "We're all domesticated animals here." She took half of the pile of ironed clothes, while Helen took the other half, and they carried them up the back stairs to each of the bedrooms.

Later, descending halfway down the front hall staircase, Kate caught sight of herself in the long thin mirror between the windows on the landing. Revolting, she thought: my suntan is fading; my hair is hanky; this navy jumper looks as if I'd been sleeping in it. "Mommy," Gabriel called, "what's going on here?"

He squatted cross-legged in the middle of the carpet of the hallway. "It's new wallpaper," she replied, descending the rest of the stairs. "But very delicate. You have to be extremely careful about it. It's a surprise for Daddy."

"Wow," said Gabriel.

She stared at him; he was the most fun of the lot. And the only one who looked like Henry. The others both looked like her. Naturally, Jonathan couldn't look like Henry. Gabriel appeared subdued.

"Did Pete tell you to leave him alone?"

"Yes."

"Are you unhappy?"

He looked up right into her face. "No." After a pause, he said, "You ask me that a lot. Sometimes I'm unhappy, and sometimes I'm happy; but most of the time I just am."

"Me too," said Kate, kneeling down and giving him a bear hug.

Without cat or apple in hand, Peggy came into the hallway. "What a difference!" she exclaimed. "It's *beautiful!*"

"It's a fox hunt," Gabriel shouted, bounding up from the floor, "and I got the fox!" His little hand slapped hard against the red and white creature running along the wall. Kate screamed and clapped her hands together. Both children look stunned. The fox was caged by an earthy handprint. "How dare you! You miserable—" Kate was gagged with outrage, "I just *told* you . . . Go to your room. You're grounded. I'll decide later whether you come down for dinner. Close your door. I don't want to see you!"

Peggy laughed at Gabriel, who was crestfallen, walking toward the stairs. Kate wheeled toward her. "And you're grounded too. How many times have I told you to put your clothes in the hamper? Do you know where your dress is? Do you know where your pajamas are?"

Peggy followed Gabriel up the stairs.

"I hate it. I hate the sight of you. I just hate it!" Kate shouted after them in her frustration.

First with a feather duster, then with a blunt knife, and finally with the use of "painter's soap," Kate removed the fingerprints. A faint crescent of the heel of Gabriel's palm remained intractable along the fox's belly. "I give up," she said quietly. "I'm through." The needles of a vicious headache started to pierce her brain, up from the nape of her neck up into her capacity to think. Prepared to suffer, she walked slowly into the large living room to see the golden balls of the clock turn under the bell jar on the mantelpiece and gently sound the signal for five thirty.

Henry parked his Mercedes alongside the gardener's truck in the driveway and walked past the front of the house toward where Peter was trimming the rose of Sharon trees between the high elms that concealed from view the house of the neighbor on the east. Henry Warner gazed at his own house as if to stroke it lovingly. His grandfather had built it. A classic red brick Georgian house, which his father painted white when he inherited it, and white it was repainted ever since. His father had destroyed the stables in 1920 to make space for the garages, and above them he had constructed a sitting room and a bedroom for his wife and himself, separating them from the rest of the house. The grandparents' master bedroom had been turned into a nursery-playroom for Henry and his brother.

Dogwood trees flourished in a wide semicircle along the walk to the front door. Henry talked with the gardener for a few minutes about fertilizer and seed for the grass and then made his way past the large screened-in porch around to the south side of the house, inhaling the acrid sweetness of the freshly mowed lawn. Up the three long stone steps, he mounted to the flagstone terrace that ran the length of the house and, stopping at the French doors to the living room, stared at the sight of his wife resting her head against the mantelpiece. Behind her, the grand piano stood open like a sheltering arm.

He studied her profile, thinking, She is a stunning woman. The word "stunning" had a much more valuable meaning for him than "beautiful"—for there was nothing about her face or figure that was merely pretty. But her appearance and the effect of her as a person were more than beautiful, in the way the Black Irish are handsome: sharply defined and strong-featured, with high cheekbones and an aquiline nose, long black wavy hair parted in the middle. She made him imagine a west country Irish noblewoman riding horses for miles along a beach where no one else ever appeared. Fierce in her pride. Fierce in her love for privacy. Fierce in her love of her family. She is, he realized, the only person I have ever known who does love herself without vanity.

He let himself in through the open door and approached her. She looked up and brought both of her hands to her cheeks as if to hide them. Her eyelids seemed heavy with sorrow. "What—what's the trouble?" he asked, sympathetic.

"I wish I were dead. I'm such a failure. This life . . ." she became speechless, holding her hands away from her with the gesture that proved there was nothing to grasp hold of. He stepped between her arms and caressed her; she rested her head against his chest. "I love you," he whispered, thinking, It is never as bad as she makes it sound. Still I love you for the exaggerations, for the hyperboles—everything in the extreme. This is why I married you: for this intensity. No one else has it as you do. Everyone else is on the outside pressing their noses against the window.

"It isn't enough," she said and then tried to laugh. Kate brought her hands up onto the flat of his back and pressed herself against him. You are the rock, she felt, and I am a balloon; and that love we speak of is the string that ties me —to what?—to life in the world. Otherwise, free-floating, weightless, I would drift off beyond the stars, disintegrate, disappear. She squeezed him affectionately.

"What happened?"

"I don't get what I want from the children and I don't know how to get it. I don't know what I should be doing. Whatever I *am* doing isn't good enough."

Henry kissed the top of her head but then through one of the archways of the living room his eye caught sight of an English hunter at a gallop astride a brown stallion in the front hallway. "My God!"

Kate followed his gaze. "The wallpaper."

"You didn't—!" he said, exulting.

"My birthday present to you. My big splurge for the year." They walked together slowly into the wide hall. He drank it all in as if breathing the purest air.

"I can't believe it." He took her hands in his and placed a kiss in each of her palms. "You *do* love me."

"It's not as if you doubted that."

"I don't know what to say."

"Tell me I'm not all bad."

He cocked his head and made a crooked smile. "Let's say, You're not *all* bad."

"Well, that's a start. I suppose I can get back to my job." She brushed her hair away from the sides of her face. "I had hoped to have my makeup on and be dressed when you arrived. I look a wreck. I need something for this headache. I thought you'd be later."

"I played only nine holes."

"Helen has to be driven to the bus stop, and Jonathan isn't back yet."

"I'll take her in my car."

"The other children are in jail." She was conscious that, by where she stood, she concealed the wounded fox. She would not tell him about it, yet. "I'll let them out and start their shower before I go to our rooms. Come up and see me sometime."

He nodded. Alone in the hallway he felt gilded by the reflected glory of the gift. The exceptional doubled value: not only that this thing of beauty should be his, here and now, and forever more, but that it came as a gift from on high, a favor, an answer to a prayer that he hadn't been aware of having prayed. That Kate knows me so well that she can choose to satisfy a desire when I hardly realized how much I lusted for it myself—that is a glory. He knew not which to extol more: his magnificent wife or this work of art. They were equally extraordinary; unique, unimaginable. He strolled up and back, from the entrance vestibule to the first step of the stairway, again and again. The tables that had stood between the arches on both sides of the hall were in the dining room. They would be too high now, they would cut off some of the landscape. We will use them somewhere else; no sacrifice. He walked back and forth. There was something that made him uneasy. The fox hunt began at the archway into the dining room, came past the arch to the little hall, then leaped across the entrance and ran along the living room walls toward the stairs where it ended with the fox. It should have been the other way, he thought; starting at the left of the entrance, running in the opposite direction, with the fox trying to get out of the front door. It didn't matter. He knew that he would never say a word about it to Kate.

It was better that there be some imperfection about it. The gods are jealous of too much happiness.

When he returned from the bus stop, Henry found Jonathan parking Kate's car in the driveway. "Hi!" he shouted. Jonathan came around and opened the door for him. "I was at the pool. I saw you at the fifth tee and waved, but you didn't see me."

"I was in solitary confinement. At least once a year I play a round by myself." They faced each other, a few feet apart.

Jonathan jerked his head up to throw the long dark bangs out of his eyes.

How good-looking he is, Henry thought. How lucky that he looks like his mother. There is not a single person in New Haven who has any reason to believe he is not my own son. It had been Kate's wish. She chose to remain in Manhattan until after the baby was born; he let out that the date of their wedding was earlier than it took place. No one had any suspicion, including Jonathan. At Kate's urging. Henry was unable to change Kate's mind when she was convinced of what would be good for the boy, which was not the case with the younger ones. He interpreted the strength of her protectiveness for him as expressing the special bond between a mother and her first child, rather than as possessive. He refused to imagine that she thought of Jonathan as "not *his,* too."

Henry gazed at the youth. How manly he had become. The undershirt he wore seemed merely a thin layer of white paint on his muscular chest; his legs were like sculpted pillars. A young stud, they're called nowadays, Henry thought.

"What are you doing this evening?"

"Going to the Road Side."

"That barn—out in Bethany?"

"Good dancing."

"And drinking?"

"Just beer."

Henry looked at Kate's white convertible. The top was down, the front fenders were filthy. "Did you drive through a dust storm?"

"I'll wash it down."

"That's a good boy." He was sorry for saying that; it sounded patronizing. The young man was too old for that. He slapped Jonathan on the back. "Do you have enough money?"

Jonathan smiled. "Never enough."

As they walked together along the covered area to the kitchen door, Henry handed him a twenty-dollar bill. "Don't tell your mother."

Lucy arrived, seventeen and nubile, hippy in tight blue jeans, and with long blond hair. She was given instructions about heating up the children's dinner. Kate was dressed in a forest-green evening gown, with thin shoulder straps, long and loose, gathered under her bosom, flowing; but she hadn't put on her makeup. Henry went up the back stairs to wash and change. Kate and he had taken the sitting room and bedroom of his parents and made them into two separate bedrooms. There was a central door between the two and they were also joined on both sides of that by the walk-through bathroom and the dressing room. Kate had chosen the inner room. "I will be your secret concubine," she said. It was the ultimate expression of their determination to respect each other's privacy. "In order to be One, at times," she had said, "let's make sure we are Two all the rest of the time." They had decorated their own bedrooms in their own ways: hers was light and cozy; his was dark and strong. What was lost or sacrificed by not sleeping together every night was made up for by the sense of freedom and newness in each coupling. Whether they made love in her bed or in his, they knew that they could retreat, retire, escape if they wanted to; neither one was "obliged" to make love, and when they did, they felt the secret charm of something slightly illicit, as if the absolute sanction that marriage was supposed to grant the desire for coupling was a danger that led to taking each other for granted, that led to boredom and to death by indifference. Kate had been given by her parents the old Socialists' touchstone, that nineteenth-century Russian novel *What Is to Be Done?* when she was sixteen; nothing in the women's liberation movement was new to her. But she knew of no other couple who had the good sense and the good fortune actually to practice the advice. Separate bedrooms meant that she was not merely a possession; and for him it had come to mean that he was a pirate who had the joy of living in a room next to his hoarded treasure.

In the Mercedes they sat beside each other, separated by the gear shift. "You look very handsome," she said. She liked to see him in black tie. It was true that he loved to dress up; Ellen Connolley knew that and insisted that for the dinner in honor of his birthday all of them would wear evening clothes.

"How's the headache?" he asked.

"Fading. Fading away. Oh, what a relief to get out of the house. You don't know how lucky you are."

"On the contrary. I do." He reached over and patted her hand. "I'm blessed." Her eyelids were now faintly taupe, accentuating her dark eyes, and there was a blush of suntan heightening her cheekbones; her black hair brushed back away from her face fell around her head in layers of waves.

She had pinned a pink tea rose to the cleft in her dark green
dress. She wore no jewelry. It was a peculiarity of hers. A way
of saying, Look at me and never think of what I own; the
rough edge of that thought was her refusal to be identified
as "the jeweler's wife." He had resented it at first but then
he learned what presents he could give her.

"Gabriel wanted to know if I really hated him or if we were
coming home tonight."

"Peggy told me she didn't want to go to camp."

"I didn't like the way Jonathan looked at Lucy."

They drove down the Ansonia Road toward the city.
"Promise me you won't drink too much," she said.

"I promise."

"You really don't hold liquor."

"I know."

"You get sleepy and sloppy; or you're hostile."

"I won't."

"Remember the other time there were just the Taylors
and us at the Connolleys' and you said, 'I'm the only man
here who didn't marry for money.'"

"Yes."

"That was a bad scene. These are our friends, and—"

Responding to the litany, as if in sacred congregation,
he concluded the injunction: "—and treat your friends as
you would your paintings; put them in their best light."

They laughed. "Oh, I'm so happy," she said, "that the wallpaper was a complete surprise."

"I adore you."

The Connolleys' house on Ellsworth Avenue looked like a Norman château. It had very little land around it, but neither the doctor nor his wife cared about gardening and he especially liked living only a fifteen-minute drive from the hospital. Huge mounds of azaleas in scarlet stood guard on either side of the entrance; otherwise there was only the green of the lawn and of the high hedges that surrounded the large house. The other houses along the avenue were equally large and impressive in their indifference to each other's architecture and in their self-sufficiency. Contiguous islands. Almost none of the owners knew any one of the other owners. All of the houses had been built in the heyday of the nineteen twenties and the Norman château was the pride of a Greek immigrant who had made a fortune in the first supermarkets in southern Connecticut. Ellen Connolley's parents bought it for them when Quentin, who had interned at Yale-New Haven Hospital, decided to settle there.

It was said of Ellen Connolley she was so ugly that she made a virtue of it. That was a little unfair. She stood in the open doorway, in a purple sari shot through with gold threads that formed themselves into griffins along the borders; on her bare arm she wore bracelets of beaten brass from India, and from her ears hung thin circles of gold along which little polished beads of rubies swung back and forth. She did have a lantern jaw and a prominent nose, but her large mouth was always so ready to laugh and her dark blue eyes were so often darting with merriment that she easily distracted one from the rather witch-like impression of her face in repose and drew people into a conspiracy to "be jolly" that endeared them to her. Her brindled hair was meant to be shaped like feathers about her skull, but she brushed it with a towel and once told her husband that she thought it looked as if she was wearing a bathing cap decorated with autumn leaves.

"You both look gorgeous!" she shouted as Kate and Henry came out of their car and approached her.

"If it isn't Madame Gandhi," Henry said, kissing her cheek.

"Happy Birthday, darling," Ellen replied. "You always smell deliciously like cinnamon and clove."

Kate stood at the top step for a moment, admiring the gown. "Ellen," she said, "your dress is magnificent."

"God sent India to protect a shapeless girl." They embraced. "Quentin's in the bird cage—creating drinks. He majored in chemistry you know." With one arm around each of them, she ushered the Warners down the hall, through the doctor's study, to the big enclosed porch. It did look like a bird cage, with glass jalousies on the three screened sides, turned horizontal now to let the breeze in. Six silent greenish-yellow parakeets fluttered about in the white wire cage shaped like the skeleton of the Taj Mahal suspended in the far corner. Quentin Connolley put the cocktail shaker down among the many-colored decanters on the glass table and held out his arms to Kate. His dinner shirt was ruffled like an eighteenth-century rake's. He was a broad, heavy man with white hair and a white beard trimmed neatly about his face, which made him look older than he was but at the same time created the impression that he was a latter-day Viking. He hugged her and hummed in her ear; he was reputed to be a ladies' man. But none of his friends knew if there was any truth in that. He shook Henry's hand with compassion. "Forty-nine," he said. "Welcome to the wake."

"At forty-nine," Henry made up on the spur of the moment, "Columbus hadn't yet discovered America."

"Right," Quentin replied. "And neither have you."

"Quentin's made manhattans," Ellen began, "but you can

have whatever you like. Except champagne; we'll have champagne at dinner."

"The Taylors are late," Quentin said.

"The Taylors are always late," Ellen added. "It's good to be able to count on certainties in life."

"Where's Raymond?" Kate asked.

"He used a marvelous expression," Quentin answered. "I asked him where he was going tonight and he said, 'Over to Jane Kelly's for dinner or something.' I really go for that 'or something.' Ah, they're so comfortable, the younger generation, about a little hanky pank."

"You're quaint," Ellen said. "He meant dinner—or supper."

A maid brought out a tray of hors d'oeuvres, offering them to each. "Hello, Margaret," Kate said familiarly. "How are you?"

"Fine, ma'am; Happy Birthday, Mister Warner."

"Why, thank you," he replied, sincerely. They had all known each other for years. Everything had been established and repeated for years. Drinking manhattans, the Warners and the Connolleys sat cushioned on the big resistant porch chairs, upholstered by images of magnolias with lacquered leaves.

Kate began, "I have a wonderful story to tell an obstetrician," drawing Quentin's attention. "I overheard Peggy and Gabriel having a conversation the other day about how babies are born. 'They don't grow in the stomach,' Peggy said. 'How do you know?' 'They come out between your legs.' Then Gabriel said, 'If they grew in your stomach they could come out your mouth.' 'Well,' Peggy said, 'that's how I know. If they came out your mouth, they wouldn't be delivered by a doctor. They'd be delivered by a dentist.'"

Under the laughter, Henry realized that Kate hadn't told him that story before. She had saved it for more of an audience. For the most appropriate audience. She was in her element. She was performing: making other people feel good. This is Kate, he thought, remembering how once Jonathan, when he was about thirteen, had asked his mother, after all the guests were gone from a garden party on their lawn one lovely summer afternoon, "How come you're so popular?" Smiling, Kate had answered, "I work at it."

"We meant to have the whole foursome tonight," Ellen said, "but I couldn't talk the Jackmans out of their cruise around the Greek islands." Henry played golf every Sunday morning with Quentin, Judge Jackman, and Conrad Taylor. Men make their connections in the world, Kate thought, then they introduce their wives and hope for the best. Kate thoroughly enjoyed Ellen, she thought Shelagh Jackman was a fool, and she found Conrad Taylor's new wife an enigma, a woman too vain and inconsequential to be happily married to a sickly older man, an intellectual with a caustic wit and crotchety habits.

"I must tell you," Ellen started, "what happened in the bookstore this morning. I went down to the Co-Op to buy that new book about whales, and I was looking around when an adorable young girl came in and asked if they had any old newspapers. She said she was training a puppy and needed a lot of newspapers. 'What kind of a dog is it?' this fey young man behind the counter asks. 'A French poodle.' 'Well, in that case,' he says, 'there are last Sunday's *New York Times*. I think he'd especially appreciate the Book Review Section.' And we all burst out laughing." Ellen did indeed have an infectious laugh and the four of them became raucous with the absurdity of it.

"Where do you come off enjoying yourselves?" Isabel Taylor asked. She stood in the farther doorway to the bird cage with Conrad indistinctly behind her.

"My darling!" Quentin barked out. "We have been drowning our sorrow for the lack of you." He leaped up and kissed her on both cheeks. "Come in. What would you like?"

Isabel was hostile and Conrad withdrawn. It was obvious they had been fighting. A most unlikely couple. Conrad Taylor came from St. Louis, by way of the University of Chicago. He had been brought to Yale to teach psychology but, early on, his talent for administration was recognized and he became Executive Vice-President for the College. He had lived for years in one of the "top management" houses on Hillhouse Avenue. His first wife was a harridan who deserted him for a Broadway producer. There was a difficult divorce and he was granted custody of their daughter, Caroline, a spiteful girl who turned out a mess, running away, taking drugs, bumming around the world. The latest incident the Warners had heard of her tawdry story was that, when she was in South Africa, she put through a collect telephone call to the President of Yale University, insisting that he tell her father to cable her more money. Conrad behaved as if he was so profoundly guilty toward her that she could do no wrong. Kate once said to Henry, "Of all the people in this world who don't know how to live, professional psychologists are the absolute worst." She cited other examples. She had a case.

Isabel was statuesque. Tall and well built with long blond hair pulled tight over her head and gathered into a smooth bun; three golden ringlets fell over each of her ears. She wore a white gown that cascaded down her powerful figure in layers, like enormous peony petals, fringed with a touch of pink. Around her neck hung a rope of pearls, and there were rings on almost every finger. Her sandals sported tiny bells on the thongs of the big toes. The Taylors had been married for three years. Conrad met her skiing at Aspen. That is, she was skiing. He was there to recuperate from the second or the third of the operations that removed half of his stomach. His ulcers were eating him alive. She had not been married before; she was in her late twenties, then, and had never known anything, after Vassar, other than playing expensive games around the world. Conrad was the only serious man she had ever met. She despised his daughter, who was only eight years younger than she. Isabel seemed to prowl around the house on Hillhouse Avenue and the rest of New Haven as a lioness might skulk through a museum after closing hours. She was caged but unappreciated.

Conrad was dressed in summer formal. When they first met, Isabel told him he reminded her of a movie actor, but she was too young to remember the name—Rudy Vallee. His wavy chestnut hair was combed back without a part; his bronzed complexion came from playing tennis every noon, but his teeth were too beautiful to be his own, and his heavy-lidded eyes bespoke a weariness that went beyond the labor of dealing with human beings. It appeared as if he were a successful man who had bought a pretty wife but, in fact, it was she who had inherited a great deal of money; he had nothing but his salary. She was vivacious and indiscreet; he was burdened and responsible.

"We are gathered together to celebrate Henry—" Ellen said, "a good man and true."

"God, spare us from that," Conrad drawled. His raspy intonation had been modeled years ago on W. C. Fields's throwaway lines.

"I've never known anyone luckier than you," Isabel said. Then she placed a kiss on Henry's cheek. It was her birthday gift. She had borne a grudge against him ever since the night he had got drunk and said something about Conrad's having married her for money.

The Taylors chose martinis to drink, and in the quiet moment as Quentin stirred the cocktails, the parakeets chirped indecipherable messages.

Ellen said, "We'll eat in a little while; but isn't the sunset lovely?" The azure of the west sky was streaked with layers of orange and lavender.

"Exquisite," Kate said. And Henry, weighing the tone invested in that one word, remembered why he had had to marry her. They were driving through Central Park in a taxi on the way to her apartment on a bleak October afternoon. The wind swished the trees up and down. "See," Kate said, "how, when the dark green leaves are lifted up, the undersides are all silver." He saw that. And he saw Kate as a diviner, a seer, as a carrier of life, as one who would infect him with the intensity of life. Her first husband was dead and she carried his child, but Henry would protect her; he would save her from loneliness and hardship and sorrow, and she would rescue him from purposelessness and superficiality. She was so independent a woman. She didn't need him, and that made him want to insinuate himself into her life. Given her strength and his strength, what could they not do together?

Conrad began a story. "One of the greatest physicists at Yale told me a tale the other day about an experience in Japan. He had been invited to lecture at the University of Tokyo. He always feels the need to go to the men's room just before he delivers a lecture. Four minutes before he was due to begin, he asked his guide where he could relieve himself, and he was discouraged. But he was persistent and, with two minutes to go, he was in one of those Japanese privies, without a seat, squatting like a frog, when he discovered that there was no toilet paper."

In chorus, Ellen and Isabel said, "Yuck!"

"What he saw before him was an artificial flower and that gave him pause; he contemplated how the leaves might feel, but he decided against them. The only paper he had on him were his lecture notes; so he took them out, scanned them, and used them for the immediate purpose. He says he gave the most inspired lecture of his career."

"Aren't academics brilliant?" Isabel asked over the laughter.

Kate felt how remote Conrad and Isabel must be from each other. She offered: "My mother would say, 'That's what you get for becoming a great physicist?' "

Yes, she thought, that *is* what my mother would say, but without the humor now. There used to be wonderful spirits and good-humored laughter in the home of her childhood, despite the earnestness of those two old Socialists, but the past decades had embittered both of Kate's parents, her mother even more so than her father.

"How is your mother?" Ellen asked.

"Sour," Kate said sadly.

Her father was a high-school teacher of modern history who achieved the distinction of running for the Lieutenant Governorship of New York on the Socialist Party ticket of 1938. When he was a young man, he had met Eugene V. Debs. Clarence Darrow befriended him. Norman Thomas, of course, visited occasionally in their house in Brooklyn Heights. Her father was a true visionary and a true fighter. But during the McCarthy period he was accused of being a crypto-Communist and was blacklisted. He had a stroke and lay half-paralyzed in his bed or in his wheelchair all the time. At sixty-seven he looked to Kate as if he were a hundred. Abandoned, not so much by old comrades—although certainly all of them were gone—as by every reason for living. Kate's mother was a nursery-school teacher. She had worked hard all her life and she would work through the coming year, at the end of which she must accept retirement at sixty-five. Henry had helped them out with exceptional medical bills, but her mother refused to take any money at all for daily expenses. Kate imagined that, when her mother was forced to retire, she would somehow have the courage to let her father die and then do away with herself.

"Speaking of Japan," Quentin said, "I had a peculiar experience in New York last week. I was at a medical convention and stayed overnight at the Algonquin—you know, not far from Grand Central. Got back there close to midnight and thought I'd have a nightcap in the little bar. The place holds only about twenty-five people. I took the last seat at a table and realized I was the only Occidental in the room. There were Japanese tourists and Japanese businessmen. The bartender and I caught each other's eye in disbelief."

Isabel Taylor said peevishly, "That war was over about thirty years ago."

"I haven't got to the point of the story yet," Quentin continued. "There was one narrow stool seat left at the end of the bar when a very Pukka-sahib-looking fellow walked in, portly, gray-haired, you know—Harvard 'thirty-three; he squeezed himself into the seat. Then he asked the Japanese next to him, 'Where are you from?' I don't remember the answer, Kyoto or Osaka. But the Harvard 'thirty-three then spoke in Japanese and—would you believe it—the Japanese answered him only in English; and that's how the conversation went on. They wouldn't speak Japanese and he wouldn't speak English."

"That's mildly amusing," Conrad drawled; he sounded as if he were grading a student's paper.

"What's new with Caroline?" Kate asked.

Conrad said, "She's living on an Indian reservation in New Mexico. How about Jonathan?"

"He'd like to ask you about a summer job at Yale," Henry said.

Conrad shook his head pessimistically. "Well, have him come talk with me." He shrugged his shoulders.

Ellen was still thinking about the Japanese in New York. "Lots of things have changed . . ." she said. She thought of an example: "Do you remember white gloves? I think for the first twenty years of my life my mother wouldn't let me do anything but take a bath without white gloves on." She tickled them all with her inviting laugh. "Now, when was the last time you wore white gloves?"

"Yes," Henry said quietly. "Many things have changed a lot."

"What are you thinking of?" Quentin asked.

"Middle age."

Conrad tried to wave it away with the hand holding his martini and spilled a little of it. "Oh, don't do that to us."

"Why not?" Kate asked. Henry may be suffering something, wanting to say something serious; it's his birthday, and we don't know what might be bothering him.

"Never mind."

"Tell us about middle age," Isabel said, as an earthling, curious about men from Mars.

"Middle age, my kitten," Henry addressed her, "is when one celery seed can ruin the rest of the dinner party for you because it is caught under your upper partial plate."

"Well, at last: there is a practical definition for the medical books," Quentin said.

We do not want to know each other, Kate felt. We do not want to know too much about each other. We want only to be amused, to be entertained. We will ask about each other's children, about each other's parents, about the dogs, or the golf game, or how "things" are going. But if we are troubled, would we be there for each other? She whispered to Henry, "You are a rock."

"What else has changed, Henry?" Conrad tried to redeem himself. "You've lived nearly as long as I have. What would you say has been the *greatest* change in the world that you've experienced on your gallop toward middle age?"

There was a respectful pause. One of Isabel's sandals jingled its tiny bell as she crossed her legs.

Henry said, "Charge accounts."

"Charge accounts?!" Ellen hooted with laughter.

"I am perfectly serious," said Henry, drawing himself up meditatively; he was preparing to deliver a speech. Quentin poured a new round of drinks for each of the guests. "I say, without hesitation, that the greatest single change in my lifetime is the proliferation of charge accounts. There are some of you," he pointed at Isabel with his slightly tilted glass, "who have never known a world without charge accounts, who cannot imagine a world without charge accounts. But you must believe me—that is the way it used to be, up to the nineteen forties. Even today, difficult as it is to believe, in most of the world other than Europe and the United States, people still have to pay for what they take, then and there, barter or hard cash. The concept of 'charging' and paying for it later has not yet taken root. But here it has—and in Canada—" he added graciously, nodding toward the darkening sunset, "and in a few spots of former British colonies about the globe."

"And why is that?" Kate asked, like a straight man feeding the next line to the raconteur.

"Because it is a substitute for religion," Henry said immediately. "Where the world has become secular, people have to trust each other as formerly they had trusted only priests and princes and divine powers. It is the ultimate victory of secularization. Our faith is in each other—that our word is as good as our bond; that all promises will be fulfilled sometime in the future. It takes up the slack in our loss of faith in anything imaginary."

"Not all of us have lost faith . . ." Ellen supplied.

Quentin corrected her casually. "We're only nominally Catholic."

"But it's nice to have in reserve," she replied.

Gently, Henry said, "For when you lose faith in other people."

"But I will tell you of the other side of that coin," Conrad said. "I see it in the students now. Where trust, faith, good will predominate there is no healthy skepticism. They take everything at face value. That's what's wrong: the passivity of good faith. They don't know what questions to ask because they can't imagine that anyone would try to take them in, or pull a fast one on them."

"But a student entering Yale," Kate said ironically, "is

opening the most valuable of charge accounts."

Only Isabel laughed. Conrad said, "Well taken. But very dangerous. I don't think it's desirable to assume the worst, any more than it is to assume the best. Not everyone is out for everyone else's well being."

"In the world that we live in . . ." Henry tried to begin. But night had fallen; Margaret stood in the doorway. Quentin lit the candles standing among the decanters on the glass table, and Ellen said pleasantly, "Let us go in to dinner."

Jonathan drove out past the golf course and turned northeast toward Bethany. The top was down, the air was mild. The darkening sky began to cloud up with filmy lengths of gauze. He checked the dashboard as the car approached the last gas station on the Rock Road. There was enough; he didn't stop. At the "Deer Crossing" sign he turned the car onto the narrow dirt road, switched off the radio, and listened to the trees waving in the breeze. He felt polished—like an apple for the teacher. He had luxuriated in a shower; he was dressed in freshly ironed faded blue jeans and a knitted white sport shirt with a royal-blue stripe around the open collar; he felt healthy. The high trees were thick with leaves above his head. There was no street light along this road. The nightclub was located about a mile ahead. It was a rough road and he drove carefully. Another car approached. He veered off and rode with two wheels raised along the bumpy high-grassed shoulder until it passed him. Soon enough he was there, facing the crudely painted sign: THE ROAD SIDE / Drinks / Live Music / Discotheque. He pulled into the dirt parking lot past the one lamp post. There must have been at least forty other cars there already. What a hideout, he thought. In the middle of no place. It literally was a barn. Probably had been a barn for a hundred years. Now it was strung with a line of yellow and green bulbs that marked the outlines of the weathered walls. Alternately yellow and green; they flickered on and off. First yellow and then green. Again and again.

Inside it felt huge. Dark. Just light enough to make your way to the long bar at one end, to make out the dancers in the middle of the floor; "and to make out," he thought to himself. He wanted to get laid. He hadn't had any action since he'd left Ann Arbor. He picked up a draught beer in a glass stein and began to move slowly among the crowd along the wall, casing them and the dancers in the center of the barn. He recognized a few old acquaintances. He smiled at Jane Kelly who was dancing. There was Charlie Ryden at the jukebox; they'd gone to Roger Sherman together. He punched him on the arm. "How's it goin'?"

"Okay," was the reply.

"Same here," Jonathan said. He didn't want conversation. He strolled up to the group on the bandstand at the far corner. The strobe lights went on and off as if there were three or four photographers taking their pictures in slow motion. An electric guitar, a drummer, a sax were young men with long blond hair; the guitarist was a girl with red hair who doubled as the vocalist. All of them wore black leather overalls and nothing else. Their arms and shoulders were bare, and so were their feet.The girl sang:

> If you don't love her,
> You better let her know;
> If you don't love her,
> You better let her go . . .

Jonathan felt the beer radiating through him, warming him. He would take his time. Turning his back to the combo, he studied the crowd. Lots of moustaches and black beards. Indian headbands. Some crew cuts. The girls' hair was long and loose—swaying, like seaweed. A lot of the guys looked skinny to him and many of the girls were too broad in the butt. They moved to this particular song like sleep walkers, swaying, pausing. Not touching. Cruising. Feeling each other out. Some had arrived there as couples who would leave with each other, but most of them were single, on the loose, wanting to make a new connection. Jonathan put the empty stein on the bandstand and stepped between a tall young man with a droopy moustache and a blond girl who might have been Lucy's sister, a little older and with a pouty mouth. "Mind?" he asked. "Go ahead," was the answer. The youth with the moustache sort of saluted her "So long." He looked tired.

They swayed opposite each other, like underwater creatures. She never changed her expression. The dancers all around them moved their arms and legs and svelte torsos as if they were each listening to their own music, solitary, unique, and yet sharing in some ancient ritual, some unspoken, unnamed ceremony. It was over. The live group took a break. The jukebox was turned on. Sergio Mendes and Brazil '66. He stood still with his hands on his hips; he jerked the dark hair out of his eyes. He stood tall. "Want a drink?"

"No," she said and turned away from him. She was gone.

Back at the long bar Jonathan slowly drank another beer. The dancers rearranged themselves with different partners. The air in the barn began to feel hot to him. Is there any ventilation? He went to the men's room. It was lighted by a pink circle of neon on the ceiling. On the wall above the urinal the graffiti read: "Want to make it a threesome with my chick?" There was a phone number under that one. "Ever suck?" "I just came in my pants." And at the bottom someone had inscribed, in small block letters: "I don't do anything." Jonathan laughed, backed up, and slipped his limp penis into the tight jeans, pointed upward toward his left hip. He was pleased that he he hadn't worn any underwear. He was pleased that he was a young dude. He liked himself. He liked the scene. He went back and danced. Hard and indifferent. And then slow and cool. With a different girl for each song. A barn dance! he thought to himself; this is the way it's always been in these four walls. Why, a hundred years ago the farm kids probably came here to sight out each other, go up in the haystacks, and have a ball. He felt the scene as if it were an orgy where you could change partners and make out with one broad after another all night long. He took a deep breath and threw his head back; his arms were jerking away from his sides, on the balls of his feet he was gliding back and forth, his shoulders swayed. The live combo was at it again, this time with rock. The girl before him had honey-colored hair tied in a pony tail that swung back and forth behind her head. She smiled a knowing smile with lips painted bright red.

The music changed. They put their arms around each other. Slow. A Burt Bacharach. The girl singer whispered into the microphone: ". . . one less egg to fry . . ."

His partner smelled sweet. He saw the glow of the strobe lights on the film of sweat, like nail polish, along her left shoulder; he felt the coolness of his own sweat on his high cheekbones. I wonder how it would taste to lick off her sweat, he thought.

"Dancing like this always give you a hard-on?" she asked.

He was suddenly conscious of her hip pressing against his erection. It burgeoned up toward his stomach. "Like it?"

"Some sausage!" she said.

"I think of it more as a lead pipe."

She was thin. She wore a halter like two sharp pointed white mountains that covered her chest and tied together behind her neck. Her back was naked. Her skirt was a blue and white plaid. Slick. He could feel her thighs through the light skirt; he flexed his thigh muscles against hers.

"Powerful!" she said, and slid her right hand between

them to stroke his hard-on. "I've got to get to know you better."

She was not exactly his type, he realized; older than he. An oval face. A high forehead. A turned-up nose and big brown eyes with long eyelids carved out of the deep sockets. She tilted her head back to look at him, her eyelids half-closed. "Bedroom eyes," he said.

"Got a bedroom?" she asked.

"Let's have a drink."

Standing at the bar, she fingered his shirt. "Nice stuff. What do you do?"

"I'm in college. Michigan."

"What are you doing here?"

"My folks live in Woodbridge."

"Hummm," she whispered appreciatively.

"You from here?" he asked.

"I'm from Philadelphia. But I haven't lived there in eight years." Eight years ago he was eleven years old, Jonathan thought. "Went to Barnard and Columbia." From along the bar rail he slipped his arm behind her. His fingertips began to play along the moist flesh over the bones of her spine. She stood still. Inviting. "I'm a researcher at Chamberlain Electronics. You know it?"

"Sure." They sipped the beers slowly, staring at each other's eyes. The lower half of her body began to sway almost imperceptibly, as though her pelvis had a mind of its own. "So you're a scientist! You must eat well."

"I'd like to eat you." He felt the surprise touch him like an electric shock.

"What's your name?"

"Joan," she answered. "Joan Rohan."

He burst out laughing. She slapped him in the ribs. "What's so funny?"

"You are a poem. Joan Rohan. You rhyme."

"Knock it off. What's your name?"

"Johnny."

"Johnny what?"

"Warner. You come here with anybody?" he asked.

"My roommate has her own car."

"I'll drive you home," he said, taking over.

"Maybe. What'll you give me for it?"

"A sausage."

"What else?"

"A joint," he said quietly. "Like to smoke grass?"

"Sure," she answered casually, as if to say, "Kid's stuff."

They left the half-full beer steins on the bar and elbowed their way toward the exit. She picked up her handbag from one of the other girls on the way. The night seemed surprisingly cool and not all that dark to them coming out of the barn. With an arm around each other they walked into the parking lot. In front of Kate's car, she pulled the pony tail up onto the top of her head with both hands and said with mock awe, "Jesus Christ! A white convertible. Swank!"

I've scored, he thought. This is going to be a good night. "You get into the back seat," he said.

"Why?" she asked as she did it. The dark seat cover felt lush to her touch.

"You take your clothes off," he was already turning the key in the ignition, "while I zoom the hell out of here." The tires screeched on a patch of gravel as he backed the car out and he drove past the barn, through the pool of light from the one lamp post, onto the dirt road. In a moment they were out of sight of the flickering yellow and green bulbs. He drove the car fairly fast past an orchard and a pasture on one side and woods along the other side, knowing that they were coming close to a dead-end cut-off. He found it and swerved to the right and drove along the rutted spur of the derelict road to a gradual stop in a round clearing surrounded by tall woods; he switched the radio on and the car lights off. Gladys Knight sang to them. The thick clouds concealed the moon. The night air was cool. His eyes slowly adjusted to the darkness.

Jonathan turned around to see the girl lying naked along the back seat. The halter, sandals, pocketbook, skirt, and a half-slip were on the floor. One hand covered her pubic hair; she was sucking the thumb of her other hand—until he looked at her, and then she laughed out loud. "Baby wants a lollypop," she said.

"How about an all-day sucker?" He flung himself over the back of the driver's seat and took her in his arms. The warmth of beer and saliva mingled in the wetness of their kiss. She clenched her teeth. He ran his tongue along the inside of her upper lip and of her lower lip, then she opened her mouth, and their tongues caressed each other. His heart pounded; his groin pounded with the pressure of his erection. But this was a special thrill in itself: she all naked and he still dressed. He fondled her breasts, slid his head down over her stomach, stroked her thighs; he felt the movements of her fingers through the sportshirt on his back. She began to lift it up along the sides of his upper body. Then she slipped both hands under his shirt and pressured her fingers up and down the hardness of his chest.

His right hand slipped between her legs and his fingertips came to play there. With everything that makes this safe, he wondered, why is it that I feel a sense of danger? Or is some kind of fear at the heart of the excitement and it never goes away? What is the danger? Consenting adults. A private place. A pill against pregnancy. A pill against V.D. For all the times I've done this why should it be that both the thrill and the danger increase? The miracle: the weight, the resistance, the response of this thin creature. I could pick her up and carry her around under one arm, he thought. But locked together like this, I feel she might destroy me. Why should that be? Because she is a stranger? But even with girls I know . . . He struggled to remember her name.

"Joan," he said. His tongue traced the outline of her ear.

"Johnny?"

Slowly and sincerely, he voiced the formula, the catchword, "You're beautiful!" His tone full of marvel and desire and hope. It always worked. It was the equivalent to what, in earlier generations, had been the value of saying, "I love you," or, at a still earlier time, what "I want to marry you," had meant. It was the sanction for license.

"Really?" she wondered, touched, reassured, haloed.

His eyes were barely open. He saw the upturned nose, the large-lidded eyes. "You *are* beautiful," he repeated. He had paid the fee. It didn't matter what he thought of her looks. He would have said the same thing if there were warts on her nose but he wanted to make love to her. It was all part of having a good time. He closed his eyes. He smelled the sweet perfume in her hair. She broke open the button and the zipper that restrained his penis. He lifted himself up slightly and she pulled his blue jeans down to his knees. They twisted their bodies simultaneously: she lay on her back and he hovered over her on his knees and hands.

"Fuck me!" she commanded. He felt as if he was glistening in the darkness from the film of sweat that slicked over him. He held her, now, with one hand behind her neck and the other in the small of her back helping her rise to meet him. "Goddamn it!" he said, as he felt the uncontrollable cascade of orgasm coursing through him, "I've got to come!"

"No," she whispered. "Hold on!" But it was too late. He shot in spasms that wrenched his body, shook him, exhausted themselves through him, until he collapsed on her, spent. His dark hair seemed to cover half his face. They felt glued together. They rested until he stopped panting.

"Too soon," she said, flatly. "I didn't come."

They separated and sat up, side by side. "I'll make it up to you. The night is young." He jerked the hair away from his eyes.

She crossed her legs and looked up at the darkness.

"Where's the pot? Or did you just make that up?"

"No. No. I've got it." His shirt was tucked up around his chest, his blue jeans fell down to his sneakers, as he leaned over the front seat and opened the glove compartment. Out of it he brought an object his father had given him for a Christmas present once: two small old French leather-bound books sewn together and hollowed out. When the front cover of the top book was opened it revealed a rectangle lined with a smooth red fabric—a hiding place, a secret compartment. That was where he kept the Acapulco Gold. He handed one of the joints to Joan and took one for himself. He started them burning from the cigarette lighter on the dashboard. They inhaled. "Ah . . ." they both said together, satisfied, relaxed. "This is the real thing," he said.

"I know the real thing when I see it," she said.

"I need about seven minutes for recovery time," he said. "The next turn is yours." They inhaled long and slowly in silence, she naked and he disheveled, side by side on the back seat.

"I feel like a bird," she said up into the circle of trees around them.

At length, he said, "I feel like a fish."

They smoked another joint each. They remembered the beer and heavy rhythm of the rock group at the night club. He turned up the volume on the car radio. They were undersea creatures wavering again to a swinging beat. He stroked her flesh, objectively, as an admiring spectator. She licked at the nostrils of his nose, his earlobes, his chin. "You ever sniff a popper?" she asked.

"No. But I'd like to."

"Wait a sec," she said, groveling on the floor to find her handbag and then to bring out a twig, a skinny stick, an inch or so long, covered in something like burlap. She snapped it under his nose for him to breathe in, then brought it to her own to inhale. He felt lifted up off the seat, he was floating.

He felt light as air. He stood up. He pulled his pants up loosely around his hips and stepped over the front seat. "Let's fly!" he said, slipping down into the front seat. "No lights," she said, "until I put some clothes on."

"What the hell for?" He reached behind him and clutched the half-slip out of her hands. "I'm only taking you someplace else to do it again."

But he didn't turn on the headlights. He felt sure of the route: round the circle, down the rough spur, left along the dirt road toward the night club, straight toward Rock Road. She was trying to put her clothes on. They passed the Road Side with its yellow and green lights winking. They were in the dark again. Jonathan made the car veer from one side to the other, curving the route back and forth. Every time she tried to lean opposite the curve, he threw her back against the seat by turning to the other side. She laughed loudly. They saw a shadowy object almost leap up at them from the shoulder of the road. The left front fender hit it head-on. The impact was much stronger than he had expected from a shadow. And the left rear wheel reared high and moved heavily over it; the car came down with a thump off the grassy shoulder. "Might have been a deer," he said, without slowing or stopping. He looked back. Joan had her skirt and the top on now and she climbed over the front seat and sat next to him. They were approaching Rock Road. "Why the hell don't you put on the lights?" she asked, dreamily.

They drove in silence, past the gas station along the main road, listening to the sounds of Aretha Franklin crooning out of the car radio. Down away from Bethany, into Woodbridge, toward the Country Club. Jonathan knew exactly where he was going. There was a thin dirt road off the highway that ran between the eleventh and the twelfth holes—Brook Road—without a house within three miles. He parked the car between the eleventh green and the twelfth tee. Eden. The clouds broke and there was a pale milky moon to light the fairways and the heavy trees, the dirt road and the dusty convertible. "Come on out," he said, leaving the car, with the keys in his hand. He opened the trunk and took out a soft large blanket. "You're going to screw me on a goddamned golf course," she said, standing up on the front seat.

"Right!" he shouted. Self-assured, in the uninhabited acres, on his father's golf course. He spread the blanket out on the eleventh green, laughing quietly to himself, swaying. Finally he said, "I've always wanted to make a hole in one right here."

"Where is that cock?" she asked.

"So you're not just dirty talk," he said.

"I mean what I say."

"Suck!"

Later, he could not recollect what else they had done except that this time she did come.

When he lay on his side along the length of her body, stroking her affectionately, she said, "Anytime, baby; anytime!"

"You are the greatest."

He forced his eyes open to look around. He was suddenly aware of the faucet and the short hose at the twelfth tee just across the narrow road. He had promised to wash down the car. "There's something I have to do," he said and he lurched up and staggered across the road. He turned the knob and the water began to flow. Players washed their golf balls and the heads of their irons here. The water gushed out around his naked feet. He pointed the hose at the front of the car and, by varying his finger grip on the nozzle, found a way to spray the stream of water far enough to hit the hood of the convertible, the fenders and the front bumper.

"What the hell are you doing?" she shouted.

"I'm peeing," he said and he laughed. Then he turned off the water and looked around for something to wipe the car down with. On the front seat he found Jane's slip, grabbed it, and started to shine up the frame and the chrome and the grill.

"You are a son of a bitch," she said.

"I'll buy you a new slip," he replied.

"You bet your ass you will!"

At length, they dressed and put the blanket back. He drove her home. They both felt numb. She lived in an apartment house of yellow brick on Crown Street, not far from the Green.

"Want me to see you to your door?" he asked. He was glazed.

"Forget it," she answered. She pulled herself together, got out of the car, and walked around to where he remained seated. "You ever drop acid?" she asked. "Not yet," he answered.

"When will I see you again?"

Jonathan thought for a moment. "I'm going away for a week or so. I'll come around when I get back."

She leaned against the car door, staring at him. "Call me at work," she said.

"Swell," he said. She held her handbag in one hand and the wet slip in the other. He thought she looked lanky.

"I really don't know anything about you," she said.

"Except what counts!" he replied with a smile, content.

Heavily, the six of them sat at the Connolleys' long dining room table as the last of the dessert dishes were removed. "Is it over?" Henry asked with a sigh.

"What a superb dinner!" Kate offered that exclamation to Ellen as if handing her a bouquet.

"Not at all," Quentin answered Henry heartily, rising, and

dropping his napkin onto the table. "We'll have after-dinner drinks in the living room. Come." They rose, taking deep breaths, moving slowly. Ellen put her arm around Henry's waist as they walked together. "What funny conversations we have," she said appreciatively.

The living room was two stories high, with rough stone walls sectioned and framed, as the wooden ceiling was, with broad oak beams. On two sides of the room an iron grillwork balcony ran along the hall to the bedrooms. The light was soft; Ellen was given to large lampshades of silk in a hue of sandy tan that complemented the walls. The big fireplace was bare. The brass poker and prongs and broom stood in a brass holder at the corner of the dark opening, but the fire-screen and the log holders had been removed for the summer. Quentin had set up the silver tray with brandy and liqueurs on a folding table in front of the fireplace. He served.

Ellen and Conrad sat together on one of the black leather sofas, opposite Isabel and Kate on a twin sofa. There was a smaller love seat covered in tan velvet directly facing the fireplace, making a cozy square area in the middle of the large room. Henry sat there looking around at the marvelous pictures on the walls: Rouault, Dufy, Matisse, Max Ernst, Klee. Ellen had been collecting for years. But their most exceptional possession hung above the mantel of the fireplace. The Connolleys owned a Rembrandt. And it was not Ellen's. Quentin had brought it back with him from Germany. He had been in the Army during the Second World War.

"Come, come, now," Quentin said, "you can't expect me to share that little seat with Henry." They rearranged themselves. Kate moved to be next to her husband. Quentin made himself comfortable alongside of Isabel. "To your good health!" he toasted Henry.

Henry smiled. He wanted to share something private with all of them. He gazed up at the Rembrandt. The old man of the oil portrait looked out, as through a dark-framed window, staring straight over Henry's head, self-contained. A golden light brightened one side of the wrinkled face. His eyes seemed to say, I have done all I could. "The most remarkable thing about Rembrandt," Henry began, "is that he left absolutely no records. And nobody who knew him ever did either. Of course, there's the official account of his bankruptcy trial. But that's all. There isn't one single letter. Rubens wrote about three thousand letters."

"Not even a postcard?" Isabel asked.

"You'd expect, at least, a note to Saskia," Henry chuckled. "Something like, 'The weather's foul. I can't get the laundry done . . .' But not even that."

Ellen asked, "What about his apprentices?"

"That's the extraordinary thing. He had about a dozen young painters a year working in his studio. Not one of them left a word about him."

"Maybe nobody understood him," Conrad drawled.

"What about all the novels . . . ?" Quentin asked.

"Pure romantic make-believe. The truth is that there's not one shred of evidence of what he was like, what he thought or cared about—in effect, who he was. He sure as hell didn't give a damn about what posterity thought of him."

Kate angled herself into the corner of the love seat in order to face her husband fully. You probably should have continued in graduate school, she thought. "Do you regret not having become a professor of art history?" she asked.

He lifted her hand from the cushion to his lips. "I regret nothing." He smiled.

"That would be the ideal life," Isabel said. "To regret nothing."

"You mean you wouldn't have it otherwise," Ellen said, and then, she turned to her husband. "What would you have become, if you hadn't been a doctor?"

"I went through my adolescence thinking I wanted to be

a professional Army man—a general. But the actual experience of a war ruined my taste for the military life."

Isabel shuddered. The others laughed sympathetically. Henry moved around offering cigars to the two men. He lit them and then one for himself as he sat back again. The ashtrays on the end tables were silver leaves resting on silver acorns. They had been bought at Warner and Son.

Isabel looked up at the Rembrandt for an instant and then turned to confront Quentin. "Did you *really* steal it?"

He flinched. "Don't say 'steal,' my dear. I 'liberated' it. Remember it was a special time. An awful lot of that sort of thing was going on."

Henry thought of Kate's criticism of his own behavior when he'd had too much to drink. "We all know each other at our worst," he said, lightly.

"Then why do we forgive each other?" Conrad asked looking at Isabel. He coughed on his cigar smoke.

"Well, how many people do we know . . . ?" Henry replied. "If you didn't forgive everybody, you'd be a hermit."

Kate disagreed but said nothing. "This time you've chosen a dilettante," her mother told her after she'd introduced Henry to her. "Last time it was a proletarian opportunist. This one is a capitalist dilettante." If she had listened to her mother she would never have married. No one would ever have been good enough.

Conrad continued to cough. Ellen said, "I'll get you a glass of water," and went out of the room. The purple sari billowed around her.

"So then the war was the turning point of your life," Isabel said to Quentin.

"I suppose so."

Henry: "I don't believe in turning points. Of course, there's the dramatic impact of outside events. But, in the essence of your life, don't you simply become more and more yourself?" He was thinking of his flower gardens.

"Your best self," Kate asked, "or your worst self?"

"The mixture," Henry answered.

When Kate had gone to Gabriel's room to tell him to take his shower, he had asked her, "Do you think I'm all bad?" "No; everybody is a mixture of good and bad," she had replied. "Is there anybody who's all good?" the imp had asked. "Yes; they're called saints." "Like who?" "Nobody we know."

Ellen returned and sat next to Conrad. He drank the water and leaned back more comfortably again. "What have you been talking about?" Ellen asked.

"Turning points," Isabel answered. "Henry doesn't believe in them."

"Of course he wouldn't. He's a man. And he stepped into his father's shoes." She chuckled, not at all unkindly, and added, "But all that will change."

"I doubt it," Kate said. "But then you don't have a daughter." She reached for a cigarette from the silver urn on her end table. Henry lit it for her. "Peggy came home from school recently with the declaration, 'I don't have to get married if I don't want to!' She's *nine.*"

"But it's true," Ellen said. She doted on Peggy. "She can become anything she wants."

"No, that's not true." Kate said. "And it's not a good idea to believe that. It only guarantees resentment. Years of resentment." She was measuring her own long hard struggle away from a childhood of idealism. It had been her parents' invocation of her future: You can become anything you want to—a lawyer, a doctor, a leader of one sort or another; but always someone who will make the world better. She hadn't wanted that. If she could have been anything at all in this life, she thought, she would have been a marine biologist. Alone. In silence. Or a pianist. Alone. Without any audience.

"I'll tell you what, Henry," she added, "if there wasn't a real turning point in my life, at least there was a gradual change that came about after we were married, somewhere in those long ten years while we waited, hoping to have another child and not having it. Gradually during those years I escaped from my parents' conception of life—of changing everything, of bringing heaven to earth, righting all wrongs, achieving justice, peace, prosperity. Very gradually I realized that the choice was between devoting yourself to changing the world or living in this world, here and now, the way it is. If you are fighting for a cause, you are not living your life. You are acting out a charade for the benefit of the abstractions you are enthralled to—or for the gratitude of an imaginary future." She was saying good-bye to her parents.

Conrad applauded quietly. "I've never heard a neater rationale for the status quo."

"The only status I'm interested in quoing is a basic human need."

"And you know what that is?" Conrad asked.

"Respect," Kate answered. "If parents don't respect their children they spend their lives trying to make them into something they aren't." She had come to the conclusion that the primary conflict in life is not between classes but between generations.

She is thinking of herself and her parents, Henry realized; not of herself and her own children. Jonathan probably ought to become an athletic coach or a golf pro, but he would suffer all the pressures of his family to train for a profession or to come into the business.

Ellen said, "It seems to me the good the women's lib movement is doing will increase respect between the sexes."

"Maybe in the job market," Kate said, "but not in human relations. It increases competitiveness and that means more selfishness."

Isabel said, "Women who were brought up with self-respect never needed the women's lib—"

"To protect them?" Kate asked. She laughed.

"Well, if I could have become anything I wanted," Isabel added, "I'd be a racing car driver."

"You are, my dear," Conrad drawled. "You are."

Kate concluded, "We all disappoint our parents; and we all disappoint ourselves. We're force-fed with the idea that we might become anything we want—and we can't."

No, Henry thought, but said nothing. He believed that almost every idea was true—at some time, and to some extent, but only partially. Nothing applied always and everywhere. We must see by fractured light, a little bit at a time.

"It's whether or not people marry and how they raise children that's at the heart of it," Ellen said, "isn't it?"

"Yes!" Kate was vehement. She had been betrayed by Roman Stanski. She had thought they were profoundly in love. She'd had a few crushes, a few romances, one affair while at Hunter College. But this was entirely different. Roman Stanski was a soldier stationed temporarily in New York toward the end of the Korean War. She was in her first year at the Columbia School of Social Work. In her first apartment by herself. When he moved in with her, she told her parents they were going to get married. She had every reason to believe it was true. He filled her with excitement.

"But the whole point of women's lib," Henry said, "seems to be a rejection of marriage and the family. It isn't seen as necessary, let alone as desirable."

"It isn't," Conrad said, casually. "But since it won't be rejected universally and simultaneously, the alternative to the extinction of the species is that the countries that go on populating like mad will, simply, take over the countries that have vasectomied themselves out of positions of power."

Ellen shivered. Quentin asked, "You can't really imagine the extinction of the species, can you?"

"Why not? We can imagine our own personal extinction. Why not for all of humanity?"

Henry saw his family gravestones, his house empty, the lawn and gardens gone to seed; everything overgrown, gradually turning to decay, to rot, to dust.

Isabel stretched luxuriantly. "I rather like the irony, in all this elegance, of imagining *doom.*"

"Most people live theirs every day," Kate surprised even herself by how dour she sounded. It was her mother's kind of remark. Her parents had loathed Roman Stanski. He stood for nothing but "making it" for "Number One." He came out of the lumpenproletariat of Eastern Europe: pig keepers in Poland, railroad engineers and factory workers in America; so unenlightened that they were too ignorant to know they were benighted. Why had she fallen head over heels in love with exactly the opposite of everything her parents respected, admired, believed in? Only to "be herself," to separate herself from them as if by surgery. He was handsome. Tall, with wavy ginger hair. So masculine. So thrilling in bed. Pleased by every simple gesture of kindness and affection. So eager to make a good life for himself. He had been a football player at the University of Pennsylvania. He planned to go to business school after the Army.

"But it's so much more satisfying to live out one's doom happily, rather than sadly," Ellen said; then she giggled. "Good Lord, I think I've made an epigram."

Conrad patted her hand. "You don't *have* to think so . . ."

"You don't *have* to have the baby," Roman Stanski had said. "I'll get the money." "But I want the baby," Kate said, in disbelief; they were in love. "It's *our* child, not just yours." "I'm not getting married," he said, "and I'm not going to take on a child." "But I thought . . ." "It was great while it lasted. But it's over. I'm being transferred to Korea; I leave in ten days. If you don't agree to an abortion, then—think of it as my gift to you." She slapped him across the face. They stood opposite each other in the middle of the small efficiency apartment on the Upper West Side, and with sangfroid he raised his large arm and slapped her across the face. "I wish you were dead," she said. "As far as you're concerned, I am." Which is what she pretended: that they had been married and he was killed in the Korean War. Three months later she met Henry Warner, at a party for a fellow student from Harvard who had been appointed an instructor of art history at Columbia, Lawrence deGroot, who was gay but kind to her because she was pregnant. They had seen him occasionally over the years. He had eventually married and had children of his own. He was a curator at the Metropolitan Museum now.

"Henry, I'm suddenly very tired," Kate whispered. "Would you mind if we left?"

"Not at all. It's very late." He stood up. "Dear people—" he began, when the telephone rang.

"At this hour!" Ellen was piqued, as if to say, For a little bit of time I had forgotten that this is a doctor's house.

Margaret called Quentin to the phone in the hallway. The others all rose, for an awkward moment, as if before parting they should hold hands in silence, but instead they were buzzing farewells at each other.

Quentin returned to the entrance of the living room, pale; he looked as if he wanted to speak but his tongue had been cut out.

"What's the matter?" Ellen asked, moving toward him.

"Raymond."

Ellen stopped.

"There's been an accident."

She brought her hands up to her mouth. "Is it bad?"

Quentin was trying to keep from crying but his face began to crumple. "I'll go see," he squeezed out; and then more strongly, "Where are the car keys?" He turned back into the hall and began to look around, when he seemed to gag and double over, and he fell to his knees on the floor. Ellen and Henry, Conrad and Kate rushed toward him. From the depths of his chest came a moan that burst into a wail. He was on his hands and knees with his head toward the floor weeping and lifted his face, streamed with tears, his open mouth contorted down into his white beard, all the muscles of his neck like taut ropes. Ellen fell to her knees before him and wrapped her arms about his head. She stroked the side of his face, weeping herself, touching his head gently. "He's . . . he's . . . he's . . . ," trying to force the word out between her sobs. "He's *dead?*" Quentin fell out of her grasp, flattening himself onto the rug as if to sink through the floor.

When Kate and Henry finally left, somehow, they drove home in a stunned silence, drove slowly in a state of shock. Kate shielded her face and continued to cry without making a sound. In all the rest of her life she would never forget the sight of Ellen suddenly standing up straight next to the flattened body of her husband; Ellen erect, as if she had been shocked to attention, in that incongruous sari, all the color drained out of her face, those slate-blue eyes blind, as if she would never see outward again, her arms fallen to her sides as if she held dead weights in each hand; that voice, almost inaudible, leaden, hollow as she said, "My only child."

Conrad had taken her in his arms.

Henry and Kate had helped to raise Quentin from the floor.

Isabel had remained in the living room, pressing herself back against the side of the fireplace, wishing she could escape through the stone wall. She was too young to be approached by death. She sought to protect herself from any contact, any infection of it. For it had come into the room, blaring, like a Nazi proclamation. It was there; the idea that

Raymond had become nonexistent. An idea that eviscerated all the others. Why is death portrayed as a black-cloaked and hooded reaper when it comes like an invisible shark, and with one bite leaves only the mind to suffer?

Conrad had held Ellen to keep her from shaking herself apart. Kate and Henry had their arms around Quentin as if they encompassed the empty space that had been Raymond. For a little while that terrible, bottomless pit of nonexistence pressed its upper rim against each of them, withdrawing all bodily warmth with the frigid fact of the loss of life, the disappearance of life: the What of death, before the gap was filled with questions of the How of death or the Why of death. Raymond was no more. A boy of twenty. He was cheated out of fifty years of grandeur and pain, of joy, of "most of the time I just am." And those who stood there in the hallway, his parents and his parents' friends, who had known him from the days when to say "Dad-dee" was a glorious achievement, felt deprived—as one complex organism from whom a tentacle had been lopped off; a feeler that would probe into the future even after they were gone. But of Raymond himself —the idea that he would have no future, that he would never see or feel or think anything ever again was an idea that each of them suffered as if their ribs had been broken by the force that blew through them and carried Raymond away.

Quentin insisted on giving Ellen a sedative. Margaret must see her to bed. He demanded to be left alone. He would drive himself to the coroner's office. He would see for himself. Conrad wedged Isabel off the wall and they were able to drive away. Henry and Kate, suddenly alone in the hallway, were left to drive home, shattered. She felt as if great spaces separated each of her bones from all of the others: opened up, exposed, vulnerable. Henry felt cauterized, as if it would be a long time before he would be able to experience any sensation again.

And then he had to drive Lucy home. She had fallen asleep

on the living room sofa. "We'll never use her again," Kate said. "The house could have burned down. The children could have choked to death, and she wouldn't have heard anything. She's good for nothing."

Henry returned under a bright moon. All of the clouds had settled along the eastern horizon. Kate stood on the landing of the front hall stairs in a yellow bathrobe that looked like an African caftan. He walked through the British fox hunting scene as if offended by an unfamiliar voice in the house. Something new and unexpected was not what he needed at the moment. Kate held out her hand until he clasped it. Together, in silence, they did what they were propelled to do out of fear, out of well-meaning, out of anxiety. They entered each child's room with the terror of finding him dead. Peggy slept surrounded by a menagerie of stuffed animals, her clothes on the floor, her school books scattered on the desk, her cat blinking at them from the rocking chair. Gabriel was curled up inside of a sleeping bag on the floor; Spanny slept on his bed. Inside their cage, the gerbils on his toy table turned their exercise wheel. But his record player was off.

Jonathan lay naked on his back, like a Michaelangelo sculpture, under a sheet up to the middle of his chest. There was the open bag that he had not unpacked. The books on the shelves. The stamp albums on the table. The pictures on the cork-board wall: the postcards, the sports medals, the aging three-by-five card that read, "I made this dot at midnight on the first day of 1962." On his desk lay the leather books with their secret compartment that Henry had given him once for a Christmas present.

They went to their own rooms. They slept the night together in Henry's bed. Kate whispered to him, as they clutched each other, "You are the best person I have ever known!"—meaning, Don't leave me, don't die; don't let it all end, for then I should have to hate you. Their faces were wet with tears. "If you die, I will never forgive you," he said, as if knowing her thought. They wrapped themselves around each other, compressed into one: their lives contracted into the intensity of the small amount of warmth they could find and protect between the two of them.

"We will do our duty, as God gives us the right to see our duty," Gabriel said.

"The 'light,' dummy," Peggy corrected.

Henry entered the breakfast room. "What's that all about?" he asked quietly.

Kate answered. "The children are learning their lines for the Pilgrim Pageant." There were rings under her eyes. But she had thrown on a sweater and skirt. "I wish the cook were back," she said. It had nothing to do with making breakfast, it meant, When she isn't away there wouldn't be the driving back and forth to the bus stop for Helen, who came and went in the cook's car.

"I'm late," Henry said. "If Jonathan isn't up by the time I leave, say good-bye for me and give him this money for the trip." He showed her an envelope with bills in it and then set it up against a pitcher on the breakfast room corner cabinet.

He embraced Kate tenderly.

"I'm sorry to be rushed like this," she said, "but I should be back before the children's bus comes. I'll talk with you later, darling."

Everything looked fragile to him: Kate hurrying out through the kitchen, Peggy munching cereal, Gabriel smiling wanly. So fragile; so easily destroyed. He touched the tops of their heads gently, without a word. Both of them looked up at him, their eyebrows raised, wondering if he was a little crazy. He laughed. Either life is there, and there is no death; or it is not there, and there is only "No More."

Jonathan entered Henry's office without being announced. Mrs. Wicks was away from her desk. The young man in blue jeans and a white polo shirt, in sneakers, his dark hair brushed back along his forehead, knocked, opened the door tentatively, said, "Dad?" cautiously. "Can I see you?" He looked around the room; there was no one else there. He saw Henry, in a dark suit, a striped shirt, a maroon tie, his reading glasses halfway down his nose, look up from the papers on his desk with surprise.

"Come in. Of course." He checked the clock between the jade urn and the golden golf ball. "It's almost noon. I thought you'd be on your way to Martha's Vineyard by now. Sit down."

Henry came around the desk and sat on the sofa. Jonathan sat at the edge of the armchair to his right. "Didn't Julian show up?" His old friend from Westport was to pick him up and they were to drive together.

"Oh, yes. He drove me down here." Jonathan looked out at the tree tops on the Green. Then his voice became very quiet. "I just don't know if I ought to go." He was holding the thumb of one hand tight in the other, on the edge of his knees, like a schoolboy in the principal's office.

Henry became concerned. "Why not?"

There was a long pause. Then almost in a whisper: "Mom told me about Raymond." His eyes filled with tears. He covered his face with both hands. Henry leaned forward and grasped the boy's knee.

"It's all right," he said. Jonathan brought out a handkerchief and wiped his eyes. "You think you should stay for the funeral?"

"It's not that." He held the handkerchief squeezed into a ball between his clasped hands. Henry stroked the knee, encouraging. "It's worse." His voice was choked.

Henry withdrew his hand. "Can you tell me?"

"I heard it on the ten o'clock news. On the radio. I was in my room. Packing. They said . . ." Now he spoke slowly and very quietly, "They said Raymond was the victim of a hit-and-run accident. Near the Road Side. In Bethany."

Henry sounded a commanding "No!" in the silent room.

"I was there. I hit something on the road. I thought it was a deer."

"No." Henry repeated, this time more softly. And again, "No," pressing his hand up against his forehead. His eyes closed. He saw Jonathan in jail; his life, like Raymond's, ruined; his family in shame; all friendships lost. Raymond was gone. But why should Jonathan be lost too? If life is there . . . His hands had gone ice cold. He put them under his legs and leaned forward, staring at his son. I will protect you. I will not let you be taken away. If he had ever had any doubt of his love for Jonathan as his son and not just Kate's, there was none now. This was his decision. He had come to him, not to Kate. "Were you alone?" he asked.

"No. There was a girl I picked up."

"Does she know you struck something?"

"I guess so. She must have felt it too. But we were both high. I mean we drank a lot of beer."

"How high?"

Jonathan hung his head. "For a little while, I was driving without the lights on."

"You didn't see what you hit."

"Right."

"You didn't stop and go back to look?"

"No."

If he had, could he have saved Raymond's life?

"Was there anyone else around?"

"No."

"Weren't there other cars on the road?"

"Not when I was driving with the lights out."

"Were you the last one to leave the Road Side?"

"No. There must have been a couple of dozen cars still there."

"Any one of them might have hit Raymond."

Jonathan cried. "But I'm afraid I did!"

Henry stood up and pulled the boy up against him. He held him in his arms until he stopped crying. "Easy," he whispered. "Take it easy." He felt the clutch of his son's arms around his back. The power of this youth. And his fear.

"Did you say anything to your mother?"

The boy sat down and wiped his eyes. "No." He gripped the arms of the chair to help control himself. "I wanted to ask your advice," he said. Pleading. He is still a child, Henry felt. Fragile. Precious. Henry felt the coffee table pressing against his legs. He stood and then began to walk up and down in the open space of the office.

"I wish Judge Jackman wasn't away," Henry said. "He would know what to do." And then suddenly he stopped and said, "But I don't think there is anything to do. You only imagine that *maybe*, perhaps, it might have been your car that hit Raymond. But you don't have any evidence for believing that. There is only the coincidence that you were at the Road Side last night—and your sense of guilt about having driven for a little while without the lights on." He didn't say, and your shame for not having gone back to see what you'd run into. "And the fact that you were high—"

"I was very high."

"Promise me you will never get that high again."

"I promise."

What is a promise? A hope. A wish, without collateral.

"But shouldn't I say something?"

"What good would it do to put yourself forward? To say that 'maybe, perhaps,' it was you?"

"I don't know."

"None. Think of what it would do to the Connolleys."

The buzzer sounded. Mrs. Wicks reminded Henry of his luncheon appointment with the auditor, Mr. Waterman. "Phone and say I'll be late," he replied.

Henry concluded, "You have no reason to believe you did it. And only harm would come of your saying you thought that 'maybe' it was your fault." But what if it truly was? "Don't say a word about it to anyone. And don't brood about it. If you hadn't heard the ten o'clock news, you'd be halfway to Martha's Vineyard by now."

"Yes," Jonathan agreed, contrite.

"I will find out if there is anything at all that ought to be done. Can we reach you if we need to talk?"

"I gave Mom the phone number for Julian's folks at the Vineyard, but I don't know who'll be there when we're out on the boat."

"That's all right. As long as there's a way to get in touch."

Jonathan stood up. He will have a good life, Henry thought. His life will not be bent out of shape, crippled. I have protected him. They shook hands.

"We'll see you in about a week," Henry said.

Slowly, and with poignancy, more than formality, Jonathan said, "Thank you."

Never in my life, Henry thought, have I felt more truly his father. I have just saved his life.

The auditor was difficult. Henry returned to his office with a list of specific items for which he needed bills and canceled checks. The I.R.S. review was intensive. Waterman needed as many records as possible. Mrs. Wicks gave him the message that Kate had called to say she was going to Mrs. Connolley's but would be home in time to take care of Helen.

The bills and the checks were not a problem; that was merely a matter of the accountant's going through the file and pulling them out. But there were innumerable instances within the gray area that would have to be defended. How much of the use and therefore maintenance of the Mercedes was business-related? How many of the parties at home were in fact designed for public relations and publicity? It was necessary to draw up guest lists. From two years ago? Yes. Complete guest lists. Henry looked carefully at Waterman, thinking, He has never drawn up a guest list for a party that took place two years ago—never in his life. It is not that Henry Warner had any desire to cheat on his income tax; but he did believe that it was appropriate to take every advantage that any ambiguity of the laws allowed. And he was unsure of how supportive Waterman would be. Then he chuckled to himself. If you don't have confidence in your accountant, you might as well go straight.

Waterman's office was in the building between Warner and Son and the post office on Church Street. So were the offices of the Consumer Fraud and Protection Bureau of the State of Connecticut, and the annex offices of the city police force, which had inadequate space in City Hall. Henry Warner ran into the chief of police in the lobby, after lunch in Waterman's office. "Hi, Henry," Barry Connors said. "How's it going?"

"Hello, Barry." They had served on the City Improvement Commission together.

"How's things?"

"Well," Henry began, somberly, "it's pretty rotten news for Dr. Connolley."

"You bet." The chief of police was a man with a long flat face and a flat nose. He wore his uniform loosely; he was losing weight. He believed that prevention was more feasible than cure.

"What can the police do?"

Barry Connors looked around the lobby, and spoke quietly, in confidence. "There's next to nothing we can do. The body was found about midnight by a bunch of kids in a car—about seven of them—who called for an ambulance. But the boy was dead on arrival. That road's pretty heavily traveled. There weren't any skid marks. Dry road. It wasn't the kind of accident that makes you think the car was damaged—you know: if the fender was dented or something like that we could put out an alert to garages. But the kid died in a freak way. His back was broken. Sort of like he was snapped. Cracked. Instantly. I don't think there's any chance of tracking down a hit-and-run like that."

"Will you put a detective on the job?"

Connors looked at him as if to say, You don't have any idea of what we need to spend our time on, do you? Dr. Connolley is a friend of yours; his son is dead, and you can seriously wonder if we're going to concentrate on finding out who did it. "It doesn't work that way," Barry Connors said. "A report will be filed. If any new evidence turns up it will be added to the file. To put it bluntly," he added, "this isn't the kind of crime that we have the need or resources to pursue."

"I understand," Henry said, sadly; happily.

Margaret showed Kate back into the bird cage where Ellen was sitting alone. The afternoon sunlight was flattened on the glass jalousies—layers of beaten gold around the screened porch.

Kate kissed her and sat next to her on the sofa. "I don't know how you can . . ." appear so placid, she thought. Both of them wore black dresses and black shoes.

"Still be alive?" Ellen half joked.

"No. I don't think that. I mean—seem calm."

"There isn't any alternative, Kate. I'm very calm." Kate wondered if she was on strong tranquilizers. "I'm really quite all right. It's Quentin who's making all the arrangements."

"How do you mean?"

"The funeral will be at noon. Tomorrow."

"Oh," she held Ellen's hand in hers. It was like the arm of Peggy's rag doll. Spongy and lifeless.

"Do you know anything more of what happened?"

"Quite a lot."

"You do?" Kate was surprised.

"At first all the police said is that he was run over on a country trail off Rock Road in Bethany. A bunch of kids called from the gas station at the crossroads there and an ambulance took him to the emergency room. But it was too late." She sighed. She did not weep; her eyes were shut.

"Then," she continued, "I had a visit from Jane Kelly. You know her?"

"No."

"Sheila Kelly's daughter. She's a very nice girl. She was all broken up. It's hideous to see a girl of eighteen all broken up." She stared suddenly at Kate who nodded agreement.

"She's a sweet girl. This is the worst thing that has ever happened to her." Ellen paused. She took a sip from the glass of water on the end table. "Raymond had been at her house for supper. Her parents are in England for two weeks. He wanted them to go dancing at a night club in Bethany, the Road Side. They took her car. Raymond stopped at a package store and bought a bottle of gin because they serve only beer at the Road Side. And for a while they had a good time dancing. But—she says—Raymond kept drinking the gin. And after a while he and she went out to the car to leave. She wanted to drive home. But he wanted to make love. And he was so drunk and sloppy and nasty to her, she became frightened. She kicked him out of the car. Can you imagine? That's what she said: she literally punched and shoved and pushed him out of the car, there in the parking lot of the Road Side. And she drove away. She went home. She was crying, all the way driving home, she said." Ellen pressed a handkerchief against her dry eyes, like a child checking to see if a scab was still there.

"Oh, Ellen," Kate said compassionately. Hadn't Jonathan been there? Had he seen Raymond?

Ellen continued. "She doesn't know what he did then, but she imagines he staggered to the road and tried to bum a ride with one of the cars leaving the place. She's so sensitive. So guilty. What if she had been willing to make love with him? He'd be alive now . . . What if she had forced him to sit still and driven him home? He'd be alive now." She began to laugh a low hollow chuckle. "It's a funny kind of guilt. It's like blaming Henry Ford for automobiles. If there hadn't been any, Raymond couldn't have been killed by a car." She gasped, and brought the handkerchief to her mouth. "It was very brave and very kind of her to come here and tell me that."

"How can you—?" Kate asked, embarrassing her friend.

"How can I what?" Ellen asked brusquely.

Bear it? is what Kate wanted to ask, but she couldn't. "How can you have listened to what she had to say, when all that matters—"

"Kate," Ellen interrupted her, "all that matters is that Raymond is no more. I haven't slept all night. I have been trying to gather him together. And you want to know the truth? I have a lot of trouble trying to find him. Oh, it's easy to remember changing diapers, and teaching him to ride a bike, and playing chess with him, and watching him win a swim meet when he was fourteen. But since then, since then . . . it is very hard to grasp him: what he cared about, who he was, what he might have become. That's where it all goes vague. You know, Kate, he never talked to me about things that were important to him. You know, I never once saw him naked after he was about ten years old!"

They cried together side by side and lowered their heads to each other's shoulders.

"You are a dear," Ellen said. "It was terribly good of you to come this afternoon." She stood up. "But you have your own children to get home to." Meaning, I want to be alone now.

Kate said, "I will be here tomorrow."

The funeral was a very dignified, very stately Mass at St. Thomas More's. There were lots of friends and many flowers. The service was in English, not Latin.

It was a clear blue-skied Sunday in June. A perfect golf day, Henry thought; but there would be no golf today. He was surprised to discover a number of women in light-colored dresses and Ellen and her mother in white. He had never before been inside the Roman Catholic Church for students and faculty at Yale, on Park Street, although he had passed it a thousand times. It was a curiously reserved Catholic gesture to New England, as if to say—from the high, plain white exterior with its modest steeple—I will not flaunt my secret. Their car was parked around the corner, on Broadway. Kate and he reached the steps just as the Connolleys and Mrs. Brandem got out of the funeral director's black Cadillac. Ellen's mother had come down from Boston alone. Her father was in a nursing home. Mrs. Brandem made Henry think of old Queen Mary; George V's Queen Mary. The Queen of his childhood. He had kept a scrapbook of newspaper clippings about their public appearances. Mrs. Brandem was over seventy, ramrod straight in a long white linen coat, with a hat wrapped around her white hair. She carried herself as if to define the word "carriage." Quentin ascended the steps on one side of her and Ellen on the other. Not one of them touched the other. But they moved as if they were one body. They ignored everyone around them: the doctors and their wives; Raymond's fellow students; Margaret; the friends of the various clubs and other organizations they belonged to. In every sense, this assembly constituted most of what they belonged to. They were gregarious and gracious people and they had built a community of loyalties and appreciations, of people who suffered for them and were there to pay tribute to them.

The casket stood before the altar, covered with a robe of white satin on which lay one wreath of fresh laurel, with tiny pink blossoms and spiky tough green leaves. Henry and Kate took seats about a third of the way back from the altar, next to the mayor of New Haven on one side and Helen on the other. The service was serene. It was not an outpouring of grief. It transcended grief. It extolled a Will beyond comprehension and the glory of submission to that mystery. Henry did not follow the forms of the prayers. He realized that he had given up the religion of his childhood so long ago he could not recapture the stages of his disengagement. It had something to do with "lack of credibility." You must go to church until you are eighteen, his father had said, and then you can decide for yourself whether you will be a member of the congregation or not. Henry never joined a church on his own. He escaped that. And still, a few days before, when his ancient uncle had given him the Bible he had felt a peculiar richness in the associations, the suggestions, the implications. Of what? Of what he had come out of, one generation after another, one century after another. Come out of—into what? Free of myths and symbols. Back where the cave men were, before the most primitive of religions. Free as a cave man. He heard again the gasp and the wail of Quentin Connolley as he fell to the floor on his hands and knees. *That* was the truth. But the other day, when he had been made conscious of his fingertips touching the Bible on his desk, when Robert Stanton was in his office: that was obscene, indiscriminate—as if he were taking strength from a forbidden source. That was unmanly. The old sources of strength had dried up. The new sources were immediate feelings, genuine feelings of involvement and devotion. He turned to look at Kate.

Her profile was sharply defined next to him. How beautiful her nostrils are, he thought. How potent is her life. "My wife is my religion," he heard as an echo in his soul.

Kate stared at the altar. This is all utterly foreign to me, she thought. And yet, something has to be done. Some ceremony, some gesture. Her idea that her body should be given to a hospital so that parts of her that were usable could be made use of—her eyes especially—and that her friends should hold a cocktail party in her honor when she died— felt, at this moment, like a joke in very bad taste. But she knew of no alternative for herself. Still, the body has to be disposed of—what a ghastly phrase! The horror of the truth has to be disposed of, or contained, or suppressed, somehow. But by this means? This rigmarole? She had been raised as an atheist by parents who had earned their atheism the hard way. She had inherited hers. She had inherited their contempt for priests and ministers and rabbis. For obfuscators. For retailers of make-believe and fairy tales. For those who say that Black is White; there is no death; there is life eternal and the only price you have to pay for the reassurance is to believe in a thousand unbelievable fictions. And still: how long did it take mankind to discover what to do with a dead body? How many centuries did it take to breed a woman like Ellen's mother, who could walk into this church dry-eyed, upright? Otherwise we would all fly apart at the sight of the truth. The truth? What truth! Her parents argued that reason arrives at the truth. The accurate assessment of cause and effect. But what difference does it make to know when and where and how Raymond died; the only important truth is that Raymond is dead. And for the rest—for the living—the only truth is that they have to accept that fact. Against their wishes. The wish that he were still alive. But wishes do not alter the fact. And all of this symbolic pretense does not alter the fact; it obscures it. It coats it in a glow of let's-pretend-it-didn't-happen. Let's pretend it will be made all right, somewhere, somehow. After a hundred times a thousand years, is this the best humanity can come up with? "Let's pretend." Why not face the fact and tear our hair out? Scream and grovel in the dirt for hatred of death; for being robbed, despoiled, cheated, maimed? That would be unseemly. And, in an instant, Kate was overwhelmed by the sense of the necessity for decorum. For restraint, so as not to offend other people's feelings—which means not to aggravate other people's fears. She covered her face with her handkerchief and wept silently.

The Mass was over.

Four members of the Yale Glee Club sang psalms, and then there were three speakers. First Father Cavanaugh, who had never met Raymond Connolley, spoke of the return of life into the bosom of God; of the mystery of the choices of the Lord; of the superiority of the Life Eternal to the Life Temporal. Kate thought that what he was saying means there are two distinct realms: the imaginary and the real. In the real there are, at this moment, people waiting in line to get onto buses, soldiers in some frightening dugout about to go into battle, women in labor, men making telephone calls about business appointments for tomorrow, children playing hide and seek, old people lonely in hospital beds, lovers in a motel room discovering ecstasy. And in the imaginary there is Raymond, clothed in gold, awaiting entry into heaven. Insane! she thought, grasping for Henry's hand and clawing her fingernails into his palm—this is real. She looked at the casket and gasped. Henry put his arm around her shoulder.

The second speaker was Dr. Waddingford of the Yale Medical School, once Quentin's mentor and now his dearest friend. A man heavy with years and an excess of weight. A learned man. He had known Raymond as a child. He spoke to his parents and to his grandmother. We are of the animal world, as well as of the spiritual, he said. We are driven by needs that are bred in the species by millennia of responses to the conditions that life seeks to satisfy. Bred finer and finer, until we have become the ethical animals that we are. And yet the biological conditions prevail. It is believed that we have evolved out of creatures of the sea come onto dry land, creatures who need the environment of the sea in which to sustain our lives, and, in respect to that, the systematic circulation of blood within our bodies is a substitute for the sea out of which life emerged. For we need that cleansing liquid medium in which to function. Tears, he said, are as the sea which washes away all sorrow. Grief, he said, is our way of coming through the separation of our hopes from those fatal events that prevent our hopes from being realized. But we operate as if—in the largest view—we were all part of an enormous imaginary organism, "the currency of life," he called it, protective, and cooperative, so that what we value in life may be sustained and enhanced.

Henry agreed, affirmatively, knowing that what he had said to Jonathan was good, was justified. Even now he was somewhere off the southeast coast of New England, sailing against the wind, full of life, ready for it.

The third speaker was Conrad Taylor, representing Yale University. He drawled less than usually. His sentences were crisp and clear. Raymond had been a student at a great college. He was a youth of very considerable promise. Serious. Dedicated to the enterprise of a liberal education, and, through that, to an enlightened life. And what did, after all, constitute an enlightened life? It was the appreciation of how all lives were interrelated, interconnected. The student is responsible to his professors, the professors are responsible to the university administrators, and they in turn are answerable to the trustees of the university, and the trustees are responsible to the world at large—a vision that was circular, for the "world at large" can call in its promissory notes, depending on how those very students performed. What they might do, what they might accomplish. It was an investment in the amelioration of thought and of life, and they were interrelated. For what improves thought betters life. And "the world at large" is the large world, the rest of the world, which is waiting, crouched in silence and uncertainty, hoping, lusting in darkness for those efforts that the dedicated would make for progress and for betterment. His speech fell apart in a warehouse of intellectual sentimentality, of liberal clichés; bits and pieces of useful tools that had not been placed in the right machine. A good young man could be helped to do good in this world, but Conrad Taylor was all caught up in the conflict between giving a recruiting speech for Yale College and giving an envoy for Raymond Connolley. He ended by saying that each student contributes to what every other student understands, what every instructor comprehends, what every trustee comes to feel responsible for. But it fell flat. The boy—the dead boy—had been metamorphosed into a type, a class, a "kind"; lost sight of, lost contact with, transformed into an idea. It was no longer Raymond Connolley he was speaking of, with a twenty-eight-inch waist and a raspy chuckle, Raymond with acne scars along his jawbone; it was youth, and hope, and the need for goodness. The words were a betrayal. By assimilating him to a generality, he had separated the living from the dead even further than he had meant to do. But the effect was clear: Raymond had ceased to be a person, a youth, a dead boy; he had become a figure of speech.

The interment took place in the Catholic cemetery of St. Vincent's. The funeral party walked from the road along an alley of high copper maples, under the batches of dark leaves like polished leather. There was only the sound of their footsteps on the pavement. The deep blue of the sky was softened by a flock of clouds. The casket had been covered by a sheet of some sort of imitation grass. To keep from giving further offense? Kate wondered. She had never seen that before. She had attended few funerals. To soften the blow still further, so as not actually to see the casket lowered into the earth inch by inch? To make believe it was not happening. Father Cavanaugh recited the last benediction. The "remains" of Raymond Connolley were lowered into the grave. But nothing remains of him, Kate felt. It is only we who remain.

They walked back, in couples, singly, or in small groups toward the line of parked cars, the cortege of dark, sleek, shiny funeral coaches, stationed close together almost like a streamlined caricature of a railroad train. As Mrs. Brandem seated herself in the first car, and Ellen and Quentin were getting in beside her, two rough-looking black boys, about eleven or twelve years old, darted through the loose crowd and flung two scarlet overripe tomatoes to splatter against the trunk of their Cadillac. One shouted, "Fuck the Pope!" and both of them ran into the street, laughing, dodging the two-way traffic, and disappeared between the houses across the road. Kate felt the hatred, the stupidity, the resentment as if she had received a body blow. The savages! How easy it was to hate them. How much easier than bending over backward to make up for three hundred years of slavery. How much easier to fight them. How? What was *she* doing with such feelings? She looked around for Helen and took her arm. Henry and she eventually drove Helen home and then went back to the Connolleys' house.

Margaret served tea at the large dining room table. Some of the men took drinks from the glass table on the screened porch. Mrs. Brandem stood before the fireplace in the living room. The Rembrandt had been removed. It was nowhere in view. The mirror in the front hall had been draped with a sheet. Ellen said to Kate, "Quentin cannot stand the sight of his face."

"Why?" Kate whispered.

"He wants to take it all upon himself. I can't help him. He hardly lets me talk to him." She was about to say, You should talk to him, but she didn't. She excused herself.

Kate joined the ladies near Mrs. Brandem, who had taken off the long linen suit coat but kept the turban-like hat on. Her chauffeur and car stood waiting in the driveway. How remarkably good-looking the woman was. Over seventy but barely lined; her jawbone firm, no sagging flesh. And then Kate remembered hearing the rumor that she had had her face lifted right after the Duchess of Windsor made doing that seem all right. She held her hands clasped before her, erect, her shoulders squared. She was not to be humbled. "God's will!" she said. Kate did not want to enter that conversation. She caught sight of Henry near one of the windows smoking a cigar and talking with Mr. Waterman, and moved away toward them; but she didn't interrupt them.

The low murmur of sorrowful voices sounded through the rooms. She caught a glimpse of Conrad; but Isabel hadn't been able to attend. Is this all we can do? Is this the best we can do for each other? Someone laughed on the screened porch and that was followed by an embarrassed quiet pause. Kate wandered through the hall, into the study, and was surprised to find Quentin there alone. They embraced each other but then he shook his head. His face was stony. He did not want to talk.

After Mrs. Brandem left, Kate returned to the living room to watch Ellen lower herself wearily onto the velvet love seat and stare blankly up to the bare wall above the mantelpiece. She was alone. Kate sat down next to her, amazed by how calm she was even now—almost as though it were no effort but rather the acting out of something rehearsed a long time ago.

"Will you tell me?" Kate asked. "Your religion really works for you, doesn't it?"

"I don't know." Ellen sighed. She was silent. "In my childhood," she began and closed her eyes. She was back in the Victorian mansion on the Fenway, back in her girlhood of white gloves. "In the house I grew up in," she said, "there was a winter garden full of rubber plants and drooping vines in pots suspended from the ceiling; it was fun to sit there and read at night. There was a curved wall of many panes of glass like a greenhouse, but the view from that corner was toward the garage and alleyway in back. I always thought it very scary at night, as if it exposed the house to dangers. And then my mother began collecting a kind of primitive art object that came from Russia. Nineteenth-century paintings on glass. Folk scenes. Simple, charming things. And she replaced the panes of the glass wall in the winter garden one by one with these paintings, as she found them. A lot of them came into the country in the twenties. Gradually they made a complete border around the curved wall, just about at eye level for me. I loved them. They were strange. But full of life. And they kept me safe. I would look at them, not *through* them into the darkness where there might be dangers. They were as far as I wanted to see."

Monday afternoon, Henry came home from the store a little early. During the hour that Kate and he sat on the terrace drinking martinis and watching Gabriel and Peggy playing at tennis in the distance, the phone rang three times in a row. In the kitchen, Helen took the first call.

A sharp-edged female voice asked, "Is Johnny there?"

Helen corrected, "Jonathan."

"Oh, it's Jon-a-than, is it?"

"Who's this calling please?"

"Joan Rohan. Is he there?"

"No. He's away just now."

"When will he be back?"

"Is this a friend of his?"

"You better believe it," was the answer.

"Well, I'm not sure. About a week."

"Really?" There was a pause. "I'd like him to get in touch with me as soon as he gets home."

Helen didn't like the tone. She said, "I'll tell him to do that," and hung up.

"Who was it?" Kate called in through the dining room.

"A girl friend of Jonathan's."

Kate resumed her seat opposite Henry, who continued his answer to the question "How did your day go?" And while Kate took no intrinsic interest in the details of personnel problems at the store, or of why a shipment of Baccarat was held up by customs, or the amount of documentation that had to be gathered together for the I.R.S. review, she wanted Henry to know that she felt with him, sympathized with him, supported him. She had no desire to speak of her own day. It had been laced with worries over the children—Jonathan off on a sailboat she had never seen, Peggy and Gabriel as ready to punch each other in the face as they were to hug and kiss. Laced with fears of loss; this life, this family secreted on this beautiful island in a world surrounded by fatal hatred and threats of violence.

The second call was from Mr. Warner's brother in Florida, Helen said. He took it on the extension in the living room. His brother's voice was throaty; he was not entirely sober. Conrad Taylor had asked during dinner at the Connolleys that gruesome night, "Can anyone of us remember the last time he went to bed *entirely sober?*" Henry's brother was embarrassing. Could he have ten thousand dollars on a short-term loan, say, sixty days? He had been playing the horses. . . . It would have been possible, but Henry knew that "loan" meant "gift," and he had made a few such presents to his brother before. Enough of such gifts. He was sorry; quietly and succinctly he gave reasons why it was not possible at this time. His brother hung up after saying, "You're a prick."

Henry felt debased. Was there any danger to his brother if the gambling debt wasn't paid off right away? He hadn't said that there was.

The phone rang again before Henry returned to the terrace. "I've got it," he called out. It was Quentin Connolley.

"Are you going out this evening?"

"No."

"Look: I'm still at the hospital. Then I'm going to take Ellen to the airport. She wants to visit with her sister in Tucson for a few days. Can I come over and see you—" there was a long pause, calculating, "about eleven? It's important to me."

"Certainly."

"That isn't too late for you?

"Not at all," Henry assured him.

"Very good!" Quentin finished. "Thanks, Henry."

By ten thirty, Kate was in a state of exhaustion. "These headaches are driving me crazy." She looked pale. The lemon-yellow bathrobe hung on her as if she was losing weight. "You're not taking care of yourself," Henry said. The children were finally asleep. The house was in order. The thought of the endless repetition of all the steps that have to be taken for the house to be "in order" made Kate's shoulders slump.

"I've got to go to sleep. But if for any reason Quentin wants to see me, too—wake me." She kissed his cheek.

Henry wandered through the house switching off lights, except for those in the hallway and the living room. He walked out onto the terrace, sipping a Scotch and water. It was still warm. The moon was bright and the stars twinkled. The lights were on in the two lamp posts along the drive from the road to the house. Quentin appeared at eleven thirty. Henry met him at the front door and they went into the living room together. Quentin did not notice the new wallpaper. "Would you like a drink?"

"No. Thanks anyway."

Quentin's face was drawn but he seemed in command of himself. The whiteness of his beard was accentuated by the cool light and the pale walls of the room. He sat in the wing chair with his back to the piano. Henry faced him from the Chippendale armchair next to the sofa. "Why did you let Ellen go away by herself?" he asked. "Shouldn't *you* go away for a while, too?"

"I will. I'm taking some time at a retreat. But it's better this way. Ellen and I are," he paused, searching for the right word, "reacting in different ways."

Grieving, Henry thought, in different ways.

"I have a favor to ask of you." Then suddenly he looked around. "Is Kate here?"

"She's gone up, but if you want—"

"No. Good. I'd just as soon she didn't know anything. I want to ask you to do a favor for me."

"What is it?"

"Get rid of the Rembrandt."

"Get rid?" Henry had the vision of burning it.

"Sell it for me."

"But I'm not an art dealer."

"And I'm not its owner."

It was Isabel Taylor who had used the word "steal"; and Quentin had flinched, after all those years.

"I stole it," Quentin said, very slowly with equal measure of importance to each word, as if repeating a confession, this time before a different tribunal. "It is one of my sins."

"Sins?" Henry felt himself withdrawing his fingertips from that old family Bible. They were about to speak with each other in different languages.

"I have committed many sins."

"This is no time for you to be counting your sins."

"This is precisely the time for me to do that." And then the doctor said something that affected Henry as if Quentin had pulled him by the hair of his head: "Raymond is dead because of my sins."

"That's ridiculous!"

Quentin said, "You're in no position to make that judgment." And then, "You don't know what you're talking about."

"How can *you?* You're not yourself."

"Are you? Are you yourself?" There was anger in his voice. "I've never been myself before this. I see myself now. I'm forced to face the facts of myself." His face was gnarled with distaste. "I hate myself." He slumped back in the wing chair, and ran his right hand through his hair. "Henry, I think I'll have that drink now. How about a bourbon on the rocks?"

Henry refreshed his own Scotch and brought Quentin's drink from the dining room. I am in the presence of a man who is suffering a religious seizure, he thought. This is irrational. I must keep myself in check.

"I have no desire to burden you with all that I have done wrong in my life," Quentin said. The word "all" took on the proportions of a mountain. "I am doing that in the right place and with the right adviser."

He is undergoing conversion, Henry realized. How had Quentin been spending the past four days?

"But I must do everything I can—wherever I can—to divest myself of sin. *My* sins. Getting rid of the Rembrandt is just one of them." He faced Henry but he was looking at an autobiography of distortions that Henry had no sight of. Malpractice? Greed? Lechery? Henry didn't want to know. Then Quentin said, "I want to buy ambulances for the fire department. They cost about thirty thousand apiece."

Would an ambulance have saved Raymond's life? Henry asked, "Does Ellen know you want to do this?"

"Yes. She thinks I'm a fool."

"I'm sorry." How weak that sounds. How can I possibly sympathize with him? This is madness. "You want to use the money from selling the Rembrandt to buy ambulances." At least he was trying to understand how Quentin's mind worked at the moment.

"That's right. As an anonymous gift. Everything has to be anonymous. I won't have my name associated with any of it."

Henry thought of Robert Stanton and the emerald earrings: no record, no bill of sale; cash; customer unknown. He asked, "How much do you think the Rembrandt is worth?"

"I don't know. A hundred thousand?"

"What?" Henry was amazed. "How much do you have it insured for?"

"I have never had it insured."

"I can't believe it." He felt the chill of the danger of exposure, naked of protection; he lived in a world of people and houses and cars and stores and inventories secured against fire, theft, and violation by the superstition of the bulletproof glass of insurance. "You never had it insured . . ."

"How could I? Wouldn't I have to show proof of ownership?"

"You might have inherited it from a great aunt."

Quentin grunted. "My great aunts worked in a laundry in Worcester."

The Siamese cat appeared in the archway. Two green lights suddenly shone at them through the cat's head. Then she turned and left them alone. Henry felt conspiratorial. "You don't want to turn it over to a regular art dealer—maybe in New York?"

"I don't want to have anything more to do with it. I don't want to have to explain myself to anyone I don't already know. I don't want to have to lie. *You* know the truth."

"All I know is that you've referred to it as loot. You brought it back after the end of the war."

"Words!" Quentin said with contempt. He stood up and began to pace back and forth in the middle of the room. "Loot. That means stolen property."

"As a fortune of war."

"*Mis*fortune. 'Brought it back'—that means smuggled it into the country. You know how I carried it back? Rolled up inside an empty Howitzer shell. A brass cartridge. Even that wasn't a *legitimate* souvenir."

Henry offered him a cigar and they both smoked. "Look: even if there are military laws against stolen goods brought back by soldiers, there must be some limit of time on them. This happened a quarter of a century ago. *More.*"

"I don't want to know what the laws are. I don't want to keep the thing anymore." Quentin continued to pace. "You know the facts. You know why I want money. You appreciate art. You know rich people. You even have a friend at the Metropolitan!"

Henry laughed. "Imagine trying to sell it to the Met."

"I didn't mean that. I mean you have know-how and you have connections. Won't you do this for me?" He was pleading. He sat down again and stared at Henry. "I can't do it on my own. I wouldn't know where to start."

"It might take a lot of time . . ."

"That doesn't matter; as long as I don't have to think about it again." Both of them concealed the self-serving concerns involved in those remarks. "You take what you like—ten percent? twenty percent?"

"Forget that."

"Then you'll do it."

"I'll try."

They were silent for a long while. Then Quentin said, "I never even liked it. I don't know why it's valuable. I took it only because someone else wanted it." He was back at the Dünning Schloss at Hoescht am Main, outside of the rubble of Frankfurt. Guard duty that last night before leave and then "rehabilitation." In the library of the great stone house his flashlight caught one of the house staff, one of the displaced persons who worked for the military government occupying the house, wedging the large frame away from the wall with a screwdriver. He attacked Quentin, knocking the flashlight out of his grip. They struggled. Quentin swung and hit him in the head with the butt of the carbine. The frame hung loose from the wall. Quentin removed the canvas himself. Back in his room, he separated the painting, one nail at a time, from the thin wooden inner frame that held it taut. He ripped up a pillow case and placed the portrait between pieces of the linen, rolled it into a tube, and placed it inside the brass cartridge artillery shell he'd been saving. He left Germany the next noon. In Paris during his four-day leave, he took the painting to the Louvre and, in high-school French, he tried to find someone who could authenticate it.

"Here," he said, drawing a faded tan envelope out of his breast pocket. "I have this," presenting it to Henry.

The stationery inside was thin as the paper used in slender editions of the Bible, turning brown along the creases of its four squares. The letterhead referred to the Bureau of European Art at the Musée du Louvre.

> To Whom It May Concern:
> I have examined the painting and believe that, in truth, it is a genuine work of Rembrandt van Rijn. I have only the *Klassiker der Kunst* to refer to at the moment. It appears to me that this work is one of the self-portraits described there —from the 1660s period. However, some of the works listed there have been subsequently dropped from the canon. Later reference works are not available here at the present time (our library has not been fully returned since the end of the war) and it deserves further research to fully establish authenticity.
>
> F. Guizot
> Curator

"It isn't without qualification, but it sounds reasonable enough. Did you pay him for it?"

"Fifty dollars . . . Don't laugh. That's about what two hundred and fifty dollars would be worth today."

Henry offered the letter back to him. "No," Quentin said, "you keep it. With the Rembrandt."

"Where is the painting?"

"In my car."

"You brought it with you?"

"Of course."

"It's in your car. In the driveway. Of my house. At midnight. And you never had it insured."

"Right."

"You felt that confident that I would take it off your hands."

Quentin smiled with satisfaction. "I know you," he said. Henry found that more amusing than he was able to understand.

"And if anything happens to it while it's in my care?"

"We'll pretend it never existed."

When Quentin had driven away, Henry found himself alone in a silent house with a "package" that was wrapped in a yellow flowered sheet, held together with strips of wide adhesive tape, leaning against the hallway scene of galloping horses at the hunt. Henry switched off the hall lights and carried the package into the living room. He set it up on the Chippendale chair and removed the "drape." He turned on the brass light over the piano and elbowed it around the wing chair so that it shone on the painting and then he proceeded to turn off every other light in the room. He found his Scotch; he sat in the wing chair; alone, awake in his house in the dark of night, his wife and children asleep; alone in the privacy of his living room in the presence of a self-portrait by Rembrandt van Rijn, 1609–1669. When Rembrandt was working on this painting, Henry thought, nomadic red Indians were setting up teepees for the night on the land where this house stands now; red Indians who had not yet set eyes on a white man; and my ancestors, the progenitors of the grandfather who built this house—Rembrandt's contemporaries—abhorred painting as idolatrous, as they did dancing and singing: distractions of the devil. What incredible transformations the world has witnessed in three centuries, in twelve or fifteen generations.

Henry sat in the shadows. The piano light illuminated the picture six feet in front of him. A human face. An old man's head and shoulders. He had never been this close to the portrait before. And at eye level. A worn face, but not crushed. The light along the temple and the cheekbone was golden and the chain around the neck glinted in the mellow light. What light? There was no way of knowing; it could be late afternoon sunlight or candlelight. The background was no garden scene glimpsed over the sitter's shoulder or even the contents of a room that indicated rich or poor. The background was a swirl of dusky light suffused into darker corners. There were no associations in which to place the human being—no time of day, no place in space. There was only the forbearance of the eyes, the measure of age, the humanity without location in time or place. An old man. A survivor. Wise. Sad. Stalwart. Is it possible that Rembrandt really cared only about the light and the shadows? The glints of gold in contrast with the sable dark shoulders and the beret-like covering of the head? No. That was the trick, the entrapment to lure the viewer into seeing this particular human being. This illusion. This oil on canvas that can be mistaken for an actual human being. It is not self-conscious. It does not suggest, "Marvel that this is an oil painting." Rather, it glories in the demand: marvel at a human being. What light years of difference there are, Henry thought, between this portrait and the smiley faces Gabriel had drawn for him as a birthday present. This was neither an artist's proclamation of his own virtuosity nor was it a statement of verisimilitude, such as, "That is exactly what Phillip II looked like." This was a silent assertion of humanism: Man, it said, is all. The human being. Neither place nor time, status nor association, matters one iota. This human being is all that matters. Human life is all that matters. Humankind is all that matters.

"What's up?" Kate asked, standing at the foot of the stairs.

"Quentin wants me to sell the Rembrandt for him," Henry answered.

"Oh. Okay. Go to bed soon. Good night, love," she said, like a sleepwalker, and left again. The cocker spaniel dogged her heels.

Raymond is dead because of my sins, Quentin had said. Poor Quentin. He wants to make sense of it. He wants to see life as a web of rewards and punishments. How he has lived his private life, he wants to believe, matters in the public world. To gauge his powers. To estimate his worth. What a delusion, Henry thought. Quentin can't let go of his son without believing that he *has* to let go of him because of things that *he* has done in the past. He wants to believe that his life controls destinies, contributes to catastrophes. Kate had told him of Jane Kelly's story. Quentin was no more to blame for Raymond's death than the inventor of gin, or the manager of the Road Side, or Columbus for discovering America. Raymond's life was cut short by a fortuitous, purposeless accident; but Quentin was determined to make sense of it. To make it appear as if it was rational by causal connections that in fact were purely imaginary. The father wants to believe that *he* is responsible for the son's death. Why shouldn't one go along with him? Did he desire it? In some hidden crevasse of his heart had he always wished his son were dead?

Henry had drunk too much Scotch. Good night, Rembrandt. He turned off the piano light and went to his bed.

Henry brought the sheet-wrapped Rembrandt into his office with him the next morning and placed it in the vault safe at the end of the room, then stared after it, contemplating the next necessity. Mrs. Wicks peered in at him. "What's the matter?" she asked.

"Nothing. I'm working."

"Oh. You looked angry."

"Well, nobody says it's easy."

They both laughed. He closed the door on her and went

to the telephone. When the call was answered, he asked for Mr. Lawrence deGroot.

"Larry! How are you?"

"Henry? Are you still alive?"

"Why not?"

"Oh, I don't know. It's just that nobody as straight as you ought to be safe and sound. What can I do for you?"

"Tell me how to get rid of a hot Rembrandt."

"You're kidding." His voice was flippant, assuming a joke.

"No. I'm not."

An entirely altered voice asked, "You're serious?" A southern voice, full of sunshine and slow movement. DeGroot came from Charleston and never changed the way he had learned to speak.

"I am serious. I have a friend who 'owns' a Rembrandt he came by illegally. He wants me to help him sell it. He needs the money. What do I do?"

DeGroot chuckled: "Why don't you buy it from him yourself?" It suddenly struck Henry that that is what Quentin might have had in mind. "I'm not in the market," he said. "Besides, I haven't a clue as to what it's worth."

"How good is it?"

"How the hell do I know?"

"What's it of?"

"An old man."

"Too bad. A nude girl would bring twice the price."

"What sort of price?"

"What's the size?"

Henry paused, looking beyond his desk to the open vault. "I'd say about two feet wide and three feet long."

"An old man . . . a self-portrait?"

"Yes."

"Is it signed?"

"Yes."

"How's the impasto?"

"The what?"

"Impasto, idiot. I thought you went to Harvard. The richness of the layers of pigment. Is it rubbed down? Overcleaned? Or still thick with the original layers of paint?"

"I'm not sure. I think it's in pretty good shape."

"I can see why you need help."

"I do."

"Bring it down and I'll take a look."

"I can't today."

"Neither can I. How's tomorrow for you?"

Henry looked at the calendar next to his phone. "All right. Tomorrow afternoon is fine."

"It's a date."

"Wait a minute," Henry said. "I can't see myself trying to walk in and out of the Metropolitan with a hot Rembrandt." He laughed.

DeGroot sounded his southern sing-song laugh. "All right. I'll meet you at the Stanhope across the street. Give me a call when you get in."

"Yes. Thanks. But wait a second. Give me some idea of the kind of money involved."

"A Rembrandt," deGroot said. "Probably a self-portrait. About two by three. In good condition. Well, anywhere between a hundred thousand and three hundred thousand. Does that tickle you?"

"In just the right places," Henry said.

"Until tomorrow, then."

"So long, Larry."

"G'bye, buddy."

Henry felt comfortable about that. The second phone call was of a different order. No lifetime of familiarity, no comfort of acquaintanceship. A little embarrassed, but for Quentin's sake, Henry dialed the number on Wall Street. He asked for Mr. Robert Stanton. A secretary with a very high-pitched British voice offered to see if, possibly, he might be in.

"Mr. Warner?" the husky voice asked cautiously.

"Yes. Mr. Stanton. I don't know if you remember—but last week. Here in New Haven."

"Don't say another word. I remember you perfectly. A most agreeable meeting."

"Good."

"Is there something I can do for you?"

"Yes. Quite unexpectedly, something extremely interesting has come up. It's not that I think it might appeal to you personally. But I thought that you might know of someone who might be attracted, someone appropriate."

"In what?"

"A Rembrandt."

There was no reply from the other end.

"An acquaintance of mine is interested in selling a Rembrandt he inherited, but only under the condition of keeping the transactions secret. A cash sale, with no records on either side. His anonymity is of the utmost importance."

"Yes, of course. I understand."

"Ah, good. I thought you would. It is a very valuable work. Either for a genuine collector or for someone who might want to donate it to a museum or a university and enjoy the tax-deductible benefit."

"I get you . . ."

"Do you know of anyone who might—" Henry was stopped in his question by Stanton's saying, "I might."

"You?"

"Yes. It's not impossible. Whereabout is the painting?"

"Well, it's here in my office."

"What kind of price did you have in mind?"

Henry paused, marshaling his self-confidence. "About a quarter of a million, give or take a little."

"What do you mean 'take'?" They both laughed.

"I mean around a quarter of a million. I know what it's worth."

"Cash," Stanton said, without tension.

"Yes."

"That might be a very interesting investment," Stanton said.

"It would be," Henry agreed. "Gilt-edged."

"It's a very attractive idea."

"Would you like to see it?" Henry asked, politely.

"Not particularly," Stanton answered, and laughed. "I don't go to look at silos of wheat, or drums of oil."

"You're kidding."

"Not at all. I'm not a collector. I'm an investor. Besides, I'm not going to be in New Haven again until next Sunday."

"Oh," Henry understood that to mean: No work is done on Sunday.

"I'll tell you what, Mr. Warner. Let me think it over for a few days. I'll call you."

"The store is closed on Sunday."

"Naturally. I'll call you before Sunday, Mr. Warner. Just let me check a few things out before then."

"Certainly."

"But don't do anything else about it in the meanwhile."

Henry was silent.

"I'm really attracted," Stanton added. "I understand the nature of the transaction."

"That's very promising," Henry Warner said, somewhat bewildered both by what he had heard himself say and by what he had listened to. "Actually I'm taking it to Manhattan tomorrow to show someone else. Perhaps we could have a short visit if—"

"Call me when you get in. Okay?"

"Yes. I'll do that."

The weather was surprisingly humid for so early in June. Henry rolled up the car window and turned on the air conditioner as soon as he reached the parkway. Still, it was a pleasant drive in the middle of the morning. He had phoned to reserve a room, on the day rate, at the Stanhope; and he found a parking space on the side street facing the enormous columned facade of the Metropolitan, flat as an operatic stage set. He hadn't visited the museum in a couple of years, although he came to Manhattan often enough. The thought of being mugged and robbed in broad daylight brought a guilty snicker to his lips as he pictured himself at the moment: neatly dressed in a seersucker suit, lugging a "hot" Rembrandt concealed in its flowered yellow sheet around the corner on Fifth Avenue.

He telephoned deGroot from the room.

"I'll be over in about fifteen minutes."

Then Henry ordered cold lobster and champagne from room service, removed his jacket, lifted the frame onto the bed, and propped it against the headboard. He left the covering over it. Why is a hotel room so sterile, he wondered, looking around at the carved white furniture, the pattern of blue and white toile scenes on the bedspread, repeated on the drapes and on the valance over the windows. The white curtains hid the view of an air shaft. Isn't it paradoxical that a room which suffers a parade of life—a different life each night—shows no signs of life? Devoid of personality. Or are we simply attuned to the wrong signs, limited only to the indicators of what matters to us: a wallet, a hairbrush, a book with an envelope as a placemark sticking out of its pages. Henry was uneasy with the lifelessness of a hotel room until he altered it with his own signs: the suit jacket over the shoulders of a chair, the long thin container of his cigars surrounded by a scattering of matchbooks on the dresser, the glass of water he'd filled in the bathroom and accidentally spilled slightly on the desk top. As he wiped up the splash with a Kleenex he comforted himself with the thought: Where there's life, there's mess.

A waiter knocked at the door and then wheeled in the table, a rectangle with a single blue iris in a tall thin vase at the center, surrounded by dishes with the lobster and garden salads. He raised the wings on each side, making it into a round table, and drew the champagne in its bucket out from a compartment under the tablecloth. As he left the room he moved sideward to make way for Henry Warner's friend who came in without knocking. "All the comforts of home," he said, admiring.

"Dr. deGroot, I presume," Henry said. They shook hands.

"*We* haven't been in a bedroom in a long time," deGroot sighed with mock longing.

"You don't change at all; you look the same as you did twenty years ago."

"Either that or you need glasses."

DeGroot, who had gone in for long-distance running at Harvard, had a slender, muscular build and he kept himself in firm condition. He had aged in a curious way: he seemed to have paled as if his color had faded from too many washings. His brown hair had become pale tan; it was down to his shoulders and wavy like an English cavalier's. His pastel blue eyes made Henry think of children's marbles held up to the sun. His taut skin, once peaches and cream, appeared now more like mellowed ivory. He had two faces. In repose it was without a line and dominated by a perky nose. But when he smiled, a wide-mouthed smile full of handsome teeth, ripples of curves shot out along both sides of his lips and a series of lines fanned out around his eyes.

"You always knew how to 'do things right,' " he said, after Henry popped out the wine cork. DeGroot held a book in one hand; the other hand rested on the table. The silk shirt he wore was itself a painting on a beige background, a gambling scene in the style of art deco; his trousers were royal blue velvet with bell bottoms.

"They let you dress like that at the Met?"

"Sho' 'nuf," deGroot answered, making fun of his own southern accent. "The old order changeth . . ."

When they had a glass of champagne raised toward each other over the table, deGroot toasted: "Here's to your life of crime."

"No," Henry replied, "I won't drink to that. Here's to—" he groped for an idea. "Here's to happiness."

"Oh, God, Hank, you're archaic."

In all naïveté, Henry asked, "Why do you say that?"

DeGroot laughed and sang the line, " 'They say that happiness is just a thing called Joe.' " They drank the champagne. "Very nice!" deGroot took a second sip and then asked, "Will it be business before pleasure or vice?"

"You want to see the picture," Henry replied.

"Not wildly; I'd like to eat lunch, too."

Henry went to the head of the bed and dropped the covering away from the Rembrandt. The old man stared out at them.

"Well, it looks like a real-ly," deGroot said, approaching it slowly. "If it is, we'll find it in Bredius." He held the book up and then dropped it onto the bed. Henry had not thought of that classic catalogue of Rembrandt since he left graduate school. Of course; it was the "basic" work on Rembrandt's paintings, published in Vienna sometime in the thirties, full of photographs and the provenance for each of the pictures. Although no question had been asked, deGroot answered, "No, I don't particularly like it." He turned away from the painting to look at the lobster, adding, "Rembrandt thought about himself too much."

"Don't we all?" Henry asked, realizing, This is small talk, this is busy work.

"No," deGroot replied. "That is the secret of my success. About ten years ago I stopped thinking about myself. 'Not me, but the wind blowing through me. . . .' "

The book lay on the bed. "Let's have lunch first and then take the plunge."

Henry sensed this was the best approach. "You're on."

Through the course of the meal they touched on each other's lives lightly, like maids carefully dusting family heirlooms. Henry spoke of the store, of his children, of the pleasures of life in New Haven. DeGroot listened to him as he would to an anthropologist just returned from Melanesia. Henry gathered that his old friend lived a life of uneasy truce with a warrior wife and children who did not touch his feelings; otherwise, he continued to be, on occasion, roaming, cruising, promiscuous. A dragonfly. When they were at Harvard, they had gone to bed twice. Henry then more free than in prep school and even more experimental. DeGroot was affectionate and accommodating. "Gone to bed" was the appropriate label, Henry thought. It is not as if they had made love; there was no love to make anything of. The experiences were not exceptional as erotic events; rather simply conditions for temporary release. A phrase Henry had read recently came to mind about indifferent sexual encounters being no more than the relief of "a genital sneeze."

"The lobster was marvelous," deGroot said. "You should fence paintings more often."

"I'm just doing a favor for a friend."

Then they turned to Bredius and, in the first section, of self-portraits, on page 39, they found a photograph of the painting propped up on the bed in front of them: the right eye looking out, with its weariness and its dignity more prominently than the left; Bredius catalogue number 43. Below the photograph was an attribution to the Gemäldegalerie in Kassel.

"How did you get it out of Kassel?" deGroot asked.

"It's a long story," Henry smiled. "And it isn't even mine." Had the people Quentin took it from *bought* it from the museum? Had it been on loan to the museum?

"Let's see what it says in the notes." DeGroot turned to the pages at the back for the references to Br. 43 which read:

> 43. *Self-portrait.* Signed: Rembrandt f. 165(4). HdG 536. Bauch 324. Painted over a female portrait in the style of the 1630s. The X-ray, showing the underlying image, is reproduced by K. Wehlte (*Verhandlungen der Deutschen Röntgengesellschaft* 25, 1932, p. 13). The picture as it stands today is difficult to judge through the thick varnish. Although belonging to the De Roever collection in 1709, the attribution to Rembrandt is not wholly convincing. *Page 39*

"Oh, my God," Henry said. "It might not be genuine."

DeGroot said, "Thick varnish? It must have been cleaned."

Henry slumped down in his chair. ". . . not wholly convincing." He looked at the empty lobster shell on his plate and saw the fire department ambulances disappearing.

"Don't despair," deGroot began, touching him consolingly on the shoulder. "Bredius doesn't have the last word. I brought him over because of all the photographs. But there's Jakob Rosenberg. That's much more recent. I'll go see what it says there. Hold the fort. I'll come back as soon as I can."

After he'd left, Henry poured the last of the champagne for himself and gazed at the portrait. What if it is a fake? What's a deception compared with grand larceny? How many people in the whole world would be able to tell the difference? Could the art gallery in Kassel have sold it because it was proved to be not authentic? How does word of this sort of thing get around in the art world? But then the entire maneuver that Henry was involved in assumed dealing with people who can be depended upon to keep their mouths shut. One turns to a Stanton or to a deGroot who are at home in the gray area, where the less said is always the better. No records. Cash. Anonymous. Still: the old order changeth . . . For the first time it suddenly struck Henry that the fact of his having gone to bed with deGroot might not be an absolute secret between the two of them. At Harvard, deGroot was not thought of as effeminate; he played it straight. Besides, with a southern accent like his, one could never tell. But twenty years later—they let you dress like that at the Met. He had grown flippant and indifferent. At this very moment he was being helpful to Henry but, at the same time, he was uninvolved. He was doing a favor for a friend. It cost him nothing. But what did he care about seriously? How much reason did he have to keep a secret about himself anymore? How indifferent was he now to keeping a secret about Henry? Still, why would he want to hurt Henry by telling *anyone*, so that somehow, some way, it might get back to his wife, his friends, his employees? And what difference would that make? To have gone to bed with another man when you were a graduate student more than twenty years ago?

DeGroot literally shocked Henry out of his thoughts, entering with the statement, "You have nothing to worry about."

"You mean the door was unlocked?"

DeGroot laughed. "Do you have anything to hide?" His glance scanned the room, ignoring the Rembrandt.

Henry realized that he actually felt frightened and tried to cover it up. Nervously, he said, "I'm not on my own turf. Big bad city and all that . . ."

DeGroot was unaffected. "Relax," he said. "You're too old to get raped." He held a brown book in his hand with the signature of Rembrandt stamped in gold on the front cover.

There was a flat manila envelope inside the back cover. "Here is the Rosenberg, 1964. Read this—" and he opened the work to a page at the back to show:

NOTE ON THE PROBLEM OF AUTHENTICITY

The Concordance of Paintings which appeared in the first edition is here replaced by the following brief lists, indicating the opinion of this author as to authenticity:

A. From the Bredius catalogue, *The Paintings of Rembrandt,* Phaidon Edition (New York: Oxford University Press, 1942), the following paintings are the only ones not accepted as authentic. In those cases where the author has not seen the original an asterisk* is added.

Bredius:

14*	127*	209	260	438	581	636*
40	136	220	273*	506	582	637
46	137	233	386	540	595	
67	147	248	421	541	597	
72*	151	254	429	556	606	
75	153*	259*	436	580	635	

"See?" deGroot asked. "Are your fears all gone? Number 43 does not appear on the Rosenberg list. *He* thinks it's authentic. Happy?"

"Relieved. Very relieved. And truly grateful to you."

"You sound too sincere, Henry. Don't get all choked up. Life is a dream."

You wouldn't let me down, Henry thought, would you? But said as casually as he could make it come out, "How can I thank you?"

"Kiss me."

Endangered, Henry looked at the closed door to the room as deGroot approached him. Their lips met; their tongue tips touched. Henry backed away. "You know what, Henry?" deGroot said with the confidence of a connoisseur. "That was really lousy." Then, blandly business-like, he tucked the

Rosenberg book under his arm and offered Henry the manila envelope. "You'll find a Xerox copy of the photograph and the provenance from Bredius there, as well as the page on authenticity. All set?"

"Yes."

"Come back in the fall. The theater season's going to start with a bang this year. Bring Kate. We'll spend an evening together." He moved toward the door. "Bring Jonathan!" he said with a leer, and disappeared.

Henry felt blessed; he was able to sleep.

As soon as deGroot left, Henry had telephoned Stanton, who agreed to meet him at four thirty. Unaccustomed to champagne at lunch, tried by the emotional charges of the past few hours, and recognizing how tired he was, Henry took off all his clothes but his underwear and lay down on the bed, crosswise, under the Rembrandt, as if it had been an icon and he stretched out on the floor before it. To his amazement he fell asleep. When he woke it was four; he washed and dressed; he called room service for Scotch and soda. He was ready, refreshed, for Robert Stanton's arrival. He was rearmed. He neatened up the bed and the rest of the room. The waiter removed the luncheon table. The window was opened to let in some fresh air. He called Kate to say he might be late. They had tickets for a Juilliard Quartet concert at Sprague Hall that evening. He suggested that they meet in the lobby, but she should go ahead to their seats if he was delayed beyond eight thirty.

Robert Stanton was punctual.

Henry had not remembered him as such a statuesque man. It was the baldness of the head and the jauntiness of the moustache that came to mind when he thought of him. But the man created an aura of enormous power in reserve, as if he towered above others and carried an invisible whip in his hand. His politeness bordered on the brusque; he was the kind of man who is accustomed to thinking about four different things at the same time.

They sipped the Scotch and soda while contemplating the Rembrandt.

"I don't know anything about art," Stanton said without apology.

"That doesn't matter," Henry replied. Did he know anything about emeralds? "There are certain things that excite the admiration and appreciation of mankind by their mystery rather than by being comprehended."

Stanton looked at him with reserve, as if to say, That was too long a sentence.

"Here is the documentation," Henry said, laying before him on the desk top the letter from Guizot in French, the Xerox pages from Bredius and from Rosenberg. Stanton read what was in English.

"That bit about painted over the portrait of a female is intriguing."

"It was very common practice in those days," Henry explained, "to use a canvas over again."

"Economical," Stanton commented.

Stanton turned his gaze back to the painting. "He wasn't an especially attractive man, was he?"

"I agree."

"But it does look as if he was willing to face a mirror and say, 'By God, that's me, here and now, isn't it?' "

"You've put your finger on it," Henry said.

"Take it or leave it."

"Yes."

"How old would you say he was then?"

"In his middle fifties." Henry realized that Stanton was

measuring himself against the appearance of Rembrandt's self-portrait—and judging himself well by comparison.

"The owner—?" Stanton began complacently.

"Must remain anonymous."

"Of course."

"But he is pressed for time." Henry wished the whole thing were already over. "He needs the money as quickly as possible."

"How much?"

"A quarter of a million."

"Too much."

"Not really, when you think of what could be done with it."

"There are limitations to what can be done, under these circumstances. Besides, I don't know whether to think of it as an investment or to give myself the simple luxury of owning it." Henry recognized that Stanton was being familiar enough with him to think out loud. "I really don't know . . ."

"What would make it worth your while?"

Stanton answered, "One hundred thousand."

Henry said casually, "No, that wouldn't be acceptable. Two hundred and twenty-five."

"One hundred and seventy-five."

They both laughed. "We've been through this before," Henry said, "haven't we?" They were accomplices.

"You mean," Stanton concluded, "it's got to be two hundred thousand."

"That's right."

"Well, I'll think about it," he said. "I'll let you know."

As things worked out, Henry was in the lobby of Sprague Hall at eight o'clock, twelve minutes before Kate arrived. "What a smashing-looking woman!" he said as he held his arms out to her.

"My darling . . ." she replied with a kiss.

There were two quartets by Bartók and one by Prokofiev.

The performances were superb. The Rembrandt was locked in the trunk of the car.

Ellen Connolley was one of the few people Kate knew who would ever appear at her house without telephoning first, and the only one she was happy to see under any circumstances. She walked into the kitchen while Helen was mopping the floor.

"Is Mrs. Warner here?"

Helen answered, "Yes," slowly, uncertain. "I think she's in the sewing room."

Ellen walked through the halls and up the stairs to find Kate in the room between Gabriel's and Peggy's bedrooms, where Kate was working at a sewing machine, surrounded, as in a nest, by knitting yarn and crocheting materials; a room decorated with macramé wall hangings. Ellen threw herself onto the chaise longue. Kate swerved around on the sewing stool.

"I thought you were in Tucson."

"I just got back."

"What can I give you? A drink? Coffee?"

"I don't want a thing." It was three in the afternoon; the children would be back any minute.

"You went to see your sister," Kate said.

"It was a mistake. She's a bitch. I'd forgotten how easy it is to dislike her. I expected some kind of compassion. She tried. But the truth is that she's much more concerned about dirt in her swimming pool than about human life. She tried, I'll admit that. But then I couldn't work up any feeling about the goddamn purity of her swimming pool. Arid-zona," she concluded. "Can you imagine a world in which your major worry is about gila monsters in the living room? Hollywood!"

"I'm sorry," Kate said.

"It doesn't matter. I just had to get away. Quentin is out of his mind."

"What do you mean?"

"It's a kind of egomania. He's taken Raymond's death on himself as if it were a personal transaction. Whatever Quentin is guilty of, *therefore,* Raymond was killed. His punishment. I've never seen anything like it before in my life. It is an absolutely self-centered suffering. He recognizes nothing else in the world as having any consequence."

Kate asked, quietly, "He had no concern for *your* feelings?"

"Oh, that!" Ellen tried to laugh. "He tries. He thinks he tries. He imagines I feel the loss too. But it's phony. It's a put-on. He's so caught up in the thought that Raymond is dead because of the way in which *he's* lived his life, that anything outside of that thought is insignificant."

Ellen's eyes were beginning to tear. "He is keeping himself from thinking about the fact that Raymond is dead by concentrating on his own sins."

Kate reached out to her. "And *you* think only about the fact that he is dead."

"Yes. Forgive me." She wiped her eyes with a handkerchief from her pocketbook.

"Oh, Ellen—"

"I'm so sorry. I didn't come here to cry. I came here because you are life."

"But Quentin . . ." Kate didn't know what she might say.

"He can't take it. He is turning himself inside out in order not to take it. His son. His only child. You know, I had a very early menopause. I'll never have another child. One child. I don't know what was the matter with me. How barren."

"Don't be absurd."

"I'm trying not to be. I think of myself as reasonable. Sensible. But my husband is transforming himself into some kind of early Christian martyr. There's no joy in his religion. Just—"

"It will pass . . ." That *is* the best we can do, Kate thought. To say, The pain will end; the knowledge will go away; it will change. Why? What if it doesn't?

"Yes. I suppose so." She repeated, "I suppose so. We've lost touch with each other. Quentin has to go through this period of believing that it's his fault. He thinks in terms of cause and effect. He wants to know 'Why?' I don't. I don't care. The only thing that matters at all is that Raymond is dead. I couldn't care less *why* he's dead." She gasped, and then repeated, as if trying to memorize a lesson, "He *is* dead."

"Ellen!" Kate wondered why she kept repeating the name. Is this some kind of invoking?

"It's all right." She was more herself now. "I'll tell you something. You want to know something sad? You know what death does even to a young man like Raymond? It's not that it keeps him from having any future. From going on to have new experiences. It stops the past from being changed. I'll never know anything more about his past than I know now. It's fixed. It's settled. He can't ever say, 'But that isn't why I did it,' or, 'That's not what it meant at all.' He can never change anybody's impression of anything. We're all limited to nothing but what we knew then—at the moment when he died. We're stuck with it. Because he's gone. Because the source of the revelations is no more. I've come to a new definition of life. Living is the source of continual revelations about the past." She wept and covered her eyes with her handkerchief.

Kate embraced her. "He was such a fine boy," she said.

Friday morning the telephone rang at the crack of dawn. Henry picked up the phone next to his bed.

"Is Johnny there?"

Henry was barely awake. "Who's calling, please?"

"Joan Rohan."

"He's on vacation—"

"Still?"

Henry found that offensive. "Yes."

"I *need* to see him."

Is she pregnant? Henry reached for a notepad and a ballpoint pen. He wrote down both her home telephone number and one at work along with the hours when she would be at Chamberlain's. "I'll give him your message."

She hung up. Henry closed his eyes and fell back on the pillow. Where did they go last night? He had drunk too much. His body felt achy. Half-dozing, he longed to soak in a hot bath. As he raised himself up on one elbow, his eyes opened slowly to be confronted by two midget Pilgrims: she in a long gray dress with a square white collar and cuffs, he in a black suit and a tall black hat with a brass buckle on it. "What the—?"

"Surprise!" Peggy and Gabriel shouted, jumping onto the bed close to him. "Last day of school!" Gabriel announced. "The Pilgrim Pageant!" Peggy cried.

"Good Lord . . ." Henry moaned as he squeezed one arm around each of them.

"You did it!" Kate said in the doorway from her bedroom. "You got dressed all by yourselves. Darlings." They jumped off the bed and hugged her. Kate had cut down an old gray linen dress of her own and had made it into the costume for

Peggy, but the outfit Gabriel was wearing came from a theatrical supply house that rented them to all the boys in the class. "Well, let's get going."

Peggy kept hugging her around the waist, pressing her face against Kate's stomach. "The last day of school!" she said. "I'm so happy!"

Henry tried to collect his thoughts while he shaved and the water filled the bathtub. There was to be a meeting with Mr. Waterman at nine thirty. What had he said about the Tax Reform Act of 1969 affecting expenses for activities unrelated to business? Then at eleven o'clock there would be the weekly meeting with department managers at the store. The Pilgrim Pageant is scheduled for one on the Green. He was lucky; he had only to walk across the street. Stanton had not called to say anything about buying the painting. It was in the safe in his office. Friday evening. He paused, looking at his reflection in the mirror. Pale. Want more sunlight. Maybe Kate and he could play a set of tennis at six. The days were growing longer. Friday night. It came clear. Bridge. The group of four couples who met for bridge once a month. Each time at the home of a different member of the group. Tonight it would be here at the Warners'. Helen was to stay late. Henry stretched and yawned. He looked at himself in the full-length mirror, thinking that he ought to fight off about five pounds. Then he slid himself into the water and scrubbed himself fully awake in the warm bath.

Kate arrived in his office at a quarter of one. "The car is fifty percent into a fire hydrant space. Do you think I'll get half a ticket?"

"I'll buy it for you."

"Big spender. It's the least we can do to be on time for the children. Come on, come on," she hurried him. "Let's go."

By what instinct, he wondered, had they each separately dressed in black and white? She in a trim suit and a bone-white blouse, nearly mirroring his. It must have been the appearance of the children in their costumes that morning and the thought of going to watch a recreation of the People of the Black and White world where there was no gray area.

At the rear of the center church on the Green, with its back to the small seventeenth-century graveyard, wooden bleachers had been set up in a semicircle. There must have been about a hundred students of the school along with teachers and as many more parents moving about and finding places for themselves when Henry and Kate arrived. The sky was a deep blue without a cloud, the air was brisk, bracing, like a perfect October afternoon rather than one in the middle of June.

The Pilgrims approached from the northwest corner of the Green, a procession of half-sized people. The boys carried rifles, the girls carried prayer books. Their ship was supposed to have landed at the corner where George Street now meets College; the river ran there in those days, from the mouth of the harbor up to the hospital, where the new highway ran now. Passers-by stopped to watch the procession. The children, from six to twelve years old, walked at a pace of practiced solemnity. It was indeed a pageant and not a play. When the classes were arranged on three sides facing the audience seated on the bleachers, spokesmen came forward, individually, made their declarations, and returned to their place in the phalanx. The Elders spoke of turning their backs on the dissensions and privations of life in the Old World. Girls spoke of the joy to be found in making the new Zion out of the wilderness. Stalwarts declared that every man would help to defend the community against the savagery of the Indians. The new community was to express the essence of their Puritanism. They were to make of themselves the embodiment of the Word of God. The words were all there; as they reasoned about the doctrines, their instructions would issue from the words. The meetinghouse would be the center of the community and the pulpit would be the center of the meetinghouse, the house of learning—here on the Green they would raise it high; here at the center of the settlement they would guard their purity. They would do no wrong; they would guard their freedom. At the point where the youngest group stated in chorus: ". . . as God gives us the light . . ." Gabriel caught Kate's eye and winked.

What madness, Kate thought, what insanity. They were no less misguided than kids who are now trying to establish hippie communes. And they didn't last much longer than those do. Those spite-filled, blinkered underdogs from Bristol and London escaping into the clutch of like-minded self-hypnotized zealots. She thought of Ellen; did they take joy in their religion? They took joy in their contempt for everyone else, and they took joy in their self-congratulation. They lived mean lives, hard lives, seeing the eye of God upon them at every instant, the eyes of the rest of the community upon them at every instant. And there was Peggy, who believed "I don't have to get married if I don't want to," saying, "Each woman will guard her chastity until God sees fit for her to be united with man in the eyes of God." Did she have any idea of what the words meant? But Peggy was earning and confirming her place in her community.

The preceptor of the sixth grade concluded the pageant by leading the classes in the last of the few psalms they sang and then summed up with clichés about the Great Tradition of encouraging independence in the new nation. Henry thought, It's all skewed. The Pilgrims cared only for their own independence; they cared nothing for anyone else. That tolerance came to predominate in this country came in spite of them and by overwhelming them with the realities of this wilderness and all the other accidents that make up a three-hundred-year history. What a brief history. Hardly civilized. A primitive country. Why do we do this? To make our children imagine that in some sense they are starting life in the New World all over again? Starting out again as Puritans, without any idea of how many complexities and subtleties they will have to discover and assimilate before they can become worldly? What a confusion of nationalism with the idea of mankind—as if human life began then and there, just three hundred years ago, on this square of a Green. We haven't the faintest idea of how our children become educated, Henry concluded. He looked at Peggy, serious, and Gabriel, smiling, and thought of Jonathan. Could he have been responsible for Raymond's death? No one will ever know.

All of the audience stood up, as the fifth-grade music teacher, a black woman, led the children in singing "The Star-Spangled Banner," a cappella.

When it was over the school year was over, and all the children shouted "Hurrays" happily and rushed to their parents, dropping their hats and stumbling over the rifles. An hour later there was to be a reception, with punch, back at the Day School and after that the children were free until the middle of September.

Henry felt deprived when he learned that Stanton had telephoned while he was out. He asked Mrs. Wicks to return the call. Mr. Stanton was on another line; he would call back. His ulterior motive involved with the negotiation made him acutely uncomfortable with the delay. If Stanton did not come through with an offer, where would he turn? He realized it had been stupid of him not to ask deGroot if he had any suggestions for possible buyers. Or was that thoroughly improper—to ask a curator at the Met for the name of someone who might be interested in buying an illegally owned Rembrandt? Probably. On the one hand, he felt offended by

Quentin's asking a favor of him that took more of his time than he ought to give it. On the other hand, it was a fantastic opportunity. He remembered to order a silver ashtray sent to deGroot in thanks for his help.

Stanton returned the call at a quarter of five. "I've been checking around, of people who ought to know," he said, taking his time, and Henry sensed that it was going to be all right. "And they tell me that the asking price is really quite fair, under the circumstances."

"I'm glad to hear that." Henry sounded reserved, not to say indifferent, as if he was trying to remember what the man was phoning about.

"Now, I'll be honest with you and say that I really don't know what the hell I'd do with it; but it is a unique chance. This sort of thing has never come my way before."

"It's a once-in-a-lifetime—" Henry was saying.

Then Stanton interrupted: "I'll take it."

"At two hundred thousand."

"Yes," Stanton agreed.

"Well, that's fine."

"So we're both pleased."

"Right."

"Now, as I mentioned, I'll be in New Haven Sunday."

"Of course, the store will be closed, but I could . . ." Instead of finishing that thought, Henry decided to say, "I'll take it home. Come to my house. In fact, come for lunch!"

"Oh, don't go to that trouble."

"No trouble at all."

"Look: Mr. Warner, we're comfortable enough with each other, aren't we, for me to say frankly—I don't want lunch. I have an appointment during the afternoon. I could come by your place; and we could, shall we say, 'make the exchange.' But I really don't want lunch. Okay?"

"Certainly." Picking up a Rembrandt for two hundred

thousand dollars in cash is just something you do on the way to—what?

"All you have to do is tell me how to find you."

Henry gave him precise directions from the parkway.

Stanton said, "I'll see you around one P.M.," and hung up.

Henry wanted to burst into song. He wanted to pirouette around his office. In his privacy behind his closed door he shouted the word "Hallelujah!" The early summer twilight seemed to gild the mahogany, the Venetian mirror, the jade urn. He thought benevolently of his brother in Florida, the school tuitions, the roof, the Internal Revenue Service. Mrs. Wicks stuck her head in. "Is everything all right?"

"Better than that," he replied. "That call you just put through was worth a great deal of money." He looked at his desk, at a Battersea box that read, *May You Be Happy,* and handed it to her. "Take this as a present." He was expansive, profligate.

"Do you mean it?"

"Don't I always mean what I say?"

"Usually—"

"Well, I certainly mean it now."

"What's going on?"

Henry smiled. "It's the last day of school."

In his bedroom, Henry dialed Quentin's phone number. At last Quentin picked up and uttered a barely audible hello. Henry said, "I've found a possible buyer . . . No, I never mentioned your name . . . Right, not in town." Weighing his words cautiously, Henry said, "I can get you one hundred thousand for it. Cash . . . I thought you would be . . . Possibly this Sunday . . . I certainly will; I don't want it to burn a hole through my floor . . . Don't mention it . . . Please don't say anything more. I think it will all be fine . . . I'll let you know right away. All right? Take care." He hung up, clever as a ten-year-old who had just pulled off a magic trick before his family's eyes.

"That's wonderful, darling," Kate said.

Henry swung around on the bed, embarrassed, to discover his wife, who stood in the entrance to his bedroom, buttoning up her dress, had been listening to his phone conversation.

"You sold the Rembrandt for Quentin."

"Yes. At least, I think so. The man who says he's buying it will come here Sunday. You don't mind, do you?"

"Why should I?"

"He'll come around noon; but he isn't staying for lunch."

"Do you want him to? We could invite him."

"No. No, it should work out just right this way."

"You're nervous. What's the matter?"

"Nervous?" He stood up. "I'm perfectly all right."

"Really? You look all uptight. Do you want a drink? You do remember the bridge club, don't you?" He nodded. "Jonathan called," she said happily. "He'll be back sometime on Sunday. Peggy and Gabriel are at the Aldermans—in Hamden—for a sleep-over to celebrate the summer vacation."

"Summer vacation?"

"Have you been drinking?"

"No!" Henry snapped out of it; he felt awkward. That was over now. He sighed. "You are lovely to look at!" A dark-haired woman with fair complexion, engaging in a long dress of chartreuse chiffon. The women of the bridge group all wore evening dresses although the men did not wear black tie. But he had to refresh himself for the evening. He felt too big for his clothes.

At dawn on Saturday, Henry walked naked into Kate's bedroom. The blinds were drawn; the air was cool. He slipped under the covers and snuggled close to her. "You're so warm," he whispered.

"You're so early," she complained.

"You're too sleepy to resist."

"You're a brute," she said, never opening her eyes.

"How'd you like a plug in the cunt?"

She laughed. "I dare you."

He held her down and made love to his wife, vigorously and quickly, like an adolescent who can't control himself. When it was over, she said, "You owe me one."

"There's always tonight," he answered.

They were relaxed. "We had a lovely evening, didn't we?" she asked.

"It was great fun."

"I wish you didn't have to work on Saturdays."

"Someday I'll learn how to 'delegate authority.' "

"You are such a dear man." She kissed him on the lips. "You make me very happy." You are spoiled and haughty and self-absorbed, she thought; but I have never met a man I liked more than you, or found more interesting than you, or trusted as much as I do you. "Will you marry me?" she asked.

"I'm thinking about it . . ." he replied. "Don't rush me."

She sat up abruptly. "I have to pick up the children."

He drew himself out of bed. "I have to go to the store."

Jonathan arrived home at about eleven Sunday morning. He had hitch-hiked. He was sun-tanned and wind-tanned; his hair was shiny, longer, drooping farther down on his forehead. Smiling. In cut-off blue jeans and white tee shirt with a knapsack over one shoulder.

"You look as though you had a wonderful time," Kate said. He is mine, she felt.

Peggy and Gabriel clung to him as if he were a jungle gym they could climb all over.

"It was great," he said.

They all gathered around the breakfast room table: Henry in a blue flannel bathrobe, Kate in her caftan, the little kids in their pajamas and fluffy slippers. Home is the sailor, home from the sea . . . Jonathan spoke of slips and squalls, and inlets, and rocky coves. Of pork and beans on tin plates, and how bright the stars shine in the night out over the black Atlantic. He was the voyager, the adventurer, daring and accomplished.

Peggy asked, "Do you still love me best?"

Gabriel said, "What did you bring me?"

They drank coffee and ate popovers with pools of butter inside them and strawberry jam. Henry told him about Joan Rohan. Kate wondered when he'd had a shower last. But soon enough the tight reunion was over. They were expecting a guest early in the afternoon. Jonathan said he'd love to play golf for a change. Peggy and Gabriel challenged each other to tennis. Even the dog and the cat wanted to be off on their own, outside, in the sparkling June day.

Henry dressed in white ducks, a navy blazer with brass buttons, and a Liberty of London ascot inside the collar of his open pink shirt. Kate wore purple slacks and a sea-green tunic made of Thailand silk; her feet were bare in sandals of thin strips of white leather. Her hair was pulled to the left side of her head and held in place with two Spanish tortoise combs. The whole atmosphere was charged with a festive quality. Jonathan was home safe and sound, the younger children, soon to go off to camp, were playing well with each other; something good had been done for Quentin; their guest was about to arrive. The day was beautiful.

Stanton arrived in a silver-gray Rolls Royce with a pale driver in black livery who actually walked around to the opposite side to open the door before Stanton emerged. He carried a leather attaché case in his hand. Henry accompanied him along the curve of dogwoods in blossom. Kate stood in the hallway, surrounded by the fox hunting scene. At the first sight of him, she wanted to escape—fly through the air, evaporate; instead she felt as if trapped between walls of glass: between her need to flee and the necessity to remain still. Revealing nothing, she was immobilized.

"Mr. Stanton," Henry announced. "My wife—Kate."

She extended her hand to Roman Stanski, touched the flesh of his palm, after twenty years. She felt the blood withdrawing from her arms and legs, rushing toward the center of her body, as if to strengthen her against a blow.

"How nice to meet you," he said politely. Did that mean Henry did not know? Stanton had not known? She thanked God that Jonathan had left for the golf course. Would he come back, by some fluke, before this man was gone?

She forced out of herself, "How do you do?"

"Won't you come in?" Henry led the way into the living room. Stanton took in the wallpaper, the staircase, the crystal chandeliers, the archways.

"Lovely," he said. "What a handsome house."

"My grandfather built it," Henry said, expansively. "I've lived here almost all my life."

"Not many men can say that," Stanton replied. He was in no hurry to make conversation. He gazed at the elegant room, the piano, the low bookcases along one wall under a group of paintings of Warner ancestors; he looked through the French doors to the terrace. Kate sat on the sofa, Stanski in the wing chair. Henry asked if they would like a sherry. Kate nodded yes. "I'd love it," Stanton said.

"I'll be back in a moment," Henry said.

They were alone. Was this actually happening? Kate wondered.

"You look wonderful," he said. Then he returned his gaze from her to the room. "You seem to have done very well."

"When did you change your name?" she asked quietly. He was completely bald; he had a moustache streaked with white. He looked ten years older than he was. Heavy. Still, he looked imposing. He was a threat.

"After the Korean War. Because of a dishonorable discharge. And for other good reasons. But I needn't have bothered. Nobody ever checks up. Did you know that? Nobody ever looks up records."

Was that a peace offering? Was he trying to tell her that he wouldn't say anything? "I'd like to believe—" she began, when Henry returned with three slender glasses on a silver circle.

"What?" he asked.

Kate said, "I'd like to believe that you will make a good home for the Rembrandt."

Stanton laughed. "I find the whole thing very amusing. Coming from humble origins, I find it more than a little— how should I put it?—*unexpected* that I should be in a position to own a Rembrandt."

"Well," Henry said, "that should only enhance the pleasure."

"I'll drink to that," Stanton said, as they raised their glasses.

Kate never took her eyes off him. I will not let him out of

my sight, she thought. I will not leave them alone for one instant. I would not trust this man any farther than I could throw him out of the house.

"Were those your children," Stanton asked, "I saw playing tennis as I drove up?"

"Yes," Henry replied.

He is vicious, Kate felt; he wants to do us harm. Her heart was pounding. Her hands were cold.

"We also have an older boy," Henry added, "but he's not here right now."

"Oh?" Stanton commented, casually. "How old is he?"

"Nineteen."

"You're very fortunate," he said.

"Do you have children?" Henry asked.

"No, I'm sorry to say. My wife was never very well."

"That's too bad. I'm sorry . . ."

Kate caught herself grinding her teeth. She remembered the slap; the betrayal; the flippancy: "That'll be my gift to you . . ."

"I suppose," Henry suggested, "that your wife is looking forward to seeing the portrait."

"No, no, she isn't," he answered. "It will be a complete surprise to her."

You are full of surprises, Kate thought, aren't you? You are unscrupulous. How did you make your big money? Out of dope, or phony stocks and bonds, or white slaves, or something worse?

Henry felt the distinct lack of warmth in the conversation. "Well, then, let me arrange for Rembrandt to make his appearance." He offered Stanton a cigar, which was declined. "It'll take me just two minutes." And he left the room.

Stanton stood up and wandered about, looking at the collection of Meissen figurines in the étagère in one corner and the score of Poulenc on the piano. "So," he said, "you have a boy of nineteen."

"Yes," Kate replied, noncommittally. She felt attacked by his mere presence. What had she done to deserve this?

"My son?"

Kate brought out a hollow laugh. "Does it matter?"

"The question calls for a simple yes or no," he said objectively.

"Yes," she said, against her will.

"Thank you."

"No thanks to you."

He faced her squarely. "You hate me."

It was all there, she realized, fully intact: the intensity of her contempt for him. How had it been preserved unchanged for all those years? Like a dagger in a secret drawer. She said, "Not without cause."

"It was all so long ago," he said.

"His name is Jonathan. He's finished his freshman year at the University of Michigan. He's an excellent athlete. He's handsome. He's good-natured. He has a splendid father. All —no thanks to you."

"You're right," he said. "And I never even thought he was born."

"You never really thought of me or of that child once— even before you walked out, did you? How easy it must have been for you; how simple. You were going off to war. Classic! You couldn't have cared less."

"I cared."

"That's phony," she said.

"What would you know?" he asked. "Just because I put on a hard front?"

"It wasn't a front; it went all the way through you."

"You will never know what I felt."

Kate asked, "Do you want me to feel sorry for you?"

Henry returned to the silence in the living room, carrying the Rembrandt in both hands. He had arranged for the clerks in his shipping department to make up a covering case. They had invented a wrapping out of styrofoam, and that enclosed the framed portrait, weightless in an all-surrounding package, with a clasp at the center like a frog on a Chinese dress. Henry opened it and displayed the painting.

"Yes," Stanton acknowledged it. "All right." He opened his attaché case on his knees and began to ladle out the packets of bills onto the end table next to him.

"You must think this quite a steal at a hundred thousand," Kate said.

"I would have," he answered in a world-weary manner; "but it's still a good buy at two hundred thousand." The cash was packed in groups of fifty thousand each. Stanton snapped his attaché case closed. He looked at his wristwatch. "I'd better be going now." He stood up. "I appreciate your hospitality, your sherry, and the pleasure of meeting your wife."

Henry nodded cordially.

"But I am pressed for time. If you'll forgive me—"

"Perhaps we'll meet again," Henry said.

"I hope so," Stanton replied amiably. "And good-bye, Mrs. Warner; thank you for your—indulgence."

Kate was unable to speak, unable to move.

Stanton never touched the painting. He called for his driver to carry it out to the car.

When they had driven away, Henry said, "What a cold fish."

Kate remained seated, nervously anxious, feeling that she had been pursued out into the woods, that her heart was pounding from the exertion of the chase—and about to be caught. Very slowly and quietly she said, "You told Quentin that you sold it for *one* hundred thousand."

"No, I did not," Henry replied, lighting a cigar. "I told him I could get one hundred thousand for him."

"Then you lied to him." Kate had the sudden fear that she might lose her sense of balance and fall over sideways. She was suffering the surreal experience of seeing the life drain out of the objects around her: the walls, the furniture, the house were becoming transparent, insubstantial, thinned away.

"I did not lie."

"You did not tell him the whole truth."

"I told him what he wanted to hear, what satisfied him."

Kate felt her life withdrawing from the outer reaches of the spaces she filled—away from Henry and the children, the dog, the cat, the cars, the garden, the lawn, the sky, rushing back into the narrow limits of her body, pulling back to safety. She sensed her world shrinking from the people and things to which she had extended herself, seeking the bare minimum: she was conscious of the invisible hairs on her arms, of her fingernails, of the combs in her hair. She pulled her legs up and sat on them, making herself smaller, less vulnerable. "Does he know you are keeping any of this money?" she asked, looking at the four stacks of bills.

"No."

"Then you've led him to believe you're going to give him whatever you get for the picture."

Henry sat down at the other end of the sofa, facing her. "I did not lead him to believe anything. I told him I could get a certain amount of money *for him,* which pleased him very much, and that is the amount he will be given."

"While you keep the rest for yourself?"

He exhaled the cigar smoke away from her, toward the terrace. "Yes."

"You intend to cheat him out of one hundred thousand dollars. You—Henry Warner." She kept her eyes on him steadily. Her hands were tucked under the sofa cushion she sat on. "Quentin Connolley—your friend."

"I grant you, I find this embarrassing. There is no reason you should have to know this. But let me make the situation clear. Quentin was in possession of a valuable object by highly questionable means, probably still quite illegally. He wanted to dispose of it immediately and for cash, which means he never wanted the legality tested, he did not want to declare ownership or pay income tax on the sale. He has his own plans for making himself feel better by the way in which he will spend the money—philanthropically. One hundred thousand suits his purposes very well.

"Robert Stanton is an operator, a speculator, accustomed to making shady deals. He has no personal desire to own a Rembrandt; he simply sees an interesting investment. It is worth two hundred thousand to him. Both of them are engaged in illegal actions—and know it. I made the connection between them. But I have done nothing illegal. Quentin is satisfied. Stanton is satisfied. There is no record, no way in which I should be implicated. I have no more cheated Quentin than I have cheated Stanton."

"But you have cheated yourself," Kate said. "You have made of yourself a cheater."

"That is a very unkind and unnecessary way for you to interpret it. As I said, there was no reason for you to have known this. If you hadn't overheard my conversation with Quentin, and if you hadn't sat here while the bastard counted out the money, you wouldn't have had any idea."

Kate completed the thought: "That what you are doing is unethical, immoral."

"No one would ever have known."

"But I know now." She was deeply grateful to him for calling the man "Stanton." That put distance between the person who left the room a mere half hour ago and the reality of Roman Stanski. It made it easier for her to confront him with the perpetration of a deception before her eyes while keeping at arm's length the reality of her own deception. He must never know. "And I wish to ask you," she said as gently as possible, "to give the two hundred thousand dollars to Quentin."

Henry crushed out the cigar in an ashtray. "I'll think about it," he said, resisting.

And I'll help you, Kate thought. We must be decent with each other or we might as well abandon each other. As it is, I've lost my foothold on life; I'm slipping. I might just fall all the way down.

Robert Stanton always rented one of the penthouse suites at the Sheraton-Plaza when he had business in New Haven, even if only for a few hours. This Sunday afternoon there was no commercial business. He had agreed to come because of a seductive telephone call. And now he was ecstatic. His driver would stand guard over the Rembrandt and the car; he would entertain himself. But he was bursting with the extraordinary news. He was the father of a son. He—childless. He—at forty-three—had just learned that there was a male child, a human being, a handsome athlete of nineteen who was his child. He had fathered a boy: vigorous, good-natured, big. He felt twice his height, twice as potent. He stripped off all of his clothes in the living room, turned on the radio to sweet music; out of his attaché case he brought a flask of Cognac and took a healthy swig. Naked he lunged toward the bathroom and showered, stroking his suds-covered body with pleasurable appreciation, humming.

When the doorbell rang, he was dried, with a fresh towel wrapped around his waist. He let the woman in and locked the door behind her. "Darling!" he shouted, threw his arms around her; held her firm with one arm around her waist, kissed her a necklace of kisses around the throat and clutched at her buttocks with his other hand.

"Lion!" she said, her head tilted back, her spine arched against his passionate pressure. "You're too much."

He hoisted her in his powerful arms and carried her into the bedroom. "Joy," he said, "I bring you infinite joy. I am filled with joy. Let me share it with you."

There were no sandals with bells on Isabel Taylor's toes today. Her long blond hair fell loose around her head. She wore ballet slippers and a dress of white satin with a sailor collar. She wore nothing under it. Stanton stripped her naked in an instant, threw back the covers of the bed, wrestled her into a position of submission and made love to her like a stallion, with her legs up over his shoulders, her hands caressing his head and the small of his back.

When it was over, she covered herself with the sheet; he wrapped the towel around his middle again and stood at the foot of the bed, staring at her, approving.

"You are fantastic," she said.

"You're not bad yourself."

He lit cigarettes for both of them and they smoked. But he could not sit down. He stalked the room.

"You're flying," she said. "What's got into you?" They had known each other for five years. They had met at Monte Carlo one summer, at a gambling table. He had become sensitive about balding and decided to shave off all the rest of the hair on his head. She was the first of the girls he was to meet who were turned on by that. She said he looked like Yul Brynner and she'd like to tan his leather. He said she was a smartass and he'd like to pull her into shape. His wife was not on vacation with him; she was an invalid. Stanton met Isabel occasionally over the years, more often after she had married and settled in New Haven.

"Of course I'm flying. This is one of the greatest days of my life." He was strutting.

"What's happened?"

He stopped at the foot of the bed and met her look. "Can you keep a secret?" He was so eager.

Silkily she said, "I am a secret."

"If I tell you something secret will you promise never to say a word about it?"

"No," she said, complacently.

He laughed. "Then I'll tell you."

"What?"

"I have a son."

Isabel thought of saying, Just one? But she let out, "No kidding."

"I just found out. Today. Right here—well, in Woodbridge. A nineteen-year-old boy. Would you believe it? I didn't know he had been born."

"Anyone I know?" she asked, casually interested.

"His name is Jonathan Warner."

She sat up, annoyed; she snuffed out the cigarette. That touched upon real life. She was not amused. "You mean, you and Kate Warner . . ." She was looking for a way to make the connection.

"No. Kate wasn't married in those days. And I wasn't either. Isn't it incredible?! I haven't even seen him. But just the idea of him—"

"Ah, machismo," Isabel said. She did not mean to condescend to him, but he was making himself ridiculous. He was barrel-chested, with no hair on his head, a man of prowess, devoted to an ailing wife, and glorious in bed. A rich man. Why did this matter so much? Then she added, "Don't get carried away."

"Have you ever seen him?"

"Yes." She was uncertain of whether she should say it, but then she added, "He looks like Kate, not like you."

All he replied was: "He's nineteen years old. . . . He's a man."

In the locker room at the golf course, the wall clock read four thirty. Jonathan was sweaty and happy; he shaved and showered and dressed in the clean blue jeans and the striped soccer shirt he had brought with him. He had played eighteen holes in sixty-eight, one of his best scores ever. Then he drove his mother's convertible into town, thinking of how eager Joan Rohan had sounded about seeing him again. Horny. Hungry for him. He tried to remember what she looked like, but he could recall only the honey-colored pony tail and the turned-up nose. She didn't ask him to meet her at her apartment. She wanted him to find her at Kaysey's restaurant and bar near where she lived. He smiled to himself. Where would they go this time? A Sunday evening. He had some money in his pocket. He was clean and strong; he hadn't had any action since that night with her before he went to Martha's Vineyard.

The light in the bar was dim but he recognized her: she was watching the crabs and a lobster in the fish tank, the bright green water lit up from behind. She looked thinner than he remembered. She was in a white sweater that revealed her little pear-shaped breasts; her hands were concealed in the pockets of her slacks. "Hi," he said patting her on the shoulder.

She twisted her shoulder away from his touch and looked at his face. Her features were expressionless.

"May I help you?" a waitress, holding menus in one hand, asked them with a pleasant smile.

"How about a booth?" Jonathan said.

They followed the waitress to the back of the restaurant to the last booth, next to the swinging doors of the kitchen, and sat down on the brown leather benches facing each other. "What would you like?"

Joan said, "Gin and tonic."

"Same here," Jonathan said. Why does she seem so distant?

"I've waited for more than a week for you to show up." Her voice was low.

"I've been away."

"Playboy," she said, flatly. They raised their glasses and drank. He discovered that she bit her fingernails.

"I came back to you as soon as I could." He smirked.

Very quietly but distinctly, as if she were laying out cards on the table before him with one word on each, she said, "You owe me a great deal of money."

"What for?"

She looked around the crowded restaurant, turned back to face him, sipped the drink again before saying, "Remember my slip?"

"Sure. I owe you a new slip."

She whispered, "I haven't washed it since that night."

"Are you sentimental?"

"Are you stupid?"

He was offended. "What's *with* you, anyway?"

"My slip is very dirty. You wiped down the car with it. Remember? You know what? There's a lot of blood on that slip."

"Blood . . . ?"

"Keep your voice down. I didn't wash it because of what I read in the paper the next day. There was a kid killed— right there—on the way to the Road Side. Raymond Connolley. Did you know that? The police don't have any idea who did it."

Jonathan felt the quickened palpitations of his heart. "So . . . ?"

"I knew you'd want to buy that slip."

"What for?"

"To get rid of it."

"I don't know what the hell you're talking about."

She sat upright. The light in the restaurant colored her face an unhealthy yellow. "Okay," she said. "I'll spell it out for you." The hissing of her words was ominous. "I figure that slip is worth twenty-five thousand dollars to you. I know who you are. Your father owns Warner and Son." Still conspiratorial, she said, "I know you killed that kid and the police would be very grateful for any information leading to . . . But we wouldn't want that to happen, would we?"

"What?"

"My going to the police."

He swallowed hard. "How could you do that?" he asked, feeling cornered. But this is make-believe. What's happening to me is taking place somewhere between old gangster movies on television and my desire to run home to my mother. This stranger is challenging my life.

"Easy," she answered. "I'd just tell the truth. And show them the slip."

"The truth? Why did you wait so long?" He swallowed the last of his drink in one gulp. "They'll want to know that." Realizing he had grasped a weapon to defend himself with, he continued, "And then there'll be what *I* tell the police. About the poppers you gave me," he whispered, "and the coke, and the LSD."

"You're making that up! It's a lie."

"Your word against mine. What would they find if they searched your apartment?"

"You don't know anything about me."

"I know you must have a taste for something expensive. I know that blackmail is a crime. You thought you had me over a barrel."

"You *did* it!"

"And you're going to prove it?"

"I've got the evidence."

"You've got a slip that needs a good washing. Maybe you ran out of Kotex."

She slumped back against the wall of the booth. "You are not going to buy it," she said more to herself than to him.

"Here," he said, as he stood up, drawing a ten-dollar bill out of his pocket, "let this take care of the drinks and help you toward a new slip."

She looked up at him full of hatred. "I'll get even with you."

Jonathan walked deliberately, slowly, through the restaurant and the bar hoping that no one would restrain him or think of pursuing him, but when he reached the College Street sidewalk he broke into a run. He was wearing sneakers. His elbows chopped at the air as if he were starting a hundred-yard dash. At the corner of Chapel Street he turned north in the street, running with the traffic, hurling himself away from the girl, the threat. He thought he might have won for now, but would she attack him again? She knew who his father was. Would she go to him? His mother's car was parked on Wall Street under an archway that connects two buildings of the Yale Art School. A man with a leathery face stood there leaning against the driver's door. Jonathan stopped cold, panting, and rested both hands on the trunk of the car. The man wore a dirty Army fatigue jacket and old khaki pants; the growth of beard on his cheeks was the same unkempt pepper and salt as the hair of his head. He asked, "What are you doing here?"

"It's my car!" Could this be a plainclothes man?

"What am I doing here?" the derelict asked.

Jonathan went icy with fear. He forced himself to approach the man, his arm outstretched, push him back, and get into the car. As he turned the ignition key, he saw the man look up to heaven, to the darkening twilight of this Sunday evening, his empty palms turned upward, and shout his plea for an answer: "What am I doing here?"

Insanity terrified Jonathan. To be touched by it, as by death, brushed by it, pierced by it, is to be infected, to run the risk of being shattered, split apart. He slammed his foot on the accelerator and the car shot off down the middle of the street.

He raced the car on Whitney Avenue, gunning the motor on toward Hamden, through Hamden toward the suburbs, before he realized he had no idea of where he was going. He stopped, put the gear in reverse, turned the car around, back toward the city. It was then after eight o'clock and beginning to grow dark. Clear dark. Night dark. Summer dark. His parents did not expect him home. He phoned them to say he had a date with a poem. Were the police looking for him? Sunday, summer night. Where was he to go? Where would he be safe? He came to the stop light at the Peabody Museum and realized that he was only a few blocks from Conrad Taylor's house. He ought to ask about a summer job: work; clean-cut; worthwhile. His father had told Conrad that he wanted to talk with him about the chances for a summer job at the university. Maybe Conrad would know of something he could do. Maybe Conrad could tie him into the real world. Whatever that was.

He turned right and drove the car up to Hillhouse Avenue and parked within a stone's throw of the house of the President of Yale. He walked past two or three other heavy homes until he came to the one that the Taylors lived in. These buildings made him think of terms like "worthy" or "pillars of society." The Taylors' house may have been built of wood in the Greek Revival period, but it looked as though it was planned to become a National Monument. He rang the bell.

Isabel opened the door. She was holding a hair brush at shoulder level. He took a step back.

"Hello, cute stuff," she said. He jerked his head up, throwing his long dark bangs back toward the top of his head.

"Hi! I wonder if Mr. Taylor is in."

"No, sweetie," she said, "he's at Berkeley for the weekend. He's giving an convocation address. Dig that!" She grasped him by the wrist and pulled him inside, shutting the door behind him. "You just come along with me." She led him through the central hall into a room that was called the Bar. He sensed both that the house was empty and that she had been drinking. She looked disheveled. Her white satin dress was rumpled and she was brushing her long blond hair idly. They have no children at home, he realized; they can give over a whole room for a Bar. "I think it's a godsend that you just dropped in like this," she said, chuckling. "A real godsend."

"How come?"

"Would you like a drink? Coke? Beer? Liquor?"

"I'd like a gin and tonic, if that's all right."

"Sure," she said, stepping behind the kidney-shaped bar in the corner. There were big lamps with dark lampshades on them. She mixed the drink for him and made another martini for herself; and then they were seated in large plaid overstuffed chairs facing each other. "Drink," she ordered.

"I'm sorry to drop in like this, without calling first."

"No, no," she said, crossing her legs, "you shouldn't be. It's destined. It's a necessary coincidence. I was talking about you with someone just this afternoon."

"You were?"

She looked at him, remembering what Stanton had said—"He's nineteen—a man"—and remembering that Stanton had never seen him.

"Yes," she said, "someone you don't know, but who was interested in you."

"Really?" He felt cold sober and fearful. Then he realized he was starving. He saw a bowl of peanuts on the bar and scooped up a handful for his supper.

Her eyes roamed lazily over his strong body. "Are you surprised that people talk about you behind your back?"

"I've never thought about it," he said.

"Are you aware that you are very handsome?"

"No," he said modestly. Next she'll ask me about what I want to "do" or what profession I'm planning to go into. "When will Mr. Taylor be back?" he asked.

"Tomorrow night." She took off her ballet slippers and wiggled her toes.

He became aware that she had nothing on under the dress. I'd better ask when I can come to see him.

"He likes you," she said.

"I like him."

"That's cozy," she said, and sipped more of her drink. "I like you too." The thought suddenly struck her how amusing it would be to have the father in the afternoon and the son in the evening.

"Who talked with you about me this afternoon?" he asked as neutrally as he could.

"Someone you don't know," she replied. "Someone who had heard of you . . ."

"Heard?" he asked. From whom? Joan Rohan? The police? "Heard what?"

"That you're a jock."

"Oh, that."

The words had different associations for her than they had for him. She tried to look at him objectively. He was, quite simply, a beautiful hunk of man. "Nineteen—a man." She recrossed her legs the other way, this time. Her short dress wrinkled back closer to her hips.

"What kind of sex do you like?" she asked.

"Sex?" he responded; he wasn't in a condition to enjoy that luxury at the moment. "The best," he laughed.

"That's ambiguous. I mean, men or women?"

She was making him uneasy. He said, "Women."

"That's nice. You always have to ask nowadays."

He felt his genitals shrivel up out of uncertainty and fear. The thought of sexual pleasure was not present in his mind. Why was she talking about it? He supposed she wanted to be titillated by an account of sex on campus, the easy sex life of students today. That's what she wants to hear, isn't it? He said, "I've had my fling."

"Is it over?" Isabel asked.

"No," he snorted. "I still like it . . ." It occurred to him that it was pornography for middle-aged people to think about the younger generation having sex.

I am unique, she thought. I left the father two hours ago and now the son is alone with me in my empty house. What can I do with him? Make of him?

"May I have another?" he asked, holding up his glass.

"Of course," she said joyfully. He walked around the bar and mixed his own drink. Isabel thought, He wouldn't be doing that if he hadn't decided to stay. She was floating, skimming the surface, sailing free. "What do you say: you and I . . ." she asked, raising her arms toward him, beckoning him to her.

He understood. He was appalled. The bar stood between them. "You don't mean that."

"I'd like it." She did not like asking for it.

"You don't mean it."

"Why not?"

Gently, he offered, "You don't know what you're saying."

"I know," she assured him. She wasn't that tight.

"You'd better go to bed," he said, sensibly.

"Not without you."

"Wrong time," he said, considerately, although she didn't appeal to him at all.

He is spurning me, she realized. Like father, like son. It was Henry Warner who had once said, "I'm the only man in this room who didn't marry for money." I'm beautiful, she thought; why does my money bring out something ugly in men? Except for Stanton. It wasn't true of him. But of the others. There was always their self-hatred about not knowing whether they wanted me or wanted only something my money could buy.

"You shouldn't act like this." He came out from behind the bar.

"Oh, now you're going to tell me how I should behave."

"I didn't mean it like that."

"The hell you didn't."

"You've had too much to drink."

"Too much for some things; not enough for others." She stood up facing him. She was weaving. He felt the slight implication that she intended to see him out of the house but she was not equal to it.

"I'll go now," he said.

"You *do* that," she said icily. "Go home to mommy and daddy."

"Well," he said, "they live there too."

"Not *your* daddy, babe."

"What do you mean by that?"

"Henry Warner isn't your father."

"Poor Isabel," he said, comfortably, "you are very, *very* drunk."

"Poor Jonathan," she replied, "you are very, *very* dumb."

"Why do you say that?"

"You wouldn't know your own father if you saw him." She rasped out a coarse laugh in appreciation of her own wit.

He said, "What the hell are you talking about?"

"Henry Warner is not your father," she said, unsteadily.

Then she sat down again. "I know who your father is."

"I don't believe you."

"I couldn't care less."

Jonathan braced himself. He spread his legs apart for better balance; he put one hand out to the edge of the bar. "Who is he?" Jonathan asked.

"Who is what?"

"My father."

"Robert Stanton."

"Who is that?"

"A man I know—in New York. A very interesting man. You ought to meet him," she laughed. "I'll give you his phone number. Try him. See if I'm right. Say *I* told you to call him."

The quiet of the afternoon at the Warners' intensified into the silence of the evening. Peggy and Gabriel had playmates visiting with them and they went their separate ways—the boys up in the tree house near the tennis court, the girls most of the time at the doll house in Peggy's room. Henry changed into old clothes and spent the afternoon gardening. Kate lay back on a beach chair in the warm sunlight on the terrace. Her eyes were closed—fearful, staring at the sight of Roman Stanski.

After the children's friends had been picked up by their parents, there was a makeshift dinner in the breakfast room in an atmosphere of uncomfortable quiet. The children did not want to face the truth of how soon they would be going away to camp. Henry felt unfairly chided and thought it better to keep his peace than to show how thorny he felt. Kate seemed afraid of speech—frightened by whatever she might blurt out. They were not so much with each other or against each other as they were enduring a waiting period. Even the dog and cat stayed in opposite corners of the room. Peggy actually said, "It feels like Free Time at school when nobody knows what to do."

In that mood the evening passed until the children finally fell asleep. Kate came back to the living room in her yellow bathrobe, with a Bloody Mary in one hand and a cigarette in the other. Henry dropped the newspaper onto the sofa next to him. "Want to see the *News?*" he asked.

"No. If you don't mind, I'd rather not. I want to play for a while." She walked toward the piano as he stood up. "I'll see you later," he said, and started to leave the room but thought better of it, came back to kiss her on the forehead. "I love you, you know."

She said, "I hope so."

He went up to his bedroom to watch a television review of the week's activities of the Judiciary Sub-Committee of the House investigating the question of impeachment.

Kate sight-read the Poulenc score that happened to be open on the piano. Then from memory she played Bach and Vivaldi, over and over. Gradually, she began to feel that her mind would be allowed to function again. Her body was here, her fingers were moving on the keys by means of some arrangement between her memory and nerves and muscles that she had no insight into. Her head was clear. Her breathing was normal. But she was conscious only of having been shaken up twice this day as she imagined a patient coming out of shock treatment must feel: ravaged, made sordid by the abuse.

Roman Stanski had been present, in this room, she told herself, because Henry Warner wanted to profit secretly from a shady deal. How could she sort that out? How could she shame him out of what he was about to do, when she had carried out a deception for as long as she had known him? "It hurt no one." That is what Henry too felt about taking advantage of both Quentin and Robert Stanton. What you don't know can't hurt you.

No one, absolutely no one in the world had known the truth about her relationship with Stanski, not even her mother. She couldn't have told her mother. During the first few weeks after he had abandoned her she imagined what might happen if she looked for compassion from her mother. Her mother would have relished the self-righteousness of "I told you so" far more than she would have sympathized. She too would have urged her to "get rid of it." That "it," then, who was to become Jonathan, now. She did not tell her mother she was pregnant until after she agreed to marry Henry; and she told her that Stanski had been killed in battle. In the agony of the month before she met Henry she had thought of suicide often enough; not of abortion. But suicide was an absurdity: she loved life too much. And "it" was part of her life; she hated Stanski but she did not hate herself. She had loved him intensely but without enough experience of the world. She was the victim of what she did not know, had not been able to judge accurately: the extent to which he loved her, how good he would be to her, how much he needed her on her terms. She had been mistaken. She had been taken in, deceived. She had been debased, made smaller, receiving from him less than she believed she deserved in return for having filled him with satisfaction which had made him larger.

Was there any possibility that it was her fault—her not being able to judge him correctly? How could she have known that he would prove insincere, callous, indifferent? She had come out of a milieu where everyone seemed to mean what they said, where the assumption of civilized life was that you appear to others as, in fact, for yourself you are. That was the nature of integrity. Between lovers, marriage is the test of the genuine, the authentic character of the relationship. Could she by any means have known—could she be held at fault for not knowing in advance—that when she thought he would be eager to marry her he would reject her? Reject her hope, her need, her wish? She could not blame herself for not knowing. It made no more sense to her than taking blame for not knowing when she would die, or not knowing anything else in the world that is unknowable by anyone before the event occurs. Her mother could pretend that she knew it would happen, but that was only because, assuming the worst would happen all of the time, it turned out that her mother was right more often than not; but not because of accurate judgment.

Stanski's rejection could not have been anticipated. It was bad luck. And then there was meeting Henry, who became her good luck—but equally accidental. Women are infinitely more subject to such vagaries of chance than men are. Of course, she could have rejected Henry, made a career for herself, brought up the child by herself. It was done even then, twenty years ago. Was it lack of courage? She never thought of marrying Henry for escape or security, let alone for the appearance of respectability, because she had always thought of herself as eminently worthy of respect. She was a good person. Henry was attractive and seductive. He courted her. He made her feel confident in him. He was not put off by the fact that she was pregnant. "Two for the price of one," he had said, laughing, happy.

No, there was more than a sexual attraction between them. He came out of an established and protected world of old money and tight family ties. Not great wealth, but high comfort; not unearned, worked at. There were many things he cared about that meant nothing to her: the formal conventions of his social class; golf, heirlooms, fine art, decorative arts. She looked across the piano to the Meissen figurines in the corner. She had felt there was something snobbish about this world of his. The correct glass for the appropriate wine. But slowly, by assimilation, she had come to understand why such things gave him pleasure, had come to even contribute to those pleasures. If she hadn't truly come to feel that way, she would never have gone to all the trouble about the wallpaper of the fox hunting scene, for example. She was no longer merely for him, she was with him. His completely private world was a refuge for her from the frenzy of the public life that her parents lived in, or imagined they lived in, while she was growing up. A refuge from all she had suffered as a schoolgirl during the McCarthy period, taunted by the dumb oxes and the bullies and the know-nothings in her class with "Here comes the Commies' kid." She had told them where to get off. And she won out—by dint of her own personality—despite her parents and despite the dumb oxes. She had made them respect her. It was the guts to do that which Henry admired. But it had taken its toll. She wanted never again to be abused by someone else's selfish passions, however nobly intended; then, longing to make her own life, she had plunged into the affair with Roman Stanski by mistake.

She came to be attracted to Henry's secure world; and he had been fascinated by her idealizing intensity. She married him because he knew what time it was without looking at a clock; and he married her because she said, if Tuesday was lovely, "This is the most glorious day there ever was"; and if Friday was fine, then, "There never was a more beautiful day in the whole world." Henry loved her passionately and then he loved her devotedly. To her complete amazement, their sexual pleasures had become, gradually, more and more gratifying. She trusted him and he guided her. They had taken their time, as if there would be no end of time. Even now, after twenty years, their love-making sometimes was more thrilling than it had ever been before. The whole quality of her life was more satisfying than it had ever been before. And yet there were all the difficulties: the disappointments with the children, the emotional strain of pressing back against their resistance, the endless rut of the household and the social routines. If she had been a revolutionary like her parents there would have been the endless rut of the public meetings, the rallies, the pamphlets, appealing for funds, the kaffee-klatsch campaigning for votes. She might have been a lawyer; she might have been a crusader.

She might have been Roman Stanski's wife. That pulled her up short. Can a woman really imagine what she would have become after twenty years of marriage to a different husband? What would she have assimilated by contagion from that? What would she have come to depend on from *him?* How different would she feel about things today, if he had married her instead of walking out?

"They're going to hang him," Henry said, standing in the archway.

"Who?" she demanded, spinning around on the piano stool to look at him, shivering suddenly, as if he had read her thoughts.

"Nixon."

"Oh, that . . ."

"The noose is growing tighter."

"Good."

She was bored with the lumbering of the whole legal process. The man was vile. A country gets the kind of government it deserves, she thought. And then, she realized, I have much more important things to think about.

"Jonathan isn't home yet."

"What time is it?" she asked.

"Midnight."

"He's young . . ."

"Do you want to go to sleep?"

"Not yet," she replied. "Do you mind?"

"No. Of course. It's been a bad day. I'm sorry . . . I wish you a good night's sleep."

"I'll see you tomorrow, darling."

"Good night."

She imagined that he would go up; instead he walked along the terrace for a while. She could see the glow of his cigar and his silhouette as he moved slowly back and forth along the flagstones. And then she saw it no longer. She was alone.

She had never expected to encounter Stanski—Stanton—again. She knew people in Manhattan who were divorced and lived within ten blocks of each other who not only never ran into each other again, but never saw anyone, never heard from any mutual friend who knew anything about the "Ex." People do disappear from your life. Why should this have happened to her? Why should she have not been left alone —successful—in denying his existence, as she had been all these years? The whole sequence of events was unimaginable: that Raymond was killed, that Quentin took it as his responsibility and asked Henry to sell the Rembrandt, that Robert Stanton had bought it. All utterly unpredictable. But it had happened. The result being Roman Stanski's presence in her living room—today. And her need to think through who she was, and what she might have been if—if. . . .

The concept of *might have been* struck Kate as the most cruel demand upon the human imagination. Our actual lives are an accumulation of costumes draped upon a clothes-horse. Can one imagine divesting oneself of all accidents—of husband, children, home, friends; reducing experience simply to being alive? What would be left?

It is possible, in thinking of the human body, to say what has to be left in order for me to recognize that I am alive at all. Kate's father had given her Dalton Trumbo's *Johnny Got His Gun* to read as an adolescent. She had never forgotten the man with no arms, no legs, no face, no ability to speak, still self-conscious, conscious of his life, of memory and of sensations. He could think, he could feel, and therefore he believed in the integrity of his physical life. That must have been what Descartes meant by the dictum, "I think, therefore I am." But this is true as a proof of bodily existence only.

What is the absolute minimum of a moral life? To be a self-respecting person and not a vegetable. Not consciousness alone. For moral integrity one must be able to say, "I think well enough of myself, therefore, I am." I am a human being, not just a breathing animal life conscious of itself. But how much of my self-respect depends on the opinion of others? On Henry, on the children, on what my friends think of me? On Henry, she thought, and how would his opinion alter if he knew that I had lied. That Roman Stanski was not dead. That he and I had not been married. That Robert Stanton who appeared here this noon was Jonathan's father. How much difference would it make? And what would his hard feelings do to her? But after twenty years together, how could she measure that? Measure where he left off feeling with her, and for her? To what degree had their feelings merged? And how could she possibly come to an accurate judgment of that in advance of its being tested?

Monday was dreadful. Henry had a full day at the store and Kate said that she could do it all herself—seeing the children off to camp; he merely hugged and kissed them good-bye after breakfast. But she had not anticipated that in the midst of everything else there would be the scene with Jonathan, who had stayed out all night.

"Where were you?" she asked. He arrived home at ten in the morning.

"Does it matter?"

She doubted that he had ever asked that question before. "No," she answered. "Are you all right?"

"I guess so."

That was off-putting. Are we no longer to be confidants? I suppose this had to come sooner or later, she thought; he is more than nineteen years old. She had to think of filling the duffel bags for the two little children, of whether the name tags were on *all* of their things; of the time for delivery at the railroad station. Helen stood next to them pretending to wash up the breakfast dishes but listening to every word.

"Come," Kate said, leading Jonathan into the dining room. They sat down opposite each other across the long table. "Is something troubling you?" she asked.

"No." He was withdrawn, distant.

"Is there anything I can do for you?" Kate asked, more gently.

"Lend me your car for a couple of days. I have to go to New York. I tried to see Conrad Taylor last night about a summer job but he's out of town. I'd like a job. Not necessarily here. I have a friend in Manhattan—Terry Lewis. His father's big in lumber mills all over New England. Maybe I can get something from him. I called him last night. He invited me down for a couple of days."

"I can't lend you my car for a couple of days," she said simply.

"Okay. I'll take the train."

"Jonathan," she reached out toward him across the table but his hands remained on his knees, "you don't really have to take a summer job. You can relax. Enjoy yourself here. You've worked hard enough . . ."

He withdrew further. "I want to," was what he said.

This is wrong; something is wrong, Kate felt, without a clue as to what it was. "What happened last night?"

"Nothing."

"The poem?"

He paused. "She turned out to be a dud."

"Too bad. There will be others." She looked at him appreciatively. "Lots of others."

"Maybe. It doesn't matter at the moment. What I want is work."

"Yes, then you should have work," she said. "You are ready for work." She loved him intensely. He was not only her first child; he was her child alone. Somehow he must know of the special bond between them. If it hadn't been for her loving him, even before he was born, he would not exist.

"I'll be back as soon as I can," he said.

Yes, she thought, I believe you, although I don't understand what is happening to you. "Do you have enough money?"

"Sure," he said.

"Why don't you help me with the little kids? When I take them to the camp train, you can find a train going to New York."

"All right," he answered, reserved, amenable, but self-protective.

It was already a hideous day.

She did it all, she who might have been a revolutionary, a lawyer, a crusader, saw to it that her two little children, adequately equipped, were delivered into the hands of the camp counselors and the camp director, and her big child found the next train going in the opposite direction, to the city. She did it as if it were a matter of arranging who sat where at a dinner party, but it wasn't. The little kids laughed and they cried, and hugged her, and had to pee; Jonathan stood stiff and remote as if he were a family retainer who was not quite bright enough to understand orders, but willing at times to do her bidding. A servant of her father's she had inherited, growing senile. It was gruesome.

Then she was alone, in the old railroad station of New Haven, Connecticut. Listening to the echo of her own footsteps. Everything about the station was handsome, once, she thought; but decline, decay had set in. That was true of the railroad station. Could it apply to her relations with her children? Within the same hour they were all gone, dispersed. At least temporarily. She should feel free and light-hearted, looking forward to being alone with her husband, her lover, the dearest man of her life. Alone together. Gratified. Liberated. They had earned it. But the thought of being alone with Henry made her uneasy. What was happening to him? And to her? She drove her car back to Woodbridge in uncertainty and fearfulness, knowing, This is not the way it should be. She drove Helen to the bus stop. And then she was by herself in the kitchen waiting for her husband to come home.

"Why are you so late?" she asked when he arrived.

"I went to see Quentin, in his office. To give him the money. He's changed. You can't imagine. He shaved off his beard! He's soft-spoken and reserved. No. I'd say he's transformed."

There was a long pause. "How much did you give him?" she asked.

"One hundred thousand."

Kate's hands were covered by two pot holders; she was about to take something out of the oven. "No," she said, and the potholders dropped from her hands onto the kitchen floor. "You cannot do this to me."

"To *you*?" Henry asked, incredulous.

"After all we talked about?"

"After all *you* had to say . . ." he answered.

"I don't believe it."

"What do you mean?" he asked.

"You cheated him," was all she could say.

"I delivered exactly what had been promised to him."

"You didn't give a damn about what we talked about."

"What we talked about?" he repeated, as if bewildered.

"Why are you acting like a moron?"

"How dare you?" he shouted.

"No," she said quietly, "you will not scream at me." And walked out of the room.

This was the form that their fights had always taken. One would challenge the other; then the volume of the voice would be raised; the other would criticize the style rather than the content; they would regroup their forces and, slowly, try to speak to each other. Once, after a bitter argument that woke Peggy late at night, she asked Kate the next morning, "Why do people shout at each other?"

"Because they want to hurt them. Shouting hurts the ears."

"If they want to hurt them," Peggy asked, "why don't they just give 'em a punch?"

"Because they still want to be civilized. Civilized people talk."

Kate stood in the center of the terrace looking out at the sky grown cloudy, smoking a cigarette, a dark figure; few of the lights were on. Henry approached slowly through the living room. He opened the French doors and let himself out near where she was standing. She did not turn; she felt his presence.

"You don't need the money," she said, quietly.

"How would you know?"

She whirled around. "You've led me to believe that you don't. That we're all right."

"You don't know anything about money," he said. "How much I make. How much I'm worth. Where you'd stand if I were to drop dead tomorrow. How you'd be taken care of. How the children would be sent through school. What the house is worth. What would become of the store."

"If I don't know that, it is entirely your fault." She felt put down; she was chattel. But she knew that whenever he had attempted to discuss such matters with her it was she who had resisted. She could no more believe in his death than she could in her own. There was no point in discussing such questions. They were morbid. She was only forty-one—three months ago.

"That's not fair," he said quietly, "and you know it."

They sat down on the ironwork chairs facing each other now, two silhouettes in the deepening evening.

"Why should you need the money: you have land you can sell, you have all sorts of ways of raising cash. Why should you need it so much that you would want it *this way?*"

"It is so easy," he answered.

"But it's so wrong."

"Ah," he intoned, sarcastically, "you are such an authority on right and wrong."

"And you don't know the difference between the two?" She felt that her life was being turned inside out; that, yes, there was a seamy side, full of loose threads, better concealed. But it is there, and she was being forced to rub her hands along the uneven edges, where the pinking shears had cut, and along the hidden line where the darts were sewn.

"Between the two," he said, "there is a gray area, where judgment is uncertain. Where the line cannot be clearly or sharply drawn. How much of the insurance on the car should be credited to business use? How many supplies from the store is it all right for me to use at home? How much entertainment is it permissible to charge to business-related expenses?"

"You're thinking of the tax review," she said.

"I'm thinking of the fact that there is a great deal of our lives that we would be willing to live on the stage of the Shubert Theater, in the presence of everyone we know; but that there is also a fair amount of what we do that takes place in the dressing rooms or in the alley behind the theater that we wouldn't want anyone else to know about, and that nobody else ought to know about. It may not be illegal; but it's none of their business."

She thought of sexual fidelity. Of the cautious and protective way in which they had come to a tacit understanding years before that he might have an affair or an occasional encounter with another woman; she was too sophisticated to imagine that it would never happen. And that was all right as long as she never knew about it, was never made to feel threatened by it. She thought no more jealously of his occasionally having another woman than she thought of his spending time playing golf.

"It's none of their business," she said, "as long as they don't know anything about it."

"Right."

"But I know about it."

"By accident."

"A curious accident: first, you called Quentin from your bedroom and then you had"—she swallowed, but must pronounce the name—"Stanton come to this house. Did you want me to find out?"

"Neither one seemed inappropriate to me at the time."

"But the combination resulted in my learning of something you didn't want me to know—that you don't want anyone to know. Because it's wrong."

"Are you my conscience?"

"That's what you married me for, isn't it?" she said sharply.

Very much in control of his anger, Henry said, "No. I married you because I thought you were wonderful—and it would fill my life with joy to be in your presence."

"Like owning a Chippendale chair that can't talk back."

He laughed. "No. I was aware that you can talk back."

"You knew that I hate liars and cheaters, and people who take unfair advantage of other people."

Slowly, he repeated: "What I am doing hurts nobody."

"It hurts me terribly!" she exclaimed.

"It's none of your business!" he shouted.

She was silent. Then she said, "The quality of your life is at the heart of my business. You are my business. The only question I can't answer for myself—because it's so horrible in its simplicity—is: How could you have done this? When did you think it out? How did it happen?"

"Too many questions at once," he said. And in a little while he explained, "If you know how to get things done in the world, it comes naturally."

"The world!" She groaned, throwing one arm to her shoulder in protection and with her other hand gesturing her rejection, her contempt. "It comes 'naturally'? You mean—this sort of thing is habitual?" She felt the invisible gauze that bound them together ripping, shredding . . . "Don't tell me that. Please!"

"I won't tell you anything you don't want to hear."

"Don't patronize me!"

"I am sorry that you found out about this and that it makes you unhappy."

"You must *not* keep that money."

"I have kept it," he said.

"I can't live with it. I can't live with anything you've come by so deceitfully." She thought of the amount it cost to send the children off to camp, of the money in her checking account, of Jonathan saying that he had enough. How much of it was dirty money? The crickets sounded intolerably noisy in the night air. The trees were listening. She stood up and went into the dining room. She poured out pink gin for both of them. Henry had followed her. They went into the living room together. Only the piano light was on. They sat at either end of the sofa, parallel, looking forward, away from each other.

"We are going to drink to keep from feeling things clearly," she said, "from understanding what is happening."

"I am feeling things clearly," he replied.

"Then what you say means that deep down you don't really care about me, care for me."

"It doesn't mean anything of the sort."

"You will not alter what you are doing, despite knowing how much it hurts me. You don't care about me enough."

"How much would be enough? Caring more about your

judgment of this matter than my own?"

She turned toward him, looked at him point-blank. She made the statement, "You are greedy. You want more than your fair share. You are like the children who don't know the limits, who have to bang their heads against something before they find out they've gone too far. Do you want to be caught? Punished? Do you need to be taken to court before you learn that you've overstepped the limit?"

"The limit of what?"

"What other people will stand for."

He snorted. "If you compare me with the children, do you want to be a mother to me, too? So that I have to come to you for approval? For a long time I've operated on the basis of self-approval. When you complain about how difficult it is to shape the children into being 'good,' what you mean is how difficult it is to make them carry out your will."

"That's how children learn to be good."

"By playing on their caring for you enough."

"Loving enough."

"Loving you more than they love themselves?"

"Yes. They can learn to love themselves later, after they've become decent human beings. Then they'll be somebody worth loving."

"You spend the first five years," Henry said, "trying to make a child self-sufficient, and the next fifteen trying to make him less selfish."

They sipped their drinks.

"It's your selfishness," Kate said, "that I'm fighting against."

"I am not being selfish." He thought of the roof, of his brother, of tuition, of clothing bills.

"You are not taking my feelings into consideration. I don't want to be married to a man who's so greedy that he'd risk his reputation, his friendships, his good name, his wife's respect for what? For a hundred thousand dollars he doesn't need." She had grown shrill with the ugliness of it.

"What I am doing," Henry replied in a level voice, "is perfectly all right."

"You are deceiving yourself. You are denying that what you're doing is immoral."

"Amoral."

She laughed. "Is that the word you've given it for sanction? To make you feel better. You know what that word means? It says"—acting out the gestures of a spastic or an idiot with her hands—"little old me, I just can't tell the difference between right and wrong."

"It isn't always so simple."

"This time it is. I don't have any difficulty with it at all. You are denying the facts. That's all it is."

"We all deny—all the time. We deny that anything undesirable will ever happen to us; we deny that accidents don't make sense; we deny that we're growing old, getting fat, going gray; we deny that there is injustice and inequality. We deny everything that would make us suffer. We deny death, disease, poverty, war, for the simple reason that, if we didn't, we would kill ourselves."

She stared at him. "A pretty speech," she said, close to a whisper. "All that to justify your doing something unethical and denying it in order to feel just fine about it."

"I love you dearly," he said, but added conclusively, "but I do not see this as unacceptable or unforgivable in the way that you do."

"You are asking me to become an accomplice, and that I won't do!"

"I'm not asking anything of the sort."

"I happen to know about it; that's the point. And if I go along with it, condone it, approve it—that will make it all right for you, won't it?"

"Yes."

"But I don't condone it. Don't you see?—it's as if I represented the rest of the world here and now. You don't have to be found out or dragged to trial, with your picture in the newspaper. You just have to recognize that while you sit there thinking you're above moral law, because you don't imagine you'll ever be found out, there *is* somebody in the world—*I*, who love you, and want to respect you—who knows that what you've done is wrong. And you can do something about it, before anything worse happens."

"What?" he asked.

"Get rid of the money. It doesn't belong to you. You shouldn't have it."

"How come you have such high standards?" He smiled at her, wanly. But he understood. The image of a picture in the newspaper had hit home. He knew the source of her anxiety. Until now he had felt she was being a shrew—that the quality of panic in her words was a gratuitous taunting of him. But she was fearful for herself. He knew how she had suffered, in the McCarthy days, from the abuse inflicted upon her. He did not want her to suffer again. Still, the possibility that what they were talking about might be made public seemed so remote, so unlikely. He resisted. His eyelids were drooping. He wanted to escape into sleep.

Kate felt that she had not altered his attitude. She had failed. Nothing was changed, except that he saw her as an enemy.

Jonathan waited until everyone except the maid had left the Lewises' apartment before approaching the telephone, and still he couldn't pick it up. He might be overheard. He would have to go out. The Lewises lived on one of the top floors of the Sherry-Netherland, and all of them had gone their separate ways after breakfast: Mr. Lewis to his office downtown; Mrs. Lewis to an organization for the benefit of the blind; Terry's younger sister to a class in some swimming pool; Terry himself to a lesson with his trumpet teacher. They were friends, but not intimates. Terry understood that he needed a "pad" in New York for a short time and was generous; but he wasn't concerned or probing. All that suited Jonathan fine. But he was unable to make the phone call from their apartment.

Out in front of the building he looked across the street and remembered the phone booths in the basement of the Plaza Hotel. He passed the line of horses and carriages with artificial flowers for decorations, waiting for riders in front of General Sherman's statue, and crossed the square to enter the hotel. It was ten o'clock in the morning. A large group of scrubby people stood about the entrance to the Palm Court in the Plaza. There were cameras pointed toward an elegant trio, seated at a near table.

"Quiet, please," implored a flunky who stood on a chair next to one of the cameras. "Take ten," he announced.

The girl in a silver lamé evening gown stood up and moved directly toward the camera and then passed it. One of the young men seated at the table turned to the other and offered him a cigarette. "That's a great-looking suit," he said. "It must be custom made."

"No," the other Beautiful Model replied, "I'd never pay more than a hundred and fifty dollars for a suit."

"Cut!" the director shouted. "You've got to put more feeling into the phrase 'more than.'"

Jonathan worked his way around the dozen or more spectators toward the staircase down to the phone booths he remembered and closed himself in behind the glass door. He took out the piece of paper on which Isabel Taylor had scribbled a phone number and stared at it on the glass shelf. Then he dialed the number.

The operator with a highly polished British voice repeated the number when she answered the call. "May I speak with Mr. Robert Stanton, please?" His Adam's apple felt especially thick in his throat.

"Who's calling, please?"

"Jonathan Warner."

"I'll find out," she said, noncommitally. But after a moment's wait, she said, "Mr. Warner, here is Mr. Stanton."

"Good morning," the older man said.

"Good morning, sir." Jonathan swallowed. Could he see this through?

"I wonder how you got this number." His voice was comfortable but with an edge of self-protectiveness on it.

"It was given to me by Isabel Taylor, Mrs. Conrad Taylor."

"Yes, of course," Stanton said, both appreciative and critical at the same time. "She is a good friend."

"Was she right in suggesting that I call you?" How much rode on that simple question: Why do you recognize my name, why are you talking with me, what the hell do we have to do with each other?

"It was very good of her. You must understand one thing, though. I never asked her to suggest that you call. That must have been her own idea."

"Yes. I'm sure it was." He could feel her presence, in the rumpled white satin dress close to him, laughing drunkenly at him. "It came up quite unexpectedly."

"Just between the two of you?"

"Yes. Mr. Taylor was out of town."

"Jonathan Warner, you say? Kate Warner's son?"

"Yes." He had no idea of what would happen next. There was a long pause.

"Are you calling from New Haven?"

"No. I'm in New York for a couple of days."

"I see. And you want to have a look at the Rembrandt?"

"What?"

"No. It's not here. It's in my apartment."

It struck Jonathan that the man was supplying him with a plausible motive for wanting to meet him.

"Yes. I'd like that," he said, weakly.

"You're an art student? Particularly interested in Rembrandt?"

There must be other people in the office with him, Jonathan realized. This was not being done for his benefit. "Yes," he said, barely audibly.

"Well, in that case, I'd be glad to have you come for a visit. Say at about five tomorrow afternoon. Is that convenient for you?"

"Yes," Jonathan said, feeling even more nervous and resentful. Is it possible that Isabel Taylor had really told him the truth? With half of his mind he had assumed that she was lying out of bitchiness.

Robert Stanton gave him the address of his apartment on Park Avenue in the sixties. "About five o'clock will be fine. I'll tell my wife you're coming for a quick drink. Okay?"

"Yes." Jonathan was almost inaudible.

"I look forward to that. Good-bye, now." He hung up. It was over. Jonathan had made the call and the man had responded as if—yes, as if—what Isabel told him might be true. His mother. A stranger. Rembrandt. Five o'clock tomorrow afternoon. How do I live until then? he wondered. He remained numbly unsure of himself there in the phone booth for a number of minutes. It seemed to him that only with great effort was he able to force himself to get up and then to move heavily up the stairs.

The television commercial crew and models were still at it. Their powerful lights caught glints of sweat on thick makeup. "Take fourteen," announced the flunky still standing on the chair. The girl in the evening gown sashayed toward the camera. The pretty boy said "That's a great-looking suit . . ."

Jonathan went out through the lobby facing the fountain on the square. I may think *they're* crazy, he realized, but they're doing it to earn a living. At least all their shit has that much purpose. I know that what I am about to do is crazy. Go visit a man named Robert Stanton on the pretext of being an art student interested in Rembrandt—and I don't know why?

Henry Warner narrowly escaped a head-on collision by a fraction of a second and the good fortune of excellent brakes. He was driving his car down the Ansonia Road toward the city, at a quarter of nine in the morning, when his left eye was caught by a brilliantly lit red cardinal in an oak tree; the morning sunlight gilded the outline of the large bird. He was not aware of the truck swinging from his right out of Overbrook Road to go up Ansonia until he came face to face with it. He avoided a crash, but, after the truck had curved around him—he could see the lips and the teeth of the driver cursing him from the open window—he felt the sweat on his forehead and palms; his body was suddenly stony.

This is probably how I will die, he thought. Someday, I will go out in front of the cottage in Maine to watch a sunset and fall off the end of the dock. Or my eyes will turn to follow a beautiful young girl bounding along the sidewalk and I'll drive the car into a lamp post. He fastened his seat belt and glided the Mercedes into movement again on the hill.

He could not remember at what point he had faded out of the conversation with Kate last night. He was in bed when he woke, but he did not remember having gone to his bed. The door to her room was locked when he tried it. He left the house without seeing her.

He knew that her argument was right but he had no idea of how to agree with her without losing face entirely. He thought it better to brazen it out. Still, his justification was destroyed. It was no longer the case that *no one* knew. Kate knew—and she was offended by it. He resented the thought of giving up a windfall of a hundred thousand dollars, free and clear—but it was no longer either clear or free. It was entangled with questions of his integrity and of her esteem.

The degree of caution that he exercised in his operations along the margins between his business life, his public life, and the life he shared with Kate, it seemed to him now, had *always* been conditioned by concern for his esteem in her eyes. Her wishes were to be respected—not because she could punish him in any of the ways a mother makes a child suffer, but because her self-respect carried with it the implication that there were limits to what she would put up with and, if the limits were exceeded, or exceeded too often, she would be free to leave, to abandon him. Of course, it occurred to him that mothers do that in the sense that they withdraw their love to punish their children; but do they ever say, "The contract is broken; it is null and void, goodbye!"? Perhaps. Kate was often enough on the verge of implying as much with their children. She did not walk out; nor did she always get her way.

When he arrived at the office, Mrs. Wicks said that Judge Jackman had phoned just a minute before he walked in.

"Oh. I didn't realize he was back already."

"He sounded very glad to be back."

"Does he want me to call him?"

"He'd like to play golf this afternoon, if possible."

Henry said, "Golf?" realizing how remote the idea was from his mind at the moment. "What day is it?"

"Tuesday."

"It's possible. Call his office and ask if he can meet me at the club at three."

In the privacy of his office, Henry found, on top of the stack of interoffice memos, separate from the morning mail, a statement from the business manager to the effect that the charges for insurance and security for the store would be increased, beginning with the new fiscal year, on July first, by seventeen percent. The amount of theft, shoplifting, and inside pilferage having increased drastically during the past year, and the costs for the installation of closed-circuit television observation having increased by a comparable percentage during the past twelve months, the rise in the rates was understandable, if not pleasant. A neat line of thought, Henry agreed with detachment, if not revulsion. The higher up you go, he thought, the shakier your dependence on a larger number of people to take care of other things. You are at their mercy. If they are not dependable, the real drawback is that you cannot do your own job. "And if I am not dependable for Kate," he recognized, "she cannot do her job."

He pushed and dragged himself through the morning. He met with Hopkins on pricing the new deliveries for the jewelry department; with the business manager about increasing fringe benefits for employees; with the buyer for the silver department, with the advertising agent, with Mrs. Wicks on correspondence. He was conscious of what was under discussion, of what decisions were made, but at a distance. He was not there. He was at the door to Kate's bedroom, his hand on the knob. He could feel the resistance of the lock through his flesh. What if one day he broke down the door and found the room empty?

The meetings continued. He observed, he conceded; but his heart was not at the store. Jonathan had gone to New York without saying good-bye; the small children were off to camp for the summer; Kate challenged him as a liar and a cheat. He had hoped to be clever, but she had "caught" him at it. It was no good. Everything was threatened. Everything that counted. He ate no lunch. He stood at the window of the office looking out at the Green—looking at the memory of the children's version of the arrival of the Pilgrims; at the imagined arrival of the original Pilgrims, thinking, How attractive is the nostalgia for simplicity, for a world of rules and regulations, clear-cut laws and customs. You would never have a doubt of the difference between right and wrong. But did such a time ever exist? Of course not. It is no more real to put it in the past, whether as a Golden Age of the gods on Olympus, or of the Noble Savage, than it is to project it into a utopian future. Perfection in human relations is as absurd an idea as a squared circle. In the real world there is only compromise with the needs and desires of one another, of here and now; and it would so be in every real world. He had always known that he could not be perfectly honest with Kate about everything. The strength she held in reserve, her independence, her privacy, consisted of her right to judge him and to leave him. In that way she was his conscience. But doesn't everybody try to cheat his conscience? To get away with something behind its back? Keeping from it things that might call forth vengeance? Therefore, he was aware of his thinking enough with her mind to decide about what things she would find unacceptable and covering them up. Her not knowing was the condition for their security, for the soundness of the high plateau they moved on, where they were together in so many ways. He was consoling himself for the loss of the hundred thousand dollars which he knew he would not retain, although he didn't know how he would divest himself of it.

At three o'clock he changed into golf clothes and was tying the laces of his shoes when Judge Jackman arrived in the locker room at the club.

"Boy, am I glad to see you!" the Judge exclaimed, shaking his hand.

"Good to see you again, Chester."

"I just want you to know I never saw one single golf course

in all of Greece," the Judge said, wallowing in his dismay.

Henry laughed.

"And they call it the source of all Western culture." The Judge smiled.

"Well, at least you survived."

"It was a trial," he joked. He began to change his clothes. "Too much beauty. Too much living in the past," he continued. "Now, imagine New Haven if its life revolved around the tourist trade that came from all over the world just to visit Judges' Cave on West Rock; that, and raising goats. Imagine!"

"Sounds healthy," Henry offered.

"Grotesque," the Judge replied. "Just try to imagine the difference between the goatherd who lives a hundred yards from the gates of Mycenae and the archaeologist from Finland or the Greek drama teacher from Hawaii who comes to gawk at the old stones every other day. Fan-tastic! I felt like an intruder at a freak show."

"Play golf," Henry demanded. "That'll clear the brain."

Chester Jackman was a man of sixty, tall and rangy, with a clean-shaven Lincoln-in-Illinois face and frame, thick lips, pouches under his eyes, bony hands with raised maps of blue veins on them. He had known Henry's grandfather when he was an adolescent and the old man, who was then in his eighties, had told him stories of the Civil War.

For the first eight holes the two friends hardly spoke to each other. At the ninth tee, after the caddies had left to look for their golf balls on either side of the fairway, the Judge stopped at the bench, said, "I think I'll catch my breath," and sat down.

"Good idea," Henry agreed, and sat down next to him. "Chester," he began lightly, "I'd like to ask you a hypothetical question."

"They're the best kind."

"You won't trouble yourself about why I'm asking, will you?"

"What's it about?"

"A legal opinion."

"Henry," the Judge began, pulling out a pack of cigarettes, "you know the old story? When two lawyers sit down to discuss a difference of opinion they get up with three opinions." He laughed to himself as if he were hearing it for the first time.

Henry laughed politely. "It's your opinion I'm interested in."

"Go ahead." He offered a cigarette but Henry declined. The old man struck a light for his own smoke and relaxed, with his elbows on his knees, looking outward, watching the caddies.

"Chester—what would you say if someone came to you with the following question: How should he advise his son who thinks that he might, possibly, have been responsible for a hit-and-run accident that resulted in someone's death? He isn't sure, by any means, that it was his fault, but he was near the scene of the accident about that time and he was high on beer, if not on other things. He was showing off for a girl and driving on a road in the woods without the car lights on. He didn't know about what happened for a couple of weeks until he gets back to town. He thinks he might have been responsible. Should he report that to the police?"

"What the hell for?" the Judge asked.

"To clear himself."

"What if he can't clear himself? He'll have an involuntary manslaughter charge brought against him, aggravated by reckless driving and drunken driving. Depending on the evidence and on the temperament of the judge—if and when the case comes to court, and do you have any idea of the backlog for court hearings?—then at the worst, if it's a first offense, he stands a chance for a three- to five-year sentence, which means he'll get out in a year and a half for good behavior. But, more likely it will be a suspended sentence on probation. It's all pointless," the Judge said. Then he moaned.

"Why do you say that?"

"The courts are overloaded with serious problems. This isn't one of them. Someone was killed. That's sad, that's bad. But punishing the driver in a hit-and-run accident? What purpose does it serve? An example to others, for deterrence?" He laughed. "Chastisement to the driver? To better him?" He snorted. "It's out of control, Henry. It's pointless. If the boy didn't mean to do it, the best you can do is to kick him in the ass and tell him to keep his lights on. Nothing the courts can do will bring the dead man back." He lifted his large head and blew out a long jet of cigarette smoke. "Nothing . . ."

"I can't tell whether you're being cynical or generous."

"Can't you?" The Judge stood up. "I never knew the difference between the two," he said, patting Henry on the shoulder. "Let's play." Everything else the Judge understood remained unsaid.

Kate was standing under one of the dogwood trees on the lawn as Henry drove up and parked in the driveway. It was twilight and rain clouds were beginning to gather in the north, airy but gray. He walked directly toward her and held out his hands but she did not take them. She was barefoot. She looked drab without makeup and with her hair unbrushed, as if she had spent the day crying or sleeping and had just awakened and wandered about, as in a dream, to find out where she was, and what she had to do.

"I picked up Helen in the morning," she said, "and I took her back in the evening; between those two major events, I have been in limbo. My children were gone, my husband was gone, and you know what I discovered?—I was gone."

"Oh, come on . . ." Henry began, putting an arm around her waist and drawing her close to him. "I'm really sorry about last night."

"How was your day?" she asked automatically, without any interest whatsoever.

"A pain," he answered, drawing her toward the house.

Her arm came around his back and they walked along together. They went through the hallway and the dining room to the terrace on the other side. They were alone. That was unusual in itself. They were still confronting each other; that was even more exceptional.

"I have done nothing about dinner," Kate said. "I can't eat. Do you need to?"

"No." Then he realized he hadn't eaten all day. "You sound glazed, Kate. Have you been drinking?"

"I haven't touched a drop. I'm perfectly sober. If I sound stupefied, it's because I am, but not because of anything other than what we've been talking about has happened to me."

"About that—" he began.

"I don't think you can ever make up for it. And I've come to the conclusion that if you don't get rid of the money then you are choosing to get rid of me. It's as simple as that."

"You haven't given me a chance." He felt her fierceness like animal claws now, poised to shred him, without listening, without waiting. "What makes you so intolerant?"

"Intolerant!" she snarled; she was fully awake now, ready to claw. "What a mealy-mouthed word! People are *tolerant* when they don't know what they ought to hate."

"You want to hate me?"

"No. I hate denial and deception. I hate getting away with murder. I hate smugness. And evil."

"I am not evil."

"You don't know what the hell you are."

"I know what you are."

"Really," she asked, imperiously. "What?"

"Holier-than-thou."

"That's a laugh."

"On the contrary. It's accurate."

"I'm not 'holy' about anything."

"Except your own idea of justice. Look, I understand you think what I've done is unfair—"

"It *is.*"

"Will you let me finish? It is. I realize that now. But everybody has his secrets."

"From his wife?"

"I suppose so."

"Well, then what? To understand all is to forgive all?"

"Why don't you wait a second? Why don't you listen?"

"I feel as though I don't have a second left."

"For what?"

"To escape."

"From me?"

"From quicksand."

"Oh, come on!"

"For a long while I've felt that I was in a rut. Now I feel that I'm in a cage—your cage—and I'm going to be smothered or drowned or something. You're going to talk me into believing that Black is White. And either I will hate you for that, or I'll . . . go to pieces."

"Nothing of the sort. It's just that everyone has secrets. Everyone knows things he'd rather no one else knew anything about."

"Everyone?" she asked. Was he implying that he had found out about Stanton and her?

"At least, I suspect so," he replied. "Jonathan, for example—"

"What? What about Jonathan?" she demanded.

Henry gagged with regret. But he couldn't keep it from

coming out now. "He thinks he might have had something to do with Raymond's death."

"What are you talking about?" She threw her arms around herself. Gentle as floating mist, a soft rain was beginning to fall, but neither of them moved.

Why had he said that? He had never intended to tell her. Now he had to go on.

"He was at the Road Side that night. He doesn't know if it was his car—"

"He told you that?"

"Yes."

"When?"

"Just before he went sailing."

"You never said a word. . . . What did you tell him?"

"To go away, not to say anything."

"Do you despise him so much for not being your own son that you would load his whole life down with that?" She felt the hair standing up on her head.

"For not being my own son?" he shouted. "What the hell do you mean? When, in all these years, do you imagine I have not thought of him as *my* son?"

"I've seen how you look at him sometimes, with that *What the devil are you doing in my house* look in your eye."

"You're mad."

"He's *my* son."

"You have to protect him from me," Henry concluded sardonically.

"You told him to keep his mouth shut and go away. You *knew* about this fear; and *that* was your advice?"

"You would have told him to go to the police?"

"Yes," Kate said.

Then he told her of the whole conversation with Judge Jackman.

"But that took place this afternoon," she said. "And you told him to go away and keep his mouth shut ten days ago."

"Does that mean I was less right than I would have been today?"

She looked at him in the darkening light, in the soft rain. "You weren't in the right either way."

"It depends on your standards," he answered.

"You've jeopardized his whole life."

"I was concerned with protecting his life."

"At what price? So that he will always feel he copped out? He evaded the consequences? Eluded them? Never faced up to what he did?"

"Might have done," Henry corrected.

"Oh, please," she begged. "If he didn't truly think it was his fault, he would never have raised the question at all."

"I don't believe that."

"How convenient. No wonder you didn't say, 'Go to the police. You must see what happens. At least you will always know that you faced up to it. No matter what the consequences.'"

"I don't think in those terms," he replied.

"You deny," she mocked him, "that anything undesirable will happen to you."

"I suppose so."

"That is contemptible."

"Of course," he said. "*Your* standards remain untarnished. The golden rule is shining golden all the time, through you, isn't it?"

"Make fun of me. I don't care. The fact is there are some basic human truths that I understand and, apparently, you do not." She turned her back on him and entered the house. He went in through the French doors of the living room, slowly, to find her standing in the center of the hallway, rigid in the center of the fox hunting scene, her arms still wrapped tight around herself as in a straitjacket.

"Don't touch me," she said, moving away from him toward the stairs. On the landing, she turned back to look at him.

"All through the day I suffered with the thought that because of what you're doing, you couldn't hurt me more. I was wrong. What you tell me now is worse." She went to her sewing room.

Henry stamped out of the house. It will still drizzling. He drove down toward the city, as far as the Sundial Bar in Westville, and drank Scotch and water, thinking, She is a spoiled brat, a fanatic, a harridan, a bitch. She is unbearable. He wanted to strangle her. The bartender and the other patrons along the long zinc-topped counter snapped around to stare at him. The glass he held was squeezed so tight it suddenly broke in his hand. Fragments of glass flew away from his fist, hitting the mirror opposite him, others skimmed along the shiny top of the bar. One triangle of glass was wedged into his palm. He was bleeding.

Kate left a note for him propped against the coffee pot, in the kitchen, so that he would be sure to find it. She wrote, "I'm going to see my mother and father. I'll stay overnight. Helen doesn't come today." It was a little past six o'clock in the morning. She raised the top on the convertible and secured it in place before she backed the car out of the garage. The dawn had turned the sky a milky white. The air was clear and cool after the rain. She felt oppressed. She wore black slacks and a zippered sweater of patchwork squares of fur. Her slender airline suitcase was on the seat next to her, along with her pocketbook.

The trip was easy. She was a good driver; there was little traffic on the highway but she drove slowly. The dogwoods along the Wilbur Cross were frothy with blossoms. Approaching the Bronx, she had to slow down. It was then about eight o'clock and she ran into the rush hour for cars moving into Manhattan. She was in no hurry. She was escaping from, not escaping to. It was even slower going through the city itself. She found herself glad for that and deliberately took the route across Central Park that led to Fifth Avenue in order to drive down her favorite street, expecting to relish the proximity of so many delights—the shops she had enjoyed the most over the years: Bergdorf's, and Bonwit's, and Saks; and along the side streets were the music shops, the bookstores, the museums. But there was no relish even in recollection. It was boring, like thinking about the good qualities of other people's children; *she* could take no pleasure in them. That wasn't where her capacity to feel was located now. She was relieved to reach lower Manhattan, finally, and drive across Brooklyn Bridge. To her amazement she lost her way and had to ask directions at a gas station. A Freudian slip, probably. She had driven this way to her parents hundreds of times. She took it as symbolic: she had lost her way.

Then she was in Brooklyn Heights approaching Willow Street. Their brownstone was four stories high, of a peculiar stratum of stone. Kate's father had told her, when she was a child, that it had the same combination of colors as the Grand Canyon at twilight, going from a yellowish hue at the top down to a maroon stone around the basement windows. It wasn't until years later that she learned he had never seen the Grand Canyon. Her parents had bought the house in the early thirties and finished paying off the mortgage thirty-five years later. There had always been a separate apartment on the fourth floor to rent out. But in the fifties they converted the third floor and rented that out as well. They occupied only the basement and first floor. Ten years ago they gave up the basement too. Kate locked her suitcase in the trunk of the car, parked a block and a half away, and walked to the stone steps and up them to the front door.

Mrs. Krevitz answered the bell and let her in. Mrs. Krevitz was the grandmother of the family living on the third floor. She looked after Kate's father, every hour or so, during the time that her mother was on her job at school in Greenwich Village. "Oh, how dee, Miz Warner," she smiled, through many missing teeth. "Nice to see you." The hallway smelled of rancid bacon fat.

"How is my father?"

"Good as can be expected." Mrs. Krevitz bent her head to one side as if listening with a good ear for any slight response. She wore bedroom slippers, a blotchy flowered housedress, and over each ear one pink curler in her gray hair.

"I'm glad to hear that. I'll be with him, now, until my mother comes back."

"Oh, it's no trouble."

"You won't have to look in for the rest of the day."

"Thank you, ma'am," she said, servile, dismissed. What must I look like to her? Kate wondered, glad that she had parked the white convertible out of sight. How offensive I must be. Mrs. Got-rocks, the jeweler's wife. She went into her parents' apartment.

It had not changed over the years. This eighteen nineties room, painted and repainted fifty times. White walls, white filmy curtains. The Navajo rug on the floor. The modest Shaker chairs and settee, like figures in a child's stick drawing. The studio couch that her mother slept on. Only the Delft tiles around the open fireplace—and they were in the house when her parents bought it—gave the room a touch of concern for appearance itself; otherwise, utility was all. And unpretentiousness. To pretend to something one was not was anathema in this household.

Books lined the walls on either side of the fireplace, as they coated all of the walls in the dining room. Her father's room was at the end of the hall beyond the kitchen. She knocked and then entered. It was even more awful than she remem-

bered. He sat curved in his wheelchair as if he were hump-
backed, his head nearly touching his left shoulder. He had
grown thin as a fifteen-year-old. She recalled how, in his
robustness, he could eat seven ears of corn in a row or drink
one tankard of beer after another. His white hair was very
thin and dull, but he was clean-shaven as ever. A neat man.
Her mother shaved him every morning. The television was
playing. She switched it off. "Daddy!" She wrapped her arms
around him and hugged him, her cheek against his cool
cheek. He wore something white over his shoulders like a
hospital gown and his legs and middle were covered with a
pale blue blanket, soft as a baby's carriage rug. His brown
eyes seemed blank, barely responsive. The flesh of his face
and his collarbones appeared to be growing transparent.
Even his nose appeared thinner, his cheeks sunken. Only the
index finger of his right hand moved. It twitched. She knelt
to kiss it. How you must suffer! she thought. It tore at her
heart. She zipped open her fur sweater and threw it down
on the bed. There was a tan silk blouse underneath. She
pulled up a straight chair to his feet, sat down, and began her
monologue.

"I'm so glad to see you. It's been weeks. But they've been
so busy. The children finishing the school year. Peggy and
Gabriel have just gone off to camp. Jonathan is back from
Michigan. Looking for a summer job. So healthy. So big and
strong. You must see him. You'd be so proud. Henry's in
wonderful shape. Of course, we drink too much and we
smoke too much—that goes without saying. But then—let's
see, he plays golf as often as he can, and I play *at* tennis with
him. We heard a magnificent concert of the Juilliard Quartet
the other night. Bartók and—I don't remember. The children were in a Pilgrim Pageant for the end of the school
year." She was suddenly ashamed. "I meant to bring you
flowers from the garden. I'm so sorry I forgot." She couldn't.
It was dawn. Henry was asleep. She might have cut a bouquet

but she turned her back on them. His flowers. "Next time," she said. Kate saw a copy of Thucydides as well as a collection of medicine bottles and pills on the occasional table next to his wheel chair. "You're not able to read, are you?" she said. "Does Mother read to you?" His eyelids drooped the message, yes. Imagine—*him* not able to read; imagine Neptune not able to swim, she thought.

He pointed with the one mobile index finger to a glass of water next to the book. Kate held it to his lips. He had almost no control over the muscles of his face. She held the back of his head with the other hand. The water dribbled down along the sides of his mouth as he drank. She patted his chin dry with the towel at the foot of the bed. Such a meticulous man. He detested a spot, a stain, dust, a slur. All this must be an incomparably worse punishment for him than death would be. He, who had moved thousands at rallies in Union Square—the orator, the teacher, the leader. Disgraced. Was there any sense in which he brought it on himself? Didn't his brilliant mind drive his light-weight body until it collapsed under the pressure? Unrelenting, always hurling himself up on toward the next foothold in the mountain climb.

They sat quietly facing each other again. The index finger pointed directly toward her.

"Me?" Kate asked, tossing her loose hair back around her head. "I'm all right." He would know she wasn't. She was sorry for pretending otherwise. "I'm in a rut. It's a very comfortable rut, but it's not good to feel that way." She sighed. "Actually, it stinks. After twenty years," she concluded, "I've come to the realization that I should never have married, never had children." She tried to laugh. "That's not what I'm good for. But then," the smile faded from her features, "I don't know what I *am* good for." She tilted her head, sadly, as if to say, What can you make of that? His blank eyes stared at her. "I'm always good for talk," she offered, patting his hand. "I always had a good mouth. Do you remember how many times we used to sit up talking, even when you came home very late at night? You and Mom and me. God, there was nothing we couldn't talk about—" Ideas. Their hopes. Debates. Current affairs. Theory. The endless engagement in interpretation. It was the breath of life. How could she ever have put it behind her? "Questions like: What is the difference between tactfulness and deception? Remember?"

Her father's eyes showed a brightness. "N, nch, on," he said.

"What?"

He tried to make the sounds clearer, as if recalling such a conversation from long ago. "In, en, hun," came out.

"Invention?" she asked.

His eyelids drooped. "In, ten, ton."

"Ah—intention! The difference is the intention. Yes, yes!" Had there ever been such a conversation when she was a child or was she fabricating this into the past? It was exactly the kind of exchange that might have taken place. . . . But we can know only our own intentions. The difference between the good will and the self-serving will is knowable only within the self. It's so easy to mislead others about your intentions. Unless caught out by cross-examination. That is why her father loved the law and believed in the procedures of the courtroom as the greatest creation of civil life. To find the truth, despite all efforts to conceal or distort it. "But can we be sure even of our own intentions?" she asked.

He seemed radiant to her. His mind was engaged. He was not a vegetable. His eyes smiled. "I love you," she said, "I want you to know—I've always loved you. Good times and bad. I'm sorry to have disappointed you. I just didn't have it in me to be otherwise." She became aware of the fact that she was crying, the wetness of her eyes clotted her eyelashes. "I'm sorry. I didn't mean . . ."

"On't rye," he forced out, in a whisper.

"Don't cry?" she repeated. Why not? Stiff upper lip? Can't

I grieve for you? This is worse than your being dead. Can't I grieve for myself? She sniffled and brought a handkerchief out of her pocketbook. "I'm sorry," she said, drying her eyes. "It's just so cruel. So unfair." She recalled, when she was at Hunter College, knowing a boy who was tape recording his grandfather's reflections on life, an old man dying, because, as he said, the man had a genuinely personal view of life. He had been a common laborer, but with an original, independent mind; he had arrived at his own wisdom. He had something to leave that was worth preserving. It was unique, the boy told her; and how many people can you say that of? It was true of her father, she thought; she knew him to be a wise man. And now he was unable to express himself, and all of that would be lost. The tears fell down the length of her cheeks, and dropped onto the knees of her slacks.

"Katie?" Her mother's voice called her up from behind.

She stood up and embraced her mother. "It's time for Dad's lunch now. You go into the living room. I'll see you in a few minutes."

A minute later, Kate backed out of the bedroom, making way for her mother carrying a small tray in her hands. There was a bowl of clear soup, a plate with tuna fish salad on it, and a glass of orange juice out of which stuck an elbow-bent clear straw. The portions were those you would serve to a two-year-old, Kate felt. She went to the bathroom to wash her hands and face.

She returned to the bedroom doorway to stand watching her mother feed her father. A third of a teaspoonful at a time. Slowly, patiently. Coaxing him. Helping him sip the juice by supporting his head tilted back. Every day, she thought. How many times a day? Is he taking less and less each day? How many days can be left? As her father was shrinking, her mother was putting on weight. She had never been a thin woman and now she was fuller than ever. The additional flesh softened the strong features of her face. It was her father's build that Kate had inherited but her mother's face: the aquiline nose, the high cheekbones, the oval contour. Her mother's gray hair was brushed straight back around her head and swirled into a French bun; she had worn it that way all of her adult life—in fashion and out and back in fashion again, although "fashion" was not a concept that disturbed her mother's mind. She wore a simple brown dress with a thin belt of the same material—a dress she might have worn at any time as long as Kate could remember. At her heart was pinned a small gold locket that had belonged to her grandmother; it had been given by an older relative to her grandmother when she emigrated from Vienna to New York.

"Now you must take a nap," Kate heard her mother say. She walked into the kitchen, not wanting to see how he would have to be helped onto the bed.

Kate had spent nearly half of her life in this apartment; she was brought here from the hospital where she was born and moved out of it only after she had graduated from college. Nothing appeared to be changed; it had always been plain, it had always been clean. But in her memory the rooms were larger and filled with the excitement of life, the excitement of people who thrilled to the possibilities of improving life, who made things happen. Of that it was empty now. Nothing could ever get better again. There was only the resigned routine of waiting for the end.

"Would you like some lunch?" her mother asked, indifferently, coming into the kitchen with the tray in her hands.

"No thanks; really. I haven't been myself lately. How are you?"

"Fine. I come from peasant stock, remember. It's your father who's descended from rabbis. I'm going to have a cup of tea. Want one?"

"Yes." She watched her mother open the door of the high glass cabinet above the sink and bring out two white pottery cups and saucers. They were Woolworth's imitation of Wedgwood, without any decoration. Could they have remained unbroken forever or were they replaced now and then by new ones from Woolworth's? "It was Josiah Wedgwood who first put into practice the idea that utensils for the poor could be made of designs as handsome as those for the rich," she distinctly recalled her father having told her. When did he say that—thirty-five years before?—sitting at this same table in this very kitchen, young, healthy, ambitious for the well-being of the working man, for progress under law, long before the world caved in and crushed him.

"Isn't it late for you to be still teaching?" Kate asked her mother.

"Not teaching. That's over. But I have to go in through this week to work on schedules for the fall classes." She brought the kettle to a boil, poured the water over one tea bag in one cup, waited, then moved the tea bag into the other cup. Waste not, want not. Then she placed the cups on opposite sides of the kitchen table. "Milk or lemon?" she asked Kate. "The sugar's on the table."

"Lemon," Kate answered. Did her mother think, after all these years, that she could change such habits, such tastes? Does anyone?

They sat down facing each other.

"I don't want you to tell me your troubles," her mother said flatly.

Kate was quick to say, "I didn't come here to do that."

"I am through with other people's troubles. As for you," she paused, holding the cup before her chin, blowing gently toward the surface of the tea, "I can't afford to think of you as anything but comfy-cozy in your elite goy hideaway."

"I am not living in a hideaway."

"You are outside of the mainstream of life. You are *hors de combat*. This country is ruled by a criminally insane President, the city of New York is sinking under its own incompetence; there are ten million people unemployed; the rest of the world bleeds in revolutions that are squashed by military fascists, or is dying in famines; and if you—who have nothing more to think about than what grades your kids will get in school or whether you ought to 'resurface' the tennis court this year—if you aren't living in a fool's paradise of a hide-away, then you don't know the difference between hide and seek."

"You make it feel so good to come home," Kate said.

"I'm not here to make you feel good." They both drank the tea in little sips.

Almost every visit began this way, Kate felt; or was it getting worse? She had never wanted to be in combat or in "the mainstream"; she did not believe anyone could tell where the mainstream was. That's always discovered after the facts. She wanted to be left alone to enjoy her life—her good fortune. Why couldn't her mother forgive her for that? She took Kate's life as a personal rejection, as a negative judgment on what she had done with her life. She wanted everyone to work for a world in which good fortune would be dispensed like food stamps to everybody.

"Everything's getting worse," her mother said. "What do you think will happen about Nixon?"

"The noose is getting tighter," Kate echoed.

"I don't think they'll impeach him. One blackguard protecting another. On the other hand—if only they had the courage to go through with it"—here she showed enthusiasm —"it might mean the revival of political morality in this country. Of a sense of responsibility to each other. This country," her voice rose, "created by men of vision, men of ideals! To think that the *Vice*-President should be caught taking payoff money for political favors, and the President . . ." Here she gave up. She could not articulate the enormity of Nixon's evil.

"I am not a political animal," Kate said.

"What kind of animal are you?"

"Ethical."

Her mother snorted. "You can't be ethical if you're not political."

"Did you really believe that your dream—a better world coming about through the election of the Socialist Party to government in this country—was ever a real possibility?"

"I did," her mother answered. "I don't any more. I don't believe that anything good will happen, any more. I think we've lost the chance. This country was created to give people a chance to escape from injustice under older systems of governments. The individual was to be given his best chance. But no one ever forgot that he was an individual inside of a society, with some degree of responsibility to all the others. Well, the demand had been too great on the side of what Others wanted of him before, and now the scales have tipped all the other way. The demand is too great for what the Self wants. Being part of a society is forgotten. People think only of rights, never of duties. Nobody gives a damn for anyone but himself."

"Nobody?"

"Nobody! I see it getting worse, year by year, in nursery school. Would you believe it? Five-year-olds. They show the difference. Oh, they can be taught a minimum of politeness —the rules of the game of getting along with others; but that's just on the surface. Their hearts have already been formed to think only of themselves, only of their own pleasure—by their parents—who, of course, live that way. They believe in nothing but the absolute supremacy of the demand for pleasure, their own prime priority for self-satisfaction. It's not that they knowingly intend to break the law; they actually believe that they alone ought to make their own laws."

"I don't think that's true of my children," Kate said.

"Really? What's the most important day in their lives?"

Kate thought for a moment before answering. "Their birthdays."

"Exactly. They celebrate themselves more than anything else in the world. What other ceremonies do they have to tie them into a world of other people?"

"Christmas. Easter. Thanksgiving. The Fourth of July."

This time her mother laughed out loud. In a slow, mockingly hollow tone she said, "Wonderful! Your children have the fringe benefits of a religion without having to earn them. Without any demand made on them to *be* religious. They don't go to church. They probably don't even know what Christmas celebrates, but they get their little hands filled with presents, nevertheless, don't they? That's how everyone in the country is raised now—to expect everything without earning anything. By their parents who believe it ought to be true." She grimaced bitterly.

"Why did you always celebrate Christmas when I was a child?"

"We chose to rebel against our parents. We knew what we were doing. We became atheists the hard way—by thinking it through. But to celebrate Christmas, for *your* sake, was to say, 'We are Americans,' not 'We are Christians.'"

"It's all so muddled," Kate said, stroking her forehead. "May I have another cup of tea?"

"Why don't you make it this time?" Her mother remained seated. "I'm tired. I'm worn down by all the foolishness. I only wish . . ."

Kate turned around from the stove where the water was coming to a boil. She was afraid of what her mother might say next. "You only wish what?"

"That I didn't care any more."

"But you do care."

"I'm alive."

"And that means to you," Kate asked, "that you have to go

on fighting to make it different, to make it more after your desire—right up to the end?"

"I don't fight it any more; I just suffer it."

Kate served them each a fresh cup of tea. They sat facing each other again, looking not quite steadily into each other's face. Her mother had never used makeup, she never smoked a cigarette, almost never drank anything but a little wine on special occasions. Nearly all the pleasures of her life were in her hopes and dreams for a different world, in which people would live lives different from those in the here and now; and all the strength of her capacity to work had gone into trying to move the world one inch closer to that goal. What if it were the wrong direction? By when could the value of her life be judged on her own terms?

Her mother suddenly said, "Don't you dare feel sorry for me."

"I do not feel sorry for you. You are one of the few people I have ever known who did exactly what she wanted to do with her life. At least, I've always thought of you that way. You can't say that of most women. Or was it because of Dad? Did you become yourself only after you married him?"

"No. We are two of a kind. We were perfectly matched. We had the same ideals and the same sort of energy. We were comrades as well as lovers. Most women can't say that either."

The word "comrades" stuck in Kate's heart. Was it possible? Unexpectedly, Kate sensed that the reason she had come on this visit, this day, was to ask the question that would run its finger along if not reopen the old wound: "Was Dad unjustly accused by McCarthy? Or is it true that he had been a Communist all along?"

Her mother nearly knocked over the tea cup pushing it away from herself. "Of course he wasn't! The Communists were totalitarian; he believed in the democratic process and

in democratic rule. He believed in persuasion and understanding, not in violent overthrow of the government."

"Then why didn't you fight it through the courts to clear
his name?"

"It was too late. The stroke had already broken him. I
couldn't do it by myself. Besides, it wouldn't have done any
good. It would have been much more pain than it was
worth."

It sounded reasonable. It was what she had always been led
to believe. But she could not or would not ask her father, and
even if she did, she did not imagine she would hear any
different answer or be made to feel any more certain. She
would probably live out her life never knowing for sure.

Softly she said, "I think I'd better go now," and rose from
her chair. Go? she wondered, go where?

Her mother said, "Be careful. I think Dad's still asleep."

Kate walked into his room cautiously. He lay on the bed
covered by the light blue blanket; only his hair, his forehead,
and the bridge of his nose were visible. I cannot even say
good-bye, she thought. But I told him that I loved him today
and it has been a very long time since I'd said that to him.
She picked up the fur sweater and her pocketbook. I may
never see him again. Each time, it is necessary to be aware
that this may be the last time I see him alive. She stroked the
arm of his wheelchair, as if to leave a message for him.

Her mother waited for her in the living room, looking as
though she were eager for the visit to be over. Eager to get
about her business. Kate put one arm around her shoulder
and kissed her cheek. Her mother did the same to her. "I love
you, too," Kate said.

"We can't do anything more for each other," was her
mother's response. Kate saw the shelves of books on the wall
behind her mother's head. "It's not owning books that matters," her father had said, "it's only what you get out of them

that counts, what they do to you. It's all in the mind."

Her mother walked with her to the front door. "Take care," she said.

"Be well," Kate replied. The door closed behind her. She stood still on the stone step for a moment, trying to remember where she had parked the car, feeling that she was alone in the world.

Jonathan Warner presented himself to the doorman at the Park Avenue address he had been given and asked for Mr. Robert Stanton punctually at five o'clock, as if this might prove to be the most significant thing he had ever done in his life. He wore a blue denim suit, a white shirt, and a dark knit tie. His fingernails were clean. His hair was brushed. His heart pounded. Should he go through with this? The elevator operator took him to the twenty-third floor. He faced a painted cornucopia on the inside of the elevator door: all the riches of a harvest spilled out before him—the dream of the Land of Cockaigne. What could the man do to him?

The door of the elevator opened directly into a wood-paneled foyer two stories high, with a circular staircase leading up to the second floor. A bland manservant, blond, in a black suit, greeted him. "Mr. Warner?"

"Yes."

"This way, please."

Through double doors, he was led into a large living room of extreme modernity: leather and chrome chairs, glass tables, floor lamps of bubbling colored lights. Pale gray walls. Purple and orange square cushions on the tan carpet. Somewhere in the spacious room a radio was tuned to a song of the Beatles from the early sixties. The light in the room was

strong: sunlight coming in through thin slats of silvery venetian blinds. Robert Stanton seemed to arise out of the floor.
He got up from a low round red leather chair that looked like
a giant apple. "Jonathan?" he asked, extending his hand. "I
am very pleased to meet you."

The young man found himself unable to say anything. His
throat seemed swollen shut. They shook hands.

"Thomas," Stanton addressed the servant, "tell Mrs. Stanton that our guest is here. What would you like to drink?" he
asked Jonathan.

"Beer," came out with difficulty.

"Fine," Stanton nodded to Thomas, who left the room.

Jonathan saw a tall, vigorous middle-aged man with a completely bald head, sandy moustache, broad shoulders; a well-
dressed, pink-cheeked man with a wide smile—as nervous as
he was. "I want you to know I'm very glad you called and
even happier that you've come. I really wanted to see you."
Stanton then added, more quietly, eyeing the doors, "You
understand that my wife knows nothing about us."

Neither do I, thought Jonathan. *What* about us? That's
what I'm here to find out.

Thomas held open the door for a woman who looked so old
that Jonathan imagined she must be Mr. Stanton's mother.
She came toward them leaning against a crooked aluminum
crutch, with a limp that Jonathan supposed went back to
childhood polio. A tiny woman in a dress of harlequin checks.
Skin and bones; the flesh of her face taut and scarred with
lines; a creature of suffering. Her gray hair was brushed up
away from her head and the sunlight streaked through it as
through a gathering of dust. "What an attractive young
man," she said smoothly in a voice that sounded of wind
tunnels and bagpipes. "How nice to see someone your age."
She sat near the giant apple on a straight chair with its back
to the window. "I don't have that chance very often. If it
weren't for television, I'm not sure I'd believe there were

any *young* men any more." The sunlight glinted on the black pearls of her earrings.

Thomas appeared with beer for Jonathan and martinis for Mr. and Mrs. Stanton, and then vanished. "Robert, do please turn off the radio," she requested. "Sit down, Mr. Warner," she insisted, pointing to a giant cherry opposite the apple. It was a squishy chair, as if the leather were stuffed full with ball bearings. "You're not from New York, if I understand correctly."

"No, New Haven."

"And you go to Yale?"

"No. The University of Michigan. I got as far away as I could."

"Did you have to escape from a beautiful mother and a cruel stepfather?" The radio music was snapped off. Jonathan caught Stanton's eye. The sun shone on his bald head. "I'm only joking," she continued. "You must realize I have no children of my own. I don't know how to talk with anyone your age."

"It shouldn't be a problem," Jonathan heard himself saying. "We speak the same language." He smiled with his lips, if not his eyes.

"Charming," Mrs. Stanton smiled; creased, wrinkled, tortured. She sipped her martini. "He's charming," she said to her husband. "And you're an art student?" turning back to him.

Jonathan drank some of the beer. "Art history," he lied, as he watched Stanton lower himself into the apple.

"That's wonderful," Stanton supplied. "I wish *I'd* had that opportunity."

His wife looked at him quizzically, but did not let her gaze linger long. "And what are you going to *do,* Mr. Warner?" she asked.

The inevitable question, Jonathan felt. What are grownups

afraid of? Supporting welfare? "I don't know yet," he admitted.

"Then why art history?" she asked.

"I love it," he answered. That is what his father would have said. His father?

"That's the best possible reason," Stanton announced. He raised his glass and toasted the young man. He was actually grinning with pleasure.

"My father studied art history at Harvard."

"What does he do now?" she asked.

"He runs Warner and Son, a store in New Haven. Our family store."

"Which sells what?"

"Jewelry. Porcelain. Silver."

"Ah, then, art history must have stood him in good stead." No one commented. "As I suppose it will you, in your turn," she added.

"You are kind," he said. Where had he learned chit-chat like this? At home? At college? At the movies?

"Not at all," she replied.

"But we're putting off the big moment." Stanton got up. "I'll bring in the Rembrandt." He left the room.

"Mr. Warner," she began a little after he was gone, "how did you know, so soon after my husband bought it, that he had a Rembrandt for you to look at?"

"Well, Mrs. Stanton," Jonathan groped, "a friend of my father's is a curator at the Metropolitan, and he told me." Jesus Christ, he wondered, how does the mind work? He hadn't thought up this lie; yet it was there on the tip of his tongue to save him.

"I see. Yes, I suppose such news travels fast in the art world."

"Oh, it does. Yes, it does."

"I was just thinking of whether we might have many such

callers as you in the future, wanting to see it. Oh, of course, not so charming as you."

Stanton returned with the portrait in hand. He set it up on the floor facing them, leaning the frame back against a leather sofa. "What do you think?" he asked.

Me? Jonathan swallowed hard. Am I supposed to think about it? "It's magnificent!" he exclaimed. He got down on his knees and looked at it from a distance of four feet. "It's just—spectacular." Must I go through with this charade?

"It's the nicest present I've ever been given," Mrs. Stanton confided to him. She finished her cocktail. "Robert," she said, supporting herself against the back of her chair and getting up, "you men may want more to drink. And I'm sure you'd like to talk a while longer. You must excuse me. I have to lie down." Stanton handed her the aluminum crutch.

Jonathan got up off his knees and shook her bony hand. "Thank you very much for your hospitality," he said.

"It has been a pleasure meeting you, young man. I wish you good luck." After she had limped a few feet away, she half turned to look at him once more and then added, "Good-bye."

When the doors closed behind her, Jonathan felt fear in the fact that he was alone with Stanton. The older man was equally uncomfortable. Both of them sat back in the peculiar chairs, staring at the Rembrandt rather than at each other.

"I have the feeling I've seen this picture before," Jonathan said.

"An interesting thing about it," Stanton said, authoritatively, "is that it's painted over another picture. There's one of a young woman under this. Apparently that was a common practice. If you were hard up for canvas money!" He laughed.

"Or if you changed your mind," Jonathan offered. He was concentrating on the portrait now. An old man. Lonely. Abandoned. Forsaken. The sad face of an old man left all alone. He shivered. I'll never be like that, he thought. The golden light made him think of the warmth of life, but here was a man in the shadows, out of it. All by himself. He turned away from the painting to look squarely at Stanton.

Neither of them spoke.

Thomas knocked at the door and entered. "Mrs. Stanton suggested that you might like to have your drinks refreshed."

"Yes," Stanton replied, without asking Jonathan.

They waited in silence until the servant had returned and left again. They sipped their drinks.

"You wanted to see me," Stanton finally said.

"You were willing to see me," Jonathan responded.

"I was eager to see you."

"Why?"

Stanton laughed. "A perfectly understandable curiosity."

"For what?"

After a pause, he answered, "To see what Kate Warner's first child looks like."

"You know my mother?"

"I knew her many years ago."

"When?"

"When I was in the Army and she was going to Columbia."

"How well did you know her?"

"We were lovers."

"Oh."

"The truth is that I loved her very much. She is a remarkable woman."

"Was she pregnant before she met my father?"

"Yes."

"Am I your child?" There was a hint of tears in his eyes.

"Yes."

Jonathan wiped his eyes on the sleeve of his jacket. They were dry now. He swallowed. "Then why aren't you my father?"

"I had to marry money," Stanton answered.

Instead of a woman, Jonathan thought. He's like Joan Rohan who would "do anything" for twenty-five thousand dollars in blackmail money. How much did Mrs. Stanton's money cost this man? What could he have felt, selling himself to her? He must have stopped feeling years before he made that deal. They looked into each other's eyes and then back at the sad silent portrait. Still, the man in the portrait held his head erect.

"Is there anything I can tell you?" Stanton asked.

"A word of advice?" Jonathan replied. "Like, 'Go into plastics!'?" The situation was suddenly funny. He had expected a cataclysm, a revelation. Something like God talking to Moses through the burning bush. But Robert Stanton was just a self-satisfied, middle-aged, wealthy man who wanted to revel in the discovery that Jonathan was his son. "Have you always known about me?" he asked, thinking, and never once tried to see me before this?

"No. I didn't know that you had been born—until a few days ago."

"If it had been up to you—would I have been born?" Where did he get the guts to ask a question like that, he wondered.

Very slowly and regretfully, Stanton answered, "No."

Jonathan could imagine the world going on after his death, but it was absolutely beyond his capacity to imagine his never having been born. "Then I owe you nothing," the young man concluded. "Do I?" He stood up. "Does anyone else know this?"

Stanton said, "Only Isabel Taylor."

"Why did you tell her?"

Now Stanton stood up. "I really don't know," he said. Then he admitted, "I had to tell somebody."

"It doesn't matter," Jonathan said. He began to move toward the doors of the room. "I'll be going now." If this man had been the father who brought me up I would be an entirely different person, he realized. But this man had not done that; and he was himself, not someone else. That was his profit on this interview. He liked himself more than he liked the idea of being someone else. He felt no fear now. He felt, This man cannot possibly harm me. Isabel Taylor wanted to hurt me by telling me about him. But she was wrong. It doesn't matter at all. Mr. Stanton is pathetic.

"Wait!" Stanton said. He looked from Jonathan to the Rembrandt, to the flowers in vases, to the walls. "I wish I could give you something."

"You can," Jonathan said.

"What?"

"Your word that you'll never tell anyone else," he said, condescending. "*I* wouldn't want it to be known."

Going down in the elevator, Jonathan felt that he could have kicked himself. He meant to find out what his parents knew about this man. Had *both* of his parents kept this secret from him—or only his mother? He had missed his chance. He pressed his hands against the elevator doors and hung his head. He would have to live with it. He felt absolutely confident that he would never, under any circumstance, let his parents know what he had happened to be told or that he had actually met Robert Stanton. They had not wanted him to know, and he would forever let them believe that he did not know anything about it. He owed them that. He felt more grown up—not because he had been let in on a secret but because he felt perfectly capable of keeping the secret to himself.

Kate drove her car up Sixth Avenue so slowly, resisting the necessity to decide where she was going, that drivers honked their horns at her to start moving at every traffic light. She could not possibly have stayed overnight with her parents; that was an absurd whim. But she had no desire to go home to Henry. She had to be alone. Approaching Forty-second Street she remembered someone, recently—who was it?—mentioning the Algonquin, and on that impulse, at Forty-fourth she turned right and pulled into the garage across the street from it, took her suitcase from the trunk, and walked over to the hotel. She had always been fond of the Algonquin. There had been many pleasant times there either before plays or after concerts. And they did have a room available. That was great luck, she felt. It was a good sign. It would clear her mind, just being in the building. Her mother hated the Algonquin—the circle of *The New Yorker* people: Benchley and Thurber, Alexander Woollcott and Wolcott Gibbs, Dorothy Parker and George S. Kaufman; trivia, gallows-humor trivia! But that's where I'm at, she felt. Do I have to go through life apologizing for it? I like fun! But my parents are evangelists; and my husband expects me to be a housekeeper and a governess and policeman. When do I get my own? When am I only myself?

An Oriental bellhop carried her bag and left the key with her. The room was almost quaint. It was a small, square room, with a brass bed, early American wallpaper, and a lamp that consisted of a brass base in the shape of a Roman column and a black shade. A silent room. She was reminded of how Henry hated the first impact of a hotel room on himself. The peculiar impression of impersonality. It never bothered her that way. But now she was trying to think with his mind. She sat down in the armchair, which was covered with a flowered chintz fabric, and looked at the empty room. No one could live in such a room for more than a day or two. It had no plants, no animals, no other people. It was as simple as that. She understood why spinsters keep cats or bachelors cultivate house plants. There must be something other than the self, which is unpredictable in your presence, in order for you

to feel alive. To feel some exchange with life. Otherwise
there is no challenge, no demand that you be alive for your
part. You need not play any part at all. You can stare at a
blank wall until you die. But if there is a cat, a child, a bego-
nia, then there are things you are called upon to do. There
is intercourse, reciprocal relations, there is uncertainty—and
that is life.

She washed up but did not change her clothes and went
down to the lounge. This was New York to Kate. She sat in
one of the overstuffed chairs, clanged the metal bell for a
waiter, and ordered a vodka and tonic. Here was the parade
of life. The director of a university press was interviewing a
young editor from a commercial publishing house. An account executive of an advertising firm was telling his date of
the hour about a think session. A would-be actress was com-
plaining about the paucity of parts to play, the poverty of the
theater season coming this fall. There was a black who looked
like a millionaire gypsy, with one gold earring, a red velvet
fedora, white brocade pants, and a jacket cut out of a Spanish
bedspread. He walked in and looked around as if he might
scatter silver coins at any moment, or burp out loud with
impunity. A presence. A power. He was greeted by the most
conventional-looking whites, in seersucker suits, probably record company executives, and he a rock music star. It was all
so funny. The decorum of so much intense and combative
private life being lived out in this scene of polite behavior in
public. The lounge at the Algonquin, New York, in June
1974.

Kate shivered with pleasure. It was wonderful to be alone.
And then a woman fell down in the narrow passage between
the elevator and the front desk, gasping: a fish out of water,
a woman in a mauve dress, with amethysts in the rings on her
fingers and along the gold chain of her necklace. A middle-
aged woman lay sprawled on her back on the carpet not
eight feet from where Kate sat. She was not drunk. The flesh

of her bare arms quivered. She was suffering a seizure of some sort. The people who gathered around her, filling the space between where Kate sat, immobile, and the woman shaking on the floor were of two kinds: those who offered help, who bent down to speak to her or took her hand in theirs; and those who hastened to disguise what was happening, conceal it. The manager who came out from behind the front desk tried to arrest the woman's seizure; the head waiter for the lounge tried to act as a screen so that no one would notice her.

We have created a civilization that can't bear to look on anything unpleasant, Kate thought; and I'm one of its victims. As soon as the elevator door opened she hurried into it, escaping up to her room. She had enough worries of her own. She couldn't think about someone else's troubles. The woman was being taken care of. But why did she feel, Kate wondered, as if any appearance of disease, suffering, or death was a personal affront? Her resentment was based on her private conception of the transactions she made with life. Not, If I am good, I will be happy; happiness depends too much on luck for that. But if I do you no harm, why should you harm me? All that matters is a fair exchange.

The silence of her room made more striking the noises of the city which permeated it. An ambulance siren, the screeching of car brakes and slamming of car doors, whistles, police sirens, the air conditioner on the window ledge, the elevator outside the door. There was a television in the room but no radio. She couldn't watch television anyway; she'd left her eyeglasses behind in the car. Kate tried to sit quietly in the chintz-covered armchair, thinking of her parents, transformed as they were by the years: her father growing smaller in his wheelchair, her mother growing heavy and more bitter with disappointment. What a shame! she thought; they'll never know how it all came out. The gamble on progress, the investment of their lives—to contribute to the amelioration of mankind. Now there are China, the Soviet Union, Cuba at one extreme; the United States at the other. Between dictatorships and chaos: there was the drama of the conflict. Who will win? Between the ant-hill and anarchy, between a minimum for everyone and the maximum for a few—how would the battle come out? *She* wouldn't live long enough to know either. How many centuries will it take? After all, it took the past four hundred years for nationalism to transform Europe out of the feudal ages; and much of the rest of the world was still feudal. Between personal freedom and social responsibility: how long will it take for a final resolution, to the end of all conflict? I don't know, she realized, and nobody else can know either. But what if there is *no* resolution? Only different kinds of governments, in the same countries, at different times? An unending game of musical chairs?

She recognized the peculiar inheritance from both of her parents that made her into what she was. Their passion and their intellect. Why should she feel offended by pain and unhappiness except by virtue of identifying herself with the lifelong efforts of her mother and father to reduce both, to contain both? She had not made those efforts herself. If she *was* holier-than-thou it was because of the self-righteousness they had earned, by what they had done. She had not been tested herself in any such firing line. Marrying Henry protected her from that; and he created an atmosphere of safety in which she could remain with her back turned to the demands of the rest of the world. Did she live "in hiding"? She had to acknowledge a revulsion on her part, a lack of sympathy for misfits and underdogs and losers, which probably grew in reaction to their excessive demand for compassion; the bleeding hearts of her parents, always ready to make every drawback or flaw into a cause. A middle-aged woman suffering a seizure on the floor of the Algonquin became "a cause": fight epilepsy; contribute to medical research; require every hotel lobby to be supplied with a registered nurse!

"You cannot be ethical without being political," Kate recalled. At what point do you stop trying to think things through farther than you have come, and act on what you already believe to be adequate? She thought of her professor of philosophy at Hunter College. Harvey Einbaum. Unforgettable name. Bearded, with curly black hair, always clenching an unlit pipe between his teeth. A craggy, sallow face like carved driftwood. He must have been in his late forties when she was one of his students in the history of philosophy. He taught that subject as he understood it: as a procession of methods for comprehending reality. But he was himself a student who had not yet arrived at an original conception of reality, and he gave Kate the impression that outside of the classroom he endured a life of suspended animation. He would wait until he *understood all* before living his own life. In the meanwhile he'd tread water, in the manner of the habits he'd learned as a child; as a nice young man. But when he'd fully made up his own mind about his own discoveries, then he would swim through life in his unique way. He would become an Original. It was as if, in order to say a kind word or a joyous word or a killing word, he must not only know every word, down to the tip of each root, but the source and nature of language itself and the complete range of the possibilities of communication. Harvey Einbaum; he would die without having spoken his own word.

Kate felt firmly, I do not have to know Everything first in order to live my own life. At each moment you start over again with what you have learned from experience and you roll with the punches. As Peggy and Gabriel were learning to do right now. You start with your intentions and you trust your feelings. But I am trying to affect Peggy's and Gabriel's feelings in order to shape their intentions in the ways I see fit, according to my expectations—as I see it in their best interests to become decent human beings. Just as my feelings were conditioned by my parents, just as Henry's were by his. By one's parents—and the rest of the world one is exposed to. Then how free are we to determine our "intentions" on our own? One more Great Thing I do not know.

How easy it would be to drown in one's own ignorance. I do not know what goes on in the world. I do not know what is going on in the room next to mine in this hotel at this moment. A lunatic may be preparing to explode a bomb. For all that I have a Good Head, how far do I need to think things through?

Kate laughed, remembering a joke her father was fond of telling in the old days. "In pre-Revolutionary Russia," it began, "Ivan and Sergei met on a street in St. Petersburg one day. 'I haven't seen you in years,' Ivan exclaimed. 'You look wonderful,' Sergei replied. 'And how is your beautiful bride?' Ivan asked. The smile was wiped away from Sergei's face. 'You don't know?' he asked. 'We had to get a divorce.' Ivan was stunned. 'But she was so beautiful, so cheerful, so loving. What happened?' Sadly Sergei explained: 'We had a long discussion, late into the night, on whether God existed or not, and *she didn't know*—either way.' "

How far we've come in three generations. "In pre-Revolutionary Russia . . ." Kate's grandparents believed in God; her parents worshiped Mankind; she believed in that knot of nature and fortune that constituted herself and her world. Is that not awe-filling enough? What would the next generation believe in? show reverence to? respect and cultivate? Just themselves? Was her mother right: are they growing up to celebrate nothing but their selfish demands for private pleasure? I will have to get along without knowing the answer to that, too; although I may live long enough to see how my own children turn out.

It suddenly occurred to Kate how hungry she was. You

can't get more basic than that. She put out her fourth cigarette in fifteen minutes. She had eaten very little during the
past two days. It was eight o'clock in the evening. She had no
desire to go out of the hotel, but she needed food.

Immediately outside of the elevator it was obvious that life
in the lobby was normal again. The epileptic woman had
been taken away. To a hospital? To one of the rooms upstairs?
Kate turned to the captain at the entrance of the Rose Room.
"I didn't make a reservation," she said.

"How many?" he asked.

"One. I'm alone."

There was a small table just a few feet from where they
stood, a circle of white tablecloth that fell to the floor. A
single red rose in a bud vase stood at the center of the table,
surrounded by heavy shiny hotel silverware, pretty plates,
and a napkin very formally pleated. She put her pocketbook
on the seat facing hers, where Henry ought to be sitting.
Henry! She had barely thought of him since driving away
from home early in the morning. But, in some sense, she felt
that all her thinking about herself this day was a way of
thinking about him as well. What would he do now about the
money? How could he risk jeopardizing everything? Even if
no one else knew, how could he live with her knowledge of
his deceit?

Kate was located facing the lounge and the lobby. She
could watch the movement of the elegant, the gaudy, and
the ordinary people who came and went, greeting and separating. The sharp faces and the soft faces. She was surrounded by other white tableclothes on tables larger than
hers. She could overhear the conversations of her neighbors.
There was an unattractive aging man in a loud plaid suit
saying, "And when I'm in L.A., I'll call you," to a bleached-
blond retired chorus girl. "Sure," she answered, "netch'-
relly!" One businessman, on the other side of her, said, "The
capital's there!" And his companion replied in a vehement

whisper, "Yeah. But who's got the balls?" Kate had the impression that the dapper gentleman seated alone in the far corner was Sir John Gielgud. All spring he had been performing in a play that was just about to close its run on Broadway. But she didn't have her glasses with her, she couldn't be sure. In through the lobby a svelte woman approached the elevator with her hand on the shoulder of a young man taller than she. A woman of thirty perhaps. She was pretty, with loose, flowing, light brown hair. Her crocheted dress was streaked with the warm pastel colors of the painted desert; it clung to her lovely bosomy figure. The young man looked like Jonathan. They turned their profiles as they stood in front of the elevator waiting for the doors to open. The young man slipped his arm around her waist. They radiated a temporary proprietary manner. It was obvious that this was a New Woman about to take this evening's "catch," picked up at some singles bar, to her hotel room for an hour. The young man's smile was smug. Neither of them spoke. Kate squinted to telescope her vision; to see the suit, the hair, the profile— to see a youth who somewhat resembled Jonathan. The couple disappeared into the elevator.

Kate suffered the frightening drop, the unanticipated plunge, as on an airplane in "light turbulence," when it unexpectedly hits an air pocket and suddenly slumps, leaving your stomach to follow later.

For two or three years she had been aware of the need to think of Jonathan as being "on his own": gradually, as he approached college, and then especially after he started there, away from home. To some degree her mind had accommodated to that change. She thought of him as trusted and of herself as not possessive. But when does one grasp such a change as an objective fact and not as a suspension of the exercise of one's own will? Kate remembered how the war against the Nazis had dominated her childhood and, although it ended when she was thirteen, it was not until she was seventeen or eighteen, walking up Fifth Avenue one day and catching sight of a poster in the Lufthansa office window —"Fly To A Vacation In Beautiful Germany"—that she grasped the truth in her own soul: the war *was* over. Thus she was struck by the sight of a young man who reminded her of Jonathan and of the fact that Jonathan was on his own, somewhere in New York, this very night. What he did was no longer up to her. Jonathan was no longer hers. He was his own.

At nine o'clock Henry could stand the quiet and the emptiness of his own home no longer. He locked up, leaving the lights on, got into the Mercedes, and took off for the club. It had been a miserable day. He awoke to find himself deserted, abandoned. In one fell swoop his wife and all three children were gone. Even the maid wasn't coming that day. There were no sounds of life in the house; and, in the most perverse way, he felt conscious of that silence during the entire working day at the office. Then he went home, alone, to confirm that fact. And it was too true. It was deadly. Until the phone rang. Peggy and Gabriel called from camp in Maine. He had forgotten his fishing rod; she was homesick, with a stomach ache, and didn't think she could live through tomorrow. He reassured them. Their mother and he would bring the fishing rod up with them in the middle of July; then they would visit the camp every Sunday. Peggy would survive. She had to; he needed to know she would be there to greet them. Them? he wondered. Would Kate be with him? Would she come home?

The clouds concealed the moon. It was a heavy June night, dark and somewhat oppressive. He drove to the club along the back roads, along Brook Road, stopping between the eleventh and twelfth holes to look to both sides at the fairways: smooth, cared for; even the trees seemed stylized, their thick foliage in rounded configurations, like trees in a painting by Grant Wood. An underrated artist. Nature is neat, he thought; and human artistry improves upon the neatness. Only human life gets messy and knows no craft for smoothing the rough edges. Only our gross hacking away with a blunt ax: trial and error. What a bore it is trying to make human life smooth, well rounded! Like trying to make a boomerang fly in a straight line.

To his surprise, the parking lot was full. It was a Wednesday night. He had completely forgotten that this was the opening of the summer season ball. Black tie. Reserved tables. Now lost was the hope for a sandwich and silence. He entered the lounge to find colored balloons attached to the ceiling and women in beautiful evening dresses flitting like butterflies all about, men he recognized from the locker room appearing like Colonel Blimps in dinner jackets. A dance band played soft music in the dining room. At least he would have a drink at the bar before driving back home.

Clarence, the black bartender, asked, "The usual, Mr. Warner?" That's comforting, Henry thought; the virtue of a routine is that you don't have to make choices as if each time were the first time. "Thank you. That's just what I'd like."

He stood at the bar, acutely uncomfortable in his sports jacket surrounded by men in summer formals. He studied Clarence at his work, turning away from the people around him.

"Rotter!" Conrad Taylor said, slapping him on the back.

"I'm awfully sorry," Henry replied.

"What happened?"

"Kate had to go to New York. And I completely forgot."

"Apparently the Connolleys did too. The Jackmans and we are alone at a table for eight. Come join us."

"No. I can't. Really. I don't feel like it. Wrong day."

"I'm sorry." Clarence gave Henry his drink and took Conrad's order of four different cocktails.

Henry said, "I read about your speech at Berkeley in yesterday's paper." How mild; couldn't he say something to make him feel good? "I take it it was a great success."

"Yes, indeed," Conrad drawled. "The former governor of California had a statistical study made and it turns out that seven people in the audience actually understood what I was talking about."

"Good for you!" Henry smiled. "Seven wise men."

Conrad did not smile. "Is anything wrong?"

"Yes," Henry replied. "But I can't talk about it."

"If you want to, will you get in touch with me?"

"Thank you. You are a friend. I'm sorry about the Connolleys. Do you know if . . ."

"Quentin's at a retreat until tomorrow."

"Good Christ."

"Yes; that's what he's there for."

"What the devil's taking so long?" Isabel asked, approaching them. "Oh, Henry! You're here after all." She looked him up and down. He felt like an intruder.

"No. I'm not. It's all a mistake."

"Come," Conrad said, carrying the drinks away on a square tray. Isabel hesitated. "I'll meet you back there," she said.

"You look great, Isabel," Henry said. She shone in an evening gown of coral color and emerald earrings with diamond pendants, her blond hair all piled up on the top of her head.

"Are you all right?" she asked, recalling how she had hated him. He realized that she had already drunk a lot.

"Yes. We just couldn't make it tonight."

"Kate all right?"

"Yes."

"Johnny-boy?"

"He's fine. As far as I know. He's in New York."

"Really?" she asked. "Learning about life?"

Henry realized that the earrings she wore were the ones he had sold to Robert Stanton. He was staring at them; he had to say, "What beautiful earrings."

"Do you like them?" She tossed her head, kittenishly. "An admirer gave them to me."

"A long time ago?"

"No. Recently." She was including him in a secret.

"You deserve admirers," he said, despising her; she should not have said that to him.

She suddenly seemed sobered and profoundly grateful. "Thank you for saying that, Henry. I really do thank you . . . I wish I were a better person." She turned and left the bar. He was free to go.

Free for what? he wondered. To return to his empty house. Yes. That is what he needed right now. Whatever was left of his own. Isabel was the special friend Stanton had given the emeralds and diamonds to. Isabel and Stanton. Did Conrad know? Why should he? Isabel could afford to buy such earrings for herself. Conrad probably had no idea. And Henry had no right to have any ideas about it at all, he believed. He felt disgusted. It was blatant. Don't they realize there are other people in the world, that it's impossible to keep such a secret? And yet I think I can keep a secret worth a hundred thousand dollars. "I wish I were a better person." Is there a word to describe a wish that cannot possibly be acted on? Is it some kind of delusion? He stalked out of the bar, through the lounge, away from the dance music and the voices, to the parking lot, revolted by himself, knowing that he had to get rid of the money. He had to redeem himself in Kate's eyes. To hell with the money.

He drove home in the knowledge that his solitude was a form of punishment. Not that all solitude is punishment—only when it's inflicted upon you. The drive calmed his spirits. He walked slowly around the house to the terrace. It had become cooler, there was a breeze from the north. If he could not recover her respect . . . He did not dare to complete that thought. But he understood intuitively: to be cut off from Kate would be to lose half of my life. Without her he would have no reflection. I have spent this whole day without her in every sense and in the uncertainty of knowing how we will behave with each other when we meet again. He lit a cigar, watched the glow of the burning tip, looked up to the clouds high in the sky, and suddenly laughed out loud.

Henry remembered meeting a man at the golf club last summer, a fellow from Austin, Texas, the guest of one of the members, who had made a big deal of telling the foursome he'd played with, over drinks after eighteen holes, that he had been in a sanitorium; he had had a nervous breakdown, been hospitalized, gone through treatments to recover, and he *had* recovered. His point was that he had been certified as sane and "How many of you can say that?" he asked. It was the same with *how much* a man wants his wife's respect. How many of us know the answer? Henry laughed to himself again. At least, I know now, he thought. There's a price tag on it. It's worth one hundred thousand dollars to me.

Kate entered the house at nine fifteen in the morning to find it empty, dropped her suitcase, returned to the car, and drove down to the bus stop for Helen, apologizing all the way back for keeping her waiting. It was inconsiderate of Henry to have left Helen like that; he had no idea of what time she would return. He must have something more important on his mind, she realized; she wanted to think well of Henry today. She wanted to be with him again. She had slept fitfully, waking frequently during the night in the hotel room, disoriented, shocked into wondering where she was each time she was unfolded into consciousness in the unfamiliar bedroom. It had been a sour night. She got up at dawn and checked out of the hotel at seven, and did not stop for coffee until she was into Connecticut, at a roadside motel near Greenwich. She wanted to be home. She wanted to love her life again. With Henry; not with Helen. Kate escaped from the maid's chatter as quickly as she could through the dining room toward the main stairway.

She stood still on the first step of the stairs and turned back, for some reason, to regard the wallpaper, the fox hunting scene. It was as if the scene meant to tell her something, wanted her to think about it for some purpose outside of herself that might be of use to her. She sat down on the stairs and contemplated the wallpaper. When Henry had taken her to Chartres, they sat side by side on hard wooden chairs in the great Gothic cathedral looking at the rose windows. "What am I supposed to see?" Kate whispered to him. "You're not *supposed* to see anything," he answered. "What is there, you see. Now make no demands on it. Expose yourself. Simply look, and wait. The question is, What does it do for you, to you? What does it say? Not what do you want to know, but what does it want to tell?" Thus did she stare at the fox hunting scene.

At nine o'clock, from his office, Henry begged Quentin's telephone answering service to have Dr. Connolley call him as soon as he came in. Quentin returned the call at ten.

"What kind of day do you have lined up?" Henry asked.

"Here until noon; at the hospital from one to five."

"Can I see you in between?"

"I don't want lunch," Quentin said.

"It's important to me."

"I'll tell you what. Stay put. I'll drop by your office sometime between twelve and one, for a few minutes, at least. Is that okay?"

"That'll be fine. I'm much obliged," Henry said, thinking, what an old-fashioned phrase. I haven't used it in years. It fits. Obligated! He was all keyed up. He knew what he was doing and why. The hundred thousand dollars was in the safe; he brought it to his desk. He engaged himself with the duties of the morning as if they were all new, he had just inherited all of his responsibilities, and he meant to find out how well he could carry them out. He would make Kate proud of him.

How quiet it is here, Henry realized at noon. Other people have started keeping radios in their offices, playing music softly as the background to everything. I wonder if I should. It eases tension. He was tense. Quentin appeared at twenty minutes of one. "I'm very grateful to you," he said, as they shook hands. "I really appreciate your coming." They sat down side by side on the sofa. Quentin continued to change. Without his beard and by steadily losing weight, he had come to look younger and stronger; everything about him was sharper and better defined: his square face, his bright blue eyes, even his white hair. The word "purer" came to Henry's mind.

"I have to make a confession to you," Henry said.

"To me?"

"It's about the Rembrandt. Your Rembrandt."

Quentin looked at the coffee table and then at the carpet between his feet. He saw himself in the Dünning Schloss, holding a carbine, the displaced person knocked out at his feet. Had he recovered? Was he dead? "What about it?"

"I didn't give you all the money."

"What money?"

"All the money I got for selling it."

Quentin turned to look at him face to face. "What are you talking about?" He sounded simple-minded.

"I gave you half of it. I have the other half here." Henry stood up, walked to his desk, took the two packets of fifty thousand dollars each out of a drawer and returned, placing them on the low table in front of Quentin. Then he sat down near him again. Quentin looked at the money dumbly.

"It's for you," Henry said.

"Why?"

"In payment for the Rembrandt."

Quentin was quiet. Then he said, "You mean you got two hundred thousand for it and you gave me only half of that?"

"Yes."

"You asshole," Quentin said.

"What?"

"You stupid asshole."

"Why?"

"You think I'd take this money? You want to make a confession? You've come to the wrong party. I don't take confessions. And I don't take dirty money to ease your conscience. What made you change your mind?"

Henry was silent.

"It doesn't matter," Quentin said, standing up. "You know what you can do with that money . . . I thought you were my friend. I thought you were an honorable man. *I* had done wrong. *I* wanted to clear myself." He took a deep breath. "I never thought you'd screw me. That's bad enough. But then to tell me, and expect me to make it all right for you by taking the goddamned money. You're out of your mind." Quentin stared at the money on the table and then at Henry. He turned and slammed the door after him as he hurried out of the office. His last words were, "You can go to hell."

Kate telephoned at three to say she was home and to ask when he would be back. Henry felt himself to be in a catatonic trance. He had not moved from the sofa since Quentin left. He saw himself as a failure and as a fool. He saw his reputation ruined and his good intentions twisted around to throw a spotlight onto his deception—for all to see. Quentin would shame him; but then, it had been Quentin's *stolen* painting that Henry had sold—he was a thief. Would Quentin tell? Henry was caught in that circle and went round and round it in his stunned mind.

"Kate?" he said, standing next to his desk.

"Yes. You don't sound well."

"I'm not. I tried to do something good and I got shot down for it."

"Come home."

"What time is it?"

"Three. I've been here all day. I thought you would have called by now."

"I didn't know when . . ." He didn't want to say *if* you'd be back.

"Henry!" Kate was alarmed. "You sound terrible. Should I come and get you?"

"No. It's all right. I'm just . . . I'm all shook up. I will come home. I want to see you. I need you. Stay there."

How peculiar, Kate felt. "Of course, I will!"

"Will you?" Henry asked.

"Come as soon as you can. Darling," she said, sincerely, "I do love you."

"Thank God," he said.

"This is absurd. Come home!"

Kate was waiting at the garage when he drove his car up their private road. She looked fresh and handsome, self-possessed. She wore a dress the color of apricots and smelled of attar of roses. They embraced. He kissed her ear. She hugged him hard. And then they walked with their arms around each other down, along the edge of the lawn, to the bench beside the tennis court and sat next to each other, close in quiet. Two ducks flew overhead. She took his hand in hers and felt the bandage on his palm. "What's this?" "Thinking of doing you harm," he replied, "wounded me." They were both silent. Finally, she said, "I wanted to run away. I wanted to leave you. But there is no place for me to go. There is no place I'd rather be. This is my life. This is where I belong."

"You are very hard," was all he could say.

"On myself, as on you. I can't be otherwise. But I can be wrong, too." They looked at each other's eyes.

"Are you forgiving me?"

"Mine is just one opinion," she admitted.

"The only one that matters to me."

"You had as much right to advise Jonathan in the way you did as I have to think otherwise."

Henry wasn't thinking of that at all. "That's just one of my imperfections," he said.

"It's the one that touches me most."

"You are too sensitive about Jonathan."

"Let's talk about you."

"I tried to get rid of the money. I tried to give the other hundred thousand to Quentin."

"That's marvelous!"

"He wouldn't take it. He made me feel like shit."

"That's *his* mistake."

"He's changed," Henry said. "He's gone pious and vengeful."

"He's suffering," she said.

"I wanted to absolve myself. He wouldn't let me."

"But you wanted to get rid of it!" Kate said joyously. "That's all that matters. You will. You could burn it, for all I care."

"You don't do that to money," Henry said.

"I could."

He laughed. "I'm sure you could—"

"You think I don't know what money's worth, what it costs to earn. I'm not that other-worldly. It's just that I also know what your self-respect is worth. I'm not 'out of it.' I know why you did it," she announced. "I understand."

"You do?" His eyebrows raised. "Tell me."

"I stared at the wallpaper in the hallway—the fox hunting scene—for an hour this morning. And then it came to me. In any society there are the most fortunate ones, whose needs are all satisfied. They are well fed, well dressed, well housed; they have the best bread and and the best circuses. Knowing what to expect, and having it under control, they feel safe and happy. But they lack the excitement of feeling alive, because they aren't exposed to dangers. They're protected from dangers, from the unpredictable. So they create imaginary dangers . . ."

Henry nodded, thinking of an actual fox hunt and not just of the scene on the wallpaper.

"Fox hunting isn't hunting for food. They're all stuffed with food," Kate continued. "It isn't hunting for fur for clothing. It's sport. It's a substitute for danger, to make them feel that they *could* hunt for food if they had a real need to. It's like saying, There are certain instincts that have to be satisfied, and if they're taken care of too easily, then it's necessary to pretend they aren't taken care of at all—to recapture that feeling of the unexpected, and of making it on your own in this world."

Henry thought, I didn't need the money, but I wanted some kind of excitement.

Kate said, "It's not that you deliberately set out to defraud other people. You acted out of some instinct for taking advantage of a situation, which has nothing to do with real needs on the surface of your life—only with the deep sense of being alive. You did it to feel *clever enough* to get away with it. But you bought the satisfaction of outsmarting others at the risk of being caught." She paused for a moment—but she was in charge of her mind at its best. "It's just that you saw a main chance and took it. That made you feel gutsy; the thrill of risking the dangers involved."

"Isn't living with you challenging enough?"

Kate ignored the flippancy of his tone. "Apparently not."

"You've always remained a mystery to me."

"That isn't enough. That puts me aside, with a label that reads 'Mystery.' But you don't come back to it every day thinking, This is the source of adventure in my life. If you did, this wouldn't have happened."

"Are you saying I take you for granted?"

"Yes. Just as I take you for granted; and that's partly why I feel that I'm in a rut."

Henry leaned forward and rested his head on his hands. "No one can be everything for anyone else."

"I know that," she said clearly and slowly, thinking of her mother and father. "But I also know that the One Most Important Person—the indispensable person—has to make you feel that he or she is what connects you with *living*. And you do it for each other."

"And that means you have to know everything knowable about the other person?"

"Not at all. I don't think the 'honesty kick' of the younger generation is appealing. I think it's foolish. And it isn't true that we have to *like* every little thing about each other. That would be a lack of taste. But I believe we want—need—to take pride in each other."

"And if we find each other wanting?"

"Then we try to help. Otherwise it's not indifference or taking the other for granted that would separate us; it's by active dislike that we'd turn our backs on each other . . ."

Henry sat up and looked her squarely in the face. "Do you still dislike me?"

"You've made it easy for me to get over that. You wanted to give the money to Quentin. You wanted to clear yourself. I'm grateful to you for being that kind of person."

"I haven't succeeded at it yet."

"You will." She took his hand in hers again.

"I'm terribly sorry," Henry said.

"Fortunately, some damage can be repaired. I want to love you again. No. That's not quite right. I don't think I stopped loving you; but I didn't like you." She laughed and squeezed his hand affectionately. "What is liking?" she asked.

Henry felt called upon. "It is," he began to pronounce, "an action of the body that says to the mind, 'I wish to be in the presence of this person or this thing, because it brings out something in me that wouldn't be felt otherwise.' "

"I *like* that," she laughed.

"I like *you,*" he said.

She let go of his hand. "I wonder if you would like me less if you knew *everything* about me."

"I could probably take everything short of a series of gory murders."

"How about a make-believe murder?" She shuddered; she had said too much. She looked up at the children's hideaway, the tree house beyond the tennis court. "Everyone does have secrets," she admitted, implying, Let them remain undisclosed.

"There is the secret that would hurt others," he said, "and the secret that would hurt only yourself—if it were known."

"Where is the line drawn between us?" Kate asked. "I don't know anymore where I stop and you begin."

"Neither do I."

The late afternoon sunlight caught Kate's eyelashes. She squinted and saw ovals of rainbows. "I think it must be time to take Helen to the bus," she said.

They stood up together and walked close to each other without touching, past the grape vines on the tennis court fence, past the violets growing wild along the edge of the dappled lawn, past the irises and the columbine, the beds of tall fritillarias, their orange bell-shaped flowers beginning to turn brown.

"Peggy and Gabriel called last night," he remembered. "Situation normal. Peggy's homesick."

"Jonathan phoned this noon," Kate supplied. "He'll be back tomorrow."

Kate took his bandaged hand in hers. She was thinking of the young man who looked a little like Jonathan getting into the elevator at the Algonquin with the woman of thirty. She said, "We have only each other."

"That's a hell of a lot."

"I want to take a long hot bath. And then I want us to make love."

"I'll break the speed limit driving Helen down."

"Don't break anything."

"Keep your secrets," Henry said. "And I'll keep mine."

"Yes."

"Unless you want to tell me. You've had a lover for five years?" She laughed. "You've been overdrawn at the bank for a month?"

"Are sex and money all you think about?"

"Nearly," he smiled.

214

Jonathan telephoned Henry's office during the next afternoon to say he was in Grand Central about to take the train for New Haven and asked if his father would be at the store at five fifteen or so when the train arrived, so that he could drive home with him. Mrs. Wicks said she didn't know. He was at his accountant's and, with the weather as beautiful as it was today, she thought he might leave early to get in at least nine holes of golf. "I'll try calling when I get there," Jonathan said. "Or I'll just take a cab home." He sounded sad.

Henry never got the message. He left Waterman's office and walked to his garage by way of the department store on Church Street where he bought an extremely elegant bottle of Kate's favorite perfume, and then he drove directly to the golf club. He asked the secretary in the office there to call Mrs. Wicks and say he wouldn't be in until tomorrow morning.

"Mr. Warner," the young girl said, consolingly, "you're one of the few members of this club who have to work on Saturdays."

He smiled. "I don't really *have* to; but it keeps me out of trouble."

When he reached home at six, Kate was alone in the kitchen, which smelled of marinated lamb, Parker House rolls, and a garlic-flavored salad dressing. "Jonathan called from the railroad station. I didn't have enough time to go for him. He'll be here any minute."

"Who's Jonathan?" Henry asked.

Kate laughed and held her arms out to him. They kissed, tenderly, appreciatively.

"This is not a peace offering," Henry said, bringing out the gift-wrapped perfume from behind his back. "It is just to intensify your fascination, oh, mystery."

"Delicious!" Kate shouted when it was unwrapped on the kitchen counter. "I won't wear anything else to bed for years." She kissed him again.

"We were all alone for *one* night." Henry fondled the thought. "We liked it."

"Jonathan is hardly ever here when he is here . . ."

"I'm not voicing resentment. I'm just saying that I like being alone with you."

"Darling, this is going to be a superb dinner and it will be ready in about fifteen minutes."

"I want to change my clothes."

When he came back, Kate said, "Do me a favor; put some music on, and light the candles."

The record player was in the corner of the living room near the telephone. Henry chose a group of Joni Mitchell records and started them. In the dining room he was surprised by what he saw. Kate always liked to take the leaves out of the large rosewood table during the summer and reduce it to a small circle. He had forgotten. She must have done that during the day, with Helen's help. The table was set for three. No place mats. Crystal, and silver, and china. A bouquet of daisies in a silver bowl at the center and, on either side of all that sophistication, his old family rustic hurricane lamps with tall yellow candles in them. He took out his cigar lighter, leaned over, and lit the candles. It was not yet dark, but the sun was lowering itself beyond the trees to the west. The light in the room was muted. The candles brightened it. The music was full of plucked heart strings.

A taxi door slammed.

"Jonathan!" Kate said, wiping her hands on a dish towel. "Hi."

"How are you?" She hugged him, cautiously. She had grasped the truth of his living his own life. There was distance between them now. He put down his suitcase and ran a hand through his long hair.

"I'm okay." He kissed her on the forehead as he had seen his father do a thousand times.

"Listen, Johnny; there isn't time for you to change. Just wash up. Dinner's almost ready."

He went through the breakfast room and the little hall to the washroom on the ground floor and freshened himself up.

Henry poured the white wine to drink with the onion soup. They were all seated together calmly at the table with the pseudo-folksongs playing in the background, when Henry asked, "What did you get out of New York?"

"I didn't get a job through Mr. Lewis, if that's what you mean."

"I didn't mean anything in particular," Henry replied. He felt the challenge of Jonathan's tone. "I know this is a lousy year for summer jobs. But then, you could work at the store, or go to Maine with us . . ."

"I realize that," Jonathan said quietly. "But I don't want to be a burden."

Kate and Henry caught each other's eye.

"There's something more important I have to do," Jonathan said.

"What?" Kate asked.

"I have to go to the police." Kate gasped. "There's something I have to get off my chest." He looked up from his plate at his mother. "Do you know . . ."

"Yes. Your father told me."

"Well, I've thought about it a lot. I don't want to be a hypocrite or a fraud. I hate frauds. I'll turn myself in and see what happens." He knew what a fraud looked like now. He had drunk beer in his Park Avenue duplex apartment and made small talk with his crippled wife.

Very quietly, Kate said, "I think that is the right thing to do." She had no idea of how it would come out. But she felt proud of him.

Henry said, "Yes. It's better that way." He was consoled by all that Judge Jackman had told him. His son was going to be a better man than he was. Henry had wanted only to evade it. Jonathan was his mother's son. He would face it head-on.

Jonathan and Henry cleared the soup bowls and the first wine glass. Kate brought out the lamb and green beans. Henry poured the burgundy. The salad appeared on crescent crystal dishes that snuggled up against the dinner plates. Henry turned the records over.

They all seemed more relaxed, confident, more engaged with each other. "This is marvelous!" Henry exclaimed.

"Ummm!" Jonathan agreed through a mouthful.

"I'm playing house." Kate laughed.

Suddenly Jonathan leaned back, threw the dark hair up from his forehead, snapped his fingers loud as a whip, and said, "I just remembered."

"What?" Henry asked.

"Where I'd seen it before." His eyes were blank. He was not looking at anything in this room.

"Seen what?" Kate said.

"The Rembrandt." Jonathan was thinking out loud. "It used to be in Dr. Connolley's living room. I'm sure it's the same picture!"

"Same as what?" Kate asked, chilled.

"As one I just saw in New York."

Frightened, Henry said, "You saw it in New York?"

"Oh, I'm sorry," Jonathan said, embarrassed, coming back to them again. "I got carried away. It's just that I thought I had seen it before, and now I remembered where."

Kate contained herself. Slowly she asked, "Where did you see it in New York?"

"At the home of a rich man who bought it as a present for

his wife." He was unexpectedly aware that he was way out on a limb that he had no desire to cling to. How could he get back?

"Robert Stanton's home?" Henry asked.

"Yes," he admitted.

How could they possibly know? Jonathan wondered. How could this have happened? He had sworn to himself never to say a word about meeting Stanton, never in his whole life. And here he was back home not more than an hour and he had blurted it out.

"What were you doing there?" Kate demanded.

"I went to see the Rembrandt," he lied weakly.

"How did you know he had it?" Kate asked.

"I didn't know you had such an interest in art," Henry said.

"I don't have."

They were all silent. No one touched the food. Henry took a sip of the wine.

"Then," Kate asked, "how can you possibly explain going to Robert Stanton's home?"

"Someone," he began limply, gazing out to the distant sky, "someone . . . told me that he was . . . my . . . father."

Kate leaped up from her chair, her napkin dropped to the floor, and she turned toward the French windows as if she might run through them without opening the doors. Henry lurched up and grasped her by the shoulders. "Take it easy," he said, and led her back to her seat.

"Are you my father?" Jonathan asked Henry.

"In every sense of the word," Henry answered, "but for the original biological seed."

"Who was the source of that seed?" Jonathan asked.

"A man," Henry answered, "named Roman Stanski, who died in the Korean War. He and your mother loved each other very much before your mother and I met. He was dead when we met, and you have been my son ever since then."

"Is it possible," Jonathan asked, "that Robert Stanton is Roman Stanski?"

Kate said, "Yes," in the same instant that Henry said, "No." They looked at each other. Jonathan laughed nervously.

"I lied to you," Kate said to Henry. "We were not married and he did not die in the war. He walked out on me."

"Stanton is Stanski?" he asked.

"Yes," she said.

"And I brought him into this house . . . ." Henry said, painfully.

"You did?" Jonathan asked.

"He came here to buy the Rembrandt," Henry answered him. Then he turned back to face Kate. "I had no idea. What you must have suffered." Kate burst into tears and covered her face with her hands.

"What difference does it make?" Jonathan asked.

Henry stood over Kate, caressing her shoulders. "Don't cry," he said, handing her his napkin. "It is the same as if he were dead. He doesn't count. He doesn't figure in our lives."

"Who told you?" Kate barked at Jonathan.

"I don't think I should answer that."

"Why not?" she said.

"It would only make for hard feelings."

"Who could possibly have known?" she asked.

Cautiously, Jonathan said, "Someone close to Stanton."

Henry suddenly stood up straight, took his hands from Kate's arms. He saw the emeralds and diamond earrings, and said, "Isabel Taylor."

"How did you know?" Jonathan asked, amazed. Kate turned to look up at Henry, who said, "She must be his mistress. Or, at least, one of his women."

"Why should she have told you?" Kate asked.

Jonathan said, "She was drunk. She felt mean. She wanted to do something to hurt me."

"Oh, my God," Kate wailed. "It's all so sordid. The Taylors!" She cringed.

"To hell with them," Henry said.

"Why had you never told me?" Jonathan asked. Henry sat down again in his chair.

"I could say," Kate began slowly, "it was for your sake. So that you'd never feel any divided loyalty or wonder about what might have been. But the truth is that it wasn't for your sake at all. It was for mine. I didn't want anyone to know I had been treated so unfairly. So brutally. I wanted you to be born; he didn't."

"I understand that," Jonathan said. "But it might have been better coming from you than from him."

"I lied to your father. I never saw any way of telling you the truth. And I never, *never* thought it would come out this way."

The back door slammed. They all turned their eyes to the kitchen. Ellen Connolley entered, suave, in a green kilt skirt and a blue sweater. In her best French, she said, "A table. May I join you?"

"Please do," Henry said. He had stood up as Jonathan did, and he came around to pull out the chair for her. She put her pocketbook on the floor next to her. "You're not eating," she observed.

"And the atmosphere is charged," Henry added. Then he returned to his place.

"Will you have some wine?" Kate asked.

"No, no, no. I don't mean to interrupt. I just couldn't keep away. So many things going on at once," she said. "I have to share them with you."

"I saw Quentin yesterday," Henry said. "He's changed, very much."

"Yes. He told me."

"About our talk?"

"Yes. He's grown nasty. I don't like it."

"He's become holy," Henry said.

"That's part of it. Oh, do go on with your dinner," Ellen said. "I'd feel like such a boor if you don't."

"We're really not hungry," Kate said.

"Pity. It looks so good. And there are so few good things in the world."

"Why do you say that?" Henry asked.

"Well, I'm taking stock. I'm thinking of closing the house. Quentin is considering going away on a mission—to someplace where there are even more natives than there are mosquitoes. And I'm considering leaving him, and spending the summer, at least, with my mother in Boston."

"I'm so sorry," Kate said.

"And then," Ellen added, "all sorts of odd things happened. Callers. Unexpected callers. I had one today."

"Like who?" Henry asked.

"A girl I'd never met before. A Miss Rohan. She came to sell me a dirty slip. A half-slip she hadn't washed for a few weeks. Very odd. She suggested that it might be worth quite a lot of money to me, but I wasn't in the market for a dirty slip."

She didn't tell them the rest: how she stood with her back to the fireplace and picked up the brass poker and said to the slender young woman, "I could break every bone in your body and get away with it. I have only to say that you broke in here in order to steal, or that you threatened me, and I'd be cleared in any court in the country—and you'd be a cripple for the rest of your life. Now you tell me the information you came here to sell me, or I'll crack your skull."

"I wasn't even in the market for dirty information," Ellen continued, "but I got it."

Jonathan was growing petrified where he sat, stony, paralyzed.

Ellen said with the casualness of disbelief, "The poor girl was under the impression that Jonathan had driven the car that killed Raymond." She stared at him uncompromisingly.

"I'm going to the police," he said. "It *might* be true."

"Spare me that," she replied, contemptuous.

"No. I mean it. I'm going."

"Don't," she commanded. "It couldn't possibly matter less. It wouldn't do anyone any good. Some damage can never be undone. But one has to make decisions on the basis of what *might* be true," she said to Jonathan, "doesn't one?"

He swallowed. "Yes."

"Yes," she repeated.

Ellen then did something extraordinary. She reached across the table to Jonathan's water glass. It was heavy crystal, the goblet cut in the shape of curved drapes. She took hold of the stem and turned the glass on its side. The water poured across the rosewood of the table and down onto his pants. His reaction was the opposite of what one might expect: he threw the napkin away from his lap onto the floor. The water poured off the table onto his crotch, soaking him. He sat there inert. Kate and Henry were stunned, speechless.

Ellen got up. "I have to start my life all over again," she said. "I have lost my only child. I may be losing my husband. I am not young. I am not good-looking. But I have my own sense of how to live. And I'll make out all right. I know what I can count on, and what I have to put behind me. And you" —she said, sweeping her gaze from Kate to Henry to Jonathan—"are among those I have to put behind me." She picked up her pocketbook. "Neither Quentin nor I ever want to see any one of you again." She walked to the archway and turned her back on them; she walked through the fox hunting scene and closed the front doors behind her.

"Ellen . . ." Kate said, as if throwing a rose into an open grave. Her eyes filled with tears.

Jonathan sat with his head hung low staring at his wet pants. Then he raised his eyes. His youthful face was long with sorrow, with shame. "May I be excused?" he asked, as he had been taught to ask a dozen years before, as he would probably never say it again in the rest of his life: as if the decision rested with others. He stood up, with his arms hanging limp at his sides. "I'll go to my room now," he said quietly. At the archway, he turned and said, "I didn't know this could feel worse than going to jail."

"There are lots of worse things," Henry said softly to Kate.

They listened to Jonathan walking up the stairs. They were alone. Neither moved to touch the beads of water that remained around Jonathan's place at the table. Henry reached out and set the water glass straight again.

"Nothing will ever be 'in place' again," Kate said.

"Don't be so grim," Henry replied.

"Let's be honest."

"Now everyone knows everything they ought to know," Henry said.

"Even if they don't want to know it."

"Yes."

It had grown dark. The black and blue of the night sky filled the view through the French doors. The candles in the hurricane lamps were no longer merely decorative, they made it possible for Kate and Henry to see each other in the gentle yellow light.

"Do you hate me?" Kate asked.

Henry gazed at her steadily. "Twenty years ago it wouldn't have mattered a tinker's dam; now it matters twenty times less."

"I lied. I was not married. He was not dead."

"Should I love you less for that?"

"It's what I always feared."

"That's silly."

"I am not a silly person," she said, passionately.

"You're wrong. That happens to be silly."

"I've suppressed this disgusting secret all these years and the best you can do is call it *silly?*" She slapped her hand down on the table.

He stroked her hand with his. "If you had told me twenty years ago I wouldn't have called it 'silly' then, because the offense would have been fresh and I would have felt the hurt with you. I would have shared your wrath. I would have supported it with you. I could have helped it fade away a long time ago. But you showed me no weakness when I was courting you. I knew only of your pride. You showed me only your self-confidence. You never asked me to buttress you in any way against having been hurt."

"I couldn't have stood your pity."

"I didn't marry you out of pity."

"But you might have, if you had known the truth then."

Henry laughed. "I understand you. For the first time, I realize that you have your vanity, too. You wanted to appear better than you are."

"Which is why you wanted to deny the truth about the money."

"I think mine's worse. I didn't want to be seen as less than I appear to be. You wanted to be thought of as more than you are."

"I didn't want anyone to know that the world had treated me so shabbily."

"You wanted to appear unblemished, untarnished."

"Yes. Because, at heart, that's how I felt."

"You give too little credit to other people's feelings."

"I don't think so. To this day, men think of rape victims as women who want to be raped."

"You weren't raped. Did you want him to walk out on you?"

"I never expected it."

"You were taken unfair advantage of. That's all."

"But it shouldn't have happened to *me!*"

"Why not?"

"Because I'm a good person. I meant what I said."

"And so the world should take you at your estimation of yourself and return only good to you." He laughed. "It doesn't always work that way." Then it dawned on him: "You had concocted that story before we ever met."

"Yes. It was for the benefit of my parents. I couldn't face them with the truth."

"Why? They're strong."

"No. You don't understand. They are very, very vulnerable."

"And very demanding. It was they who led you to believe that you got what you deserved; so, if you were taken advantage of, that meant there was something lacking in you—it was your fault. You must have warranted it, somehow. That's how life makes judgments on people."

"Yes," she said, sadly. "I would have lost their respect; and I never would have gained yours."

"You're not talking about respect or even admiration," he said in a sharper voice. "It's so exaggerated. You mean adoration. You sound as if you wanted to be adored—worshiped—for being perfect."

"I've lived with you for twenty years, worrying in my most private thoughts that this moment might take place someday. Imagining that no, my parents are not wrong, and, if you found out, it would all collapse. You would think as little of me as Stanski did—and as I did when he abandoned me."

"When I met you, you didn't 'think little' of yourself."

"That was a front. I put on a good act. Over the years, very gradually, I came to feel that I had grown into the part. I had earned your devotion, not just lucked into it."

"That's how I came to feel, too."

"You always led me to believe," Kate said, "that there was so much going on in your life—you could take me or leave me."

He gasped. "Two nights ago I wondered how I could go on living if you didn't come home."

"When we met," she said, "I was pregnant with another man's child."

"That didn't deter me. I made love to you while Jonathan was in your womb."

"Did that excite you? The thought of another man's child there?"

He paused. "I don't know. *You* excite me. I haven't thought of 'another man . . . there' in decades."

"I can't bear that. The idea that anyone else might think about me making love with someone other than you. I'm sure that's why I could never have told Jonathan. It's obscene. People thinking about that . . ."

"Jonathan isn't shocked by the idea of people making love."

"Jonathan doesn't know anything about love. He knows only about sex. You know what? His generation is going to do away with marriage. And do away with having children. And that will be the end of their world."

"We've come a long way from the fact that Stanski is alive, and that Jonathan and I know about him now—Stanton—and that it doesn't matter one hoot or holler in hell. It doesn't matter at all."

"Doesn't it?"

"People don't change that much."

She looked away from him to the bowl of daisies. "What will you do about the money?"

"I'll get rid of it," he assured her.

Very slowly and very stately, with a sense that all this was like being told by a panel of doctors, No, you do *not* have terminal cancer, after all, Kate looked at Henry's face and gratefully said, "Thank you."

Then she stood up. "Now, I'd like to go upstairs and see if I can help Jonathan in any way." She could say no more. She could only feel, I hope I can. But even if I can't, then, I'm going to my bedroom and I'm going to think about my wounds, and his, and yours. I'm going to wait to see what out of all this life might remain unbroken or might be put back together again. I'm going to wait, silent and patient. And I'll see if in the future the one man to whom I have pledged my life will see fit to—to share my isolation with me . . . She looked at the table, the uneaten meal, the water on the rosewood around Jonathan's dinner plate and ignored them all.

"We don't know how much we can take," she said.

"Some things are better left unsaid," he replied.

"Yes," Kate agreed. "The difficulty is in knowing which ones."

She bent down to kiss Henry on his cheek and then she was gone.

He got up and blew out one of the half-burned candles. He picked up the other hurricane lamp and walked around the ground floor, locking doors, turning out the lights in the kitchen, in the halls, in the living room, turning off the silent record player. Back in the main hallway he stood still and stared about him at the fox hunting scene, an artist's vision of a fox hunting scene, in the mellow candlelight.

We have created a civilization, he realized, that is so committed to safety and comfort that we protect everyone we can from any feeling of real danger. No more wild beasts in the wilderness. We are concerned with making it all so easy that there are only make-believe challenges left to excite us. All our surface needs have been taken care of; we have satisfactions without uncertainties. The rest is sport. He looked carefully at the figures of the fox hunters. Young or old, fat or thin, they were winners; they were on top of the heap; they were kings of the hill on an outing, for fun, for a thrill —the way married men seduce other men's wives—for the sake of the game. Will the younger generation do away with marriage? What good is a marriage? We no longer care about who is the father of our children. Children? Why not stop having children? They will not make us feel potent by the largeness of their numbers; they will not help us till our fields; they will not care for us in old age. We have driven out the bitter truth from every aspect of our lives, so that no one will suffer, no one will feel deprived. We have sex without any intention of having children—for the fun of it only. We carry out ceremonies without any meanings: safer that way. We maintain forms without any content. We make marriages with no terms to the contract: more comfortable that way. The knife's edge is never at our throats. Therefore, we drive cars on dirt roads, in the darkness of night, with the car lights off. We bait ourselves.

With the hurricane lamp in his hand Henry turned toward the stairs. The candlelight drew his eye to the indelible trace of Gabriel's handprint under the red fox.

ABOUT THE AUTHOR

Morris Philipson is the author of five novels: *Bourgeois Anonymous*, *The Wallpaper Fox*, *A Man in Charge*, *Secret Understandings*, and *Somebody Else's Life*. Born in New Haven, Connecticut, he holds degrees from the Universities of Paris, and Chicago, as well as Columbia University. After working in trade publishing in New York, he became Director of the University of Chicago Press in 1967, a post he has held for some thirty-odd years. Philipson has written short stories, articles, and reviews, and has edited a number of books, including a volume on Leonardo da Vinci. He has also published a biography of Tolstoy and a study of Jung. His numerous awards include a PEN "Publisher Citation"; in 1984 he was made a Commander of the Order of Arts and Letters by the French Minister of Culture.